Ecstatic Witchcraft

About the Author:

Fio Gede Parma (they/them) is a Balinese-Australian queer witch and award-winning author. They are the author or compiler and editor of 8 books including *The Witch Belongs to the World, Elements of Magic, Magic of the Iron Pentacle, Magic of the Pearl Pentacle*, and *Ecstatic Witchcraft*.

Fio has been brought into the mysteries of four witchcraft traditions and has initiated witches into Wildwood, Reclaiming, and Anderson Feri traditions. They are a hereditary healer, seer, diviner, and magic-maker, and their Balinese and Irish, Scottish, Welsh, and English ancestries deeply influence their life and Craft.

They have taught hundreds of classes, courses, intensives, and WitchCamps in five continents and continues to mentor, work with, and teach with some of the leading lights of witchery, magic, activism, decolonisation, and artistry worldwide.

You can find out more at fiogedeparma.com

Ecstatic Witchcraft

Magic, Philosophy & Trance in the Shamanic Craft

Fio Gede Parma

Foreword by Lee Morgan

Chicago, IL

Paperback ISBN: 978-1-959883-27-2
Library of Congress Control Number on file.

Cover design by Kain Morgenmeer.
Typesetting by Gabriella De La Hoya.

Published by:
Crossed Crow Books, LLC
6934 N Glenwood Ave, Suite C
Chicago, IL 60626
www.crossedcrowbooks.com

Printed in the United States of America.
IBI

This book is dedicated to three beings.
Indah, Koda, & Jaya: this is, in part, some of their inheritance.
If they should need the magic, may it always be theirs. x

Acknowledgement of Country

I acknowledge and pay respects to the Gadigal and Bidjigal Peoples of the stolen and unceded lands I write these words within. I acknowledge your Elders, past and present, and all the immense work of survival, affirmation, and celebration of your Sovereignty of People and Country that confirms you as the right and true custodians of these lands. I acknowledge the Old People, the Song Lines, and the Dreaming. I acknowledge all Indigenous and First Nations peoples everywhere, who survive and live full and complex lives in the face of colonial violence and imperialist oppression. May Indigenous people everywhere know justice and peace.

Acknowledgements

I want to acknowledge and thank Elysia Gallo—editor par excellence—at Llewellyn Worldwide for taking a chance on me back in 2007 with my first manuscript, and for several more manuscripts which became published books, including the first edition of *Ecstatic Witchcraft!* I also want to thank Lee Anderson, whose skillful editing of this new Crossed Crow Books edition helps to breathe new life into this book!

To Blake Malliway from Crossed Crow Books for reaching out and suggesting this re-issue! I was so proud of this book in 2012, and I am even prouder of it now. Thank you for this opportunity.

To the Wildwood Tradition of Witches: you are my home and I adore our magic and have deep trust in the power of what we and our Mysteries do together. So much of the magic that I teach and write about is inspired and supported by you. To all of the initiates and Firebrand priestexes of our Tradition, and especially to James, Molly, Hannah, Laura, and Jarrah, the trailblazers of our beloved Covenant.

To all those Witches and spirit-workers who undertook the Shamanic Craft apprenticeship, and especially to Pipaluk, who was my first long-distance apprentice and who has become a skilled and dedicated teacher of magic in the world.

To my grandparents of beloved and mighty memory, for the gifts you have endowed me with in this current life and the yearning for the Mysteries you have inspired within me.

To my mother, Ros; my father, John; and sister, Noni: the first family I knew and loved.

To Phyllis Curott and Starhawk: your words and wisdom inspired me to become a writer.

CONTENTS

Foreword

Ecstasy is both a gateway that can be opened with her own most wild but also most cultural forms of methodology, and a destination that is creeping up on all of us. Some of us will only reach that moment on the edge of the death. Witchcraft is about being too impatient for that. Witches court that moment. When we get to the moment of ecstasy, we often re-meet ourselves all over again with a sense of divine revelation. This is not a narcissism in our nature—quite the opposite. It is about seeing that we were always an out-breath of something far older and larger.

When you look up ecstasy in the dictionary, the simplest truth about it is experiencing a breathless moment of being absorbed by one thing, to the extent that the rest of seeming-reality is dropped through your fingers like so many grains of sand. In many spiritual traditions, these sand grains are discarded in favour of what appears to sit behind them. But witchcraft is cheekier than that. From a witchcraft perspective, both the sand and what lives behind it sparkles into being, exuding a feral quality of musk and madness, one that whispers that this one thing the dictionary speaks of is also The One Thing. This great interconnected consciousness seems at first to sit just out of sight, but bursts through unexpected; other times, She comes through a shared design that could also be called the mind of God Herself, or the great being that in this book is sometimes called the All-Self.

Anyone Marked, or chosen, or found by witchcraft might be able to relate to the feeling of home-coming that led me to first pick up Carlo Ginzburg's *Ecstasies: Deciphering the Witches' Sabbath*. Although it was a scholarly text, I just knew from the title that he had grasped something about the meat and bones of the craft. By choosing this title, Ginzburg automatically connected witchcraft with what might be termed a "shamanistic background." Mircea Eliade described shamanism as a technique of *ekstasis,* and explicitly made this connection between witchcraft and the deep trance flirtations with the All-Self that manifest in various shamanistic traditions. Ginzburg evoked this to describe the flight of the *benandante* and *mazzeri* in a way that opened up a space.

Fio Parma's book also followed in this tradition in my reading life. After all the ecstatic moment of the Grand Sabbat, the fundamental experience when the walls in our perception come down and The Art reveals itself as something truly artistic, something truly inspired…. Is this not the very heart of witchcraft? During these moments the genesis of magic is revealed, what Fio refers to here as "the world of infinite possibility." For modern readers, it might even evoke the sense of the branching realities that are suggested by quantum mechanics: the idea that there is a you living in the experience you would like to manifest in your sorcery, as well as every other possible reality.

Such an idea—one taken seriously by physicists like Oxford University's David Deutsch and also Sean Carroll—makes it seem worthy of considering if magic has always been about pulling possibilities through the wall between versions of yourself. When we ward a space, do we protect it from other less desirable realities seeping through? What if there is a you out there somewhere not constricted by the limiting stories you've been taught to tell about yourself? What if the true artistry of the Now, that is also the future weaving itself, is to thread them around until one becomes their own All-Self? Such questions seem a necessity to anyone alive at this perilous moment of terror and insight.

This reality of infinite possibilities is not a form of positive thinking at all then; it is something based on some very well-considered principles. As Fio puts it: "This experiential paradigm goes hand in hand with the concept of plurality and the idea that multiple realities may exist simultaneously." In this way, you could even reach towards the definition for magic having something to do with a craft that sits beside the theories that are emerging about reality in our lifetimes. The work of Laurie Cabot also took these emerging ideas about synchronicities into account, where her books regularly talk about magic being an expression of our most mysterious scientific observations and theories.

Having an ecstatic experience can help to break the mental shackles that stop people from being able to grasp those possibilities, to even see them clearly as existing at all, let alone embodying them. It is one thing to believe there are multiple versions of reality where all things exist, and another to be able to draw on the power of those realities. The person thus inspired by an experience of insight generally must then reach for a framework, what I like to call a narrative structure, one that can hold and explain that experience, otherwise the power of it tends to slip away. Fio attempts to do this here in this book, and I think that's really valuable because obtaining a moment of true *ekstasis* is only one part of the process of transforming your life.

Having been privileged enough to experience Fio in moments of possession by spirits and gods I have a strong sense of how these techniques, but also these philosophies can break open a pathway for such things. There is something about possession, about being made one with a being that has laid their identity down in sacrifice before that of a larger story—or what we generally call a god—that opens the person to the idea of immensity. In doing so, one often opens to their own immensity.

A whole wild hunt's worth of ancestors speak through this creature we call Fio, and it's been a joy to me to both learn and teach, and the third thing that is a combination of both, from, with, and to them. They are responsible for a great deal of True Seeing that has guided my hand and that of my witch kin over the years. It is my hope that Fio's artful words are able to poke some holes between the threads in the tapestry of you and your many iterations, that blessings slide through, but also that the structure of the practices supports you as you attempt this metamorphosis.

—Lee Morgan

Preface

This book is an accompaniment to my previous book, *By Land, Sky & Sea: Three Realms of Shamanic Witchcraft* (which I will sometimes refer to as *By Land, Sky & Sea* within this book). However, it is not a direct sequel; they are tied together through subject matter alone. Though this book is presented as a grounding in a particular paradigm and philosophy of Witchcraft, it requires at least some contextual familiarity with Witchcraft as a spiritual tradition. Many of the topics within these pages are deeply confronting and can be dangerous. To read on is to acknowledge Witchcraft as a true wisdom tradition, abiding only by the precept that *total freedom equals total responsibility*. I shall leave the ethics to the deeper selves in all of you.

This book was written as an alternative to Witchcraft and Wicca books that introduce the seeker to a world of ritual and ceremony, correspondences, and overtly Hermetic overtones. Though there is nothing inherently wrong with this style of book, I believe it is essential to first orient oneself to cosmological, philosophical, and spiritual understandings before entering the realm of ritual. Without knowing why we cast a Circle (and other ritual steps) and truly connecting with that implicit meaning, ritual merely becomes a series of empty gestures, words, and movements. Ritual should be alive with the innate magic which is its fuel; it should sing with emotion and effectively link us with our psyches, transforming us. This is the deep power of ritual.[1]

Ecstatic Witchcraft is the product of 35 years of growing up in a spirit-working animistic family, 25 years of conscious spiritual growth, eighteen

---

[1] It is also important to understand that, through years of conducting ritual and integrating the Ways into your life, you will soon come to realise that there is never an end to the depth of insight you will behold related to any and everything. The Circle may be one thing one day but take on an entirely different meaning the next. The path of the Witch who ignites their awareness is endless in this way.

years involvement with what has become the Wildwood Tradition of Witchcraft, intense spontaneously derived and consciously facilitated shadow-work, and a triple-descent journey which punctuated the mythic influence of the Dark Ones in my life.

I am an initiated priestess of the Wildwood Tradition of Witchcraft, which emphasises the Shamanic foundation of the Craft and seeks to revive and celebrate it in the modern day. We consider Witchcraft a vital and ever-renewing tradition with deep, primordial roots. A tree may not grow toward the limitless heavens unless it is firmly entrenched within the Earth. So it is with the spirituality of the Witch. Without our Mother, we may not ascend the World Tree to know the delights of the heavens. If we do not first nourish ourselves and bear our grounding, we may never aspire to travel elsewhere or be strong and lucid enough to cultivate conscious experience. Start where you are.

Within these pages, you will find an outline for Shamanic Witchcraft apprenticeship. This course material is designed to ground and orient a Witch in the Shamanic Craft and on the pathway toward Shamanic apprenticeship, which in my mind can only be forged between self (the apparently autonomous, independent individual) and the spirits, or self and All-Self. Each chapter provides theory, tools, and discourse on the various elements of Shamanic Witchcraft. I have defined Witchcraft as an "ecstasy-driven, Earth-based, Mystery tradition," which I have unpacked in my previous works. However, I feel the need to explain what I mean by Shamanic Witchcraft as distinct from the broader concept of Witchcraft today, especially in the so-called West.

The first book to truly open me to the reality that, at its core, Witchcraft was and is the survival and shapeshifting of European Shamanic traditions was Kenneth Johnson's *Witchcraft and the Shamanic Journey.*[2] The author goes into great depth and detail concerning the records of the Witch trials and, through an unbiased and comparative religious lens, unearths a well-rounded theory that speaks of Witchcraft's origins in the Shamanic traditions. Johnson refers to the night battles of Carlo Ginzburg fame (the Italian *Benandanti,* "the Good Walkers"), Joan of Arc, and the nature of "crisis cults" such as the development of Haitian Vodou in response to slavery and the Ghost Dances of numerous Indigenous tribes in the so-called United States, including the Northern Paiute and Lakota. Perhaps Witchcraft, as it exists in scattered remnants

---

[2] Crossed Crow Books, 2023.

even to this day, was once a crisis cult originating in the fourteenth century during social and political unrest. This certainly has parallels with the ideas raised by *Aradia, or the Gospel of the Witches* as received by Charles Leland in the nineteenth century from the Tuscan Witch Maddalena. The Shamanic Craft I am speaking of is a revisioning and reclaiming of the older ways of seership, healing, and travelling between the worlds with the aid of our spirit-allies. In many ways, the historical and derivative conclusions drawn by Sorita d'Este and David Rankine in their wonderful book,[3] *Wicca: Magical Beginnings,*[4] may highlight the differences between a Witchcraft which is decidedly ceremonially oriented, and Shamanic Witchcraft. In fact, as I will discuss in the following introduction, Ceremonial Wicca and Shamanic Wicca are the two strands Raven Grimassi of beloved memory refers to when observing the trends of Craft practice and belief.

The Shamanic Craft I participate in is a philosophy and path which embraces the ecstatic, the wild, the gnostic (lowercase "g"), the transformative, and the visionary. A Shamanic Witch is born to their fate and, through countless threshold moments (rites of passage/initiation), embraces the art of evolutionary consciousness so that a deepening of the spiral-soul may take place. Essentially speaking, a Shamanic Witch is a Wild Witch: one who dwells by the precipice, on the edge, with one foot in this world and one in the next. We are given to magic, and magic is given to us. Nature is the foundation for Spirit, the essence of nature is magic, and the magical arts aid our reunion with Spirit as a whole being. Nature is our sacred foundation; magic is our sacred charge.

There are several key concepts within this definition:

• **Ecstatic, wild, gnostic, transformative, and visionary:** A Shamanic Witch embraces ways and methods which dissolve self as bound by

---

[3] In "Conclusions," d'Este and Rankine offer five possible histories for the development of the British Wiccan tradition: that "Wicca is a continuation of the grimoire tradition." that Wicca descends from a Victorian ceremonial magic system; that Wicca is the sole creation of Gerald Gardner and his co-conspirators; that Wicca is the direct survival of (a) British folk magic; and that Wicca is the "final form" of a European Witchcraft tradition with roots in the Aegean and Mediterranean. Of these five hypotheses, d'Este and Rankine opt for the viability of the first, complemented by the second.

[4] Avalonia, 2008.

the limited ego and societally imposed boundaries (ecstatic), evoke the untamed spirit within the human (wild), and bring true knowledge of Self (gnostic). All of this is deepened through the cycle we call life, death, and rebirth (transformative) and is affirmed by the Witch's gift to see and encounter the raw vividness of the world(s) (visionary).

- **Born to their fate and through countless threshold moments (rites of passage/initiation):** Most, if not all, Witches agree that a feeling of "home-coming" is a highlighting factor of returning to or arriving at the Craft. One traditional teaching regards that all Witches have always been so, reincarnating into new lives as Witches. It is a belief shared by Witches of a variety of traditions and lineages; Gardner often spoke of this in his published works and interviews. Once a Witch, always a Witch. All of this points to the older belief of reincarnation through the tribal or family line.

Briefly, on the topic of initiation:

A Shamanic Witch is not brought into a tradition necessarily made of organized covens, but a tradition of spirit-allyship or land guardianship and the gift of knowing the worlds and the roads between them. Self-initiation, in the strictest sense of the term, is absolutely viable but is the outcome of several other threshold moments in which the aiding and familiar (family) spirits work to empower, orient, and ground the Shaman/Witch in the here and now. The Circle is cast through this process, and upon reaching the point of origin, a true revolution of spirit takes place. There is a deepening, and the spiral begins.

The hereditary Craft and the Witches therein are not always genetically related to the family at large; individuals may be "adopted" into family traditions if there is significant interest either way and the individual fits appropriately within the family tradition. If a soul has returned but has not been born into the ancestral line, the individual's fate can still be intuitively or experientially read, and an adoption will take place. Ideally, at least in the older traditions of Craft, any initiatory ritual, threshold moment, or transition stands in for an adoption ceremony. In this context, an initiation is a decision on the part of the existing coven or family to accept a new-old soul into the family or tradition. The initiation brings the individual into the current of the tradition and energetically and spiritually connects them with the Gods, totems, and spirits that guide and oversee the tradition.

The Spiral-Soul

As mentioned above, initiatory experience naturally opens our awareness to the deeper reality of the Spiral-Soul. The Spiral-Soul is described in many traditions, but not necessarily in the same manner. We often hear it called the "Triple Soul" in the Reclaiming and Feri Traditions. I connect the Three Souls with the Three Worlds of Land, Sky, and Sea and understand these souls to be distillations of those worlds within us as well. When the Star Self (Sky), the Talking Self (Land), and the Shadow Self (Sea) are aligned and in wholeness, evolutionary consciousness becomes the illumined pathway of Self, and we are Self-initiated.

Wild Witch

"Wild" often equals primal to those who hear it; it signals raw and pure nature as it is rather than the romanticised version of nature that is exclusively pleasant and lovely. When we consider that there is no separation and the mirror of nature is also the mirror of our internal Divinities, one can then assert that if we have undergone the Elemental purification of walking life's path in honour and integrity, we partake in that holy Mystery which says, "Here lies the way to ascension (the road to God), here lies the way to decadence (the road to oblivion), and here lies the road to the Faerie Country (the road to magic)." The Witch, honouring their spiral nature, will often simply walk in the direction of the middle-way (the Faerie Road) because they know, intrinsically, that a road or path is never one-dimensional and will eventually turn and twist and bend: the Crooked Path. And here, we find the element of risk which makes our journey worthwhile, for without it, we have sacrificed nothing: the Mystery. To be wild and, thus, to be a Wild or Shamanic Witch is to honour the pledge to the Mysteries of the Eternal Question and to embrace it as the forever way to God, oblivion, and Faerie.

The Shamanic Witch, in my mind, consists of four definitive qualities:

1. Our ways and lore form from ecstatic methodology, wild being, gnostic philosophy, transformative longings, and visionary impetus.
2. We are born and made Witches, not necessarily through heredity, but through the pacts we make with Self to learn more deeply than it is possible and to embrace the Fate of homecoming, purpose,

and the integrity of being made worthy through challenge to change—initiation.

3. We embrace our soul's (and, thus, the world's) spiral nature—the triplicity of self—which, by its very numerological value, speaks of breaking duality and reconciling the loathing of opposites by melding them.

4. We proudly and passionately embrace the wilderness within and allow it free reign, not because it would be decadent or indulgent to do so, but because it is the way of nature and the Road to God, oblivion, and Faerie are one and the same.

I wrote this book to fill a void which is smoothly disappearing as of late. Authors and teachers such as Veronica Cummer, Janet Farrar, Gavin Bone, Raven Grimassi, Christopher Penczak, and R.J. Stewart have paved the way. I thank them, for I stand on the shoulders of giants, as do we all.

Therefore, I dedicate this book to the giants, the titans, and the raw forces of nature, which share so much with the Shamans. And may it be forever so.

Introduction to the New Edition of *Ecstatic Witchcraft*

I write now on the unceded and stolen traditional lands of the Gadigal and Bidjigal Peoples. I must first acknowledge and honour the Elders—past and present—of the Gadigal and Bidjigal. The British Crown invaded, colonised, and still occupies these lands. I honour the strength and survival of First Nations and Indigenous communities and cultures here and everywhere in the face of attempted genocide.

When I first imagined writing *Ecstatic Witchcraft*, I was in my early 20s, married, and living in a different city and state. Over a decade has passed—as well as five big moves to five different cities and countries—since that time, but reflecting on this book and what it meant (and might still mean) for me and others brings me into a deep space of surrender, excitement, and willingness.

Ecstatic Witchcraft is still very much what I do. Originally, the title I had put forth for the publication was *The Wild Witch,* but one of my Ravens (there's always several) suggested the title that made the most sense. I had used the phrase in the book multiple times as well, of course. I connect my experience and understanding of Ecstatic Witchcraft with Shamanistic cosmologies and spirit work. I was not and am not original in this, though in the current discourse fuelled by various social media platforms, this is no longer popular.

Historically and folklorically, scholars have argued for the connection between what some in the so-called Western world call "Shamanism" and what we call "Witchcraft." In some ways, both are highly charged and nebulous terms; in other ways, they seem definitive and certain with very specific associated images, tropes, and emotions. I still think that many aspects of Witchcraft become illuminated and more complexly contextualised by understanding what Shamanistic spirit-workers and community priests do and how they do it. The notion that a Witch is only a malevolent, night-flying, shapeshifting sorcerer and a Shaman is a tribal wise person who only heals for the good of the group is a reductive binary that does not represent these histories or cultures accurately. Things are much wilder in actuality, as are the realities of cultural exchange, fusion, appropriation, and the legacies of imperialism and colonisation.

Is Witchcraft "Shamanism"? No, I don't think I could say that because Shamanism, as we regard it today, is the result of hundreds of years of imperialism, colonialism, and misunderstandings of indigenous Siberian religion and culture. It is also true that we have co-evolved a term—*shaman* or *shamanic/shamanistic*—that sometimes suits various ethnic and indigenous communities and spirit-workers and has been in established cross-cultural usage for decades. Does the Witchcraft I know have Shamanistic elements? Yes. Does being a Witch mean they practice a Shamanistic spirituality? Well, that depends on the Witch and their magic and spirits.

The Witchcraft I practice has always involved ecstatic states, community healing, priestessing, mentoring, initiatory mysteries, and honouring the ancestors and spirits. The Witches I know and love are all participating in something like this. We journey to the otherworlds; stalk our shadows; dance with our demons; wrestle with societal monsters; transform illness; blast and hex empire; connect through food, mutual aid, and obligation; conjure spirits and make love with them; and cast spells for ourselves and people who come to us. We help solve situations, bind those who abuse and bully, divine the past and the future, find what is lost or forgotten, and venerate saints and old Gods. Sometimes, we oracle with and by powers of the Gods and Spirits, opening as vessels for them to act through in this world. This is Ecstatic Witchcraft.

There are methods and processes included in this book that are still a part of my practice. Others have evolved or dissolved. There are significant threads of personal and mystical insight that I had forgotten I put into this book...but here they are. They remind me of where I've been, and perhaps they'll remind you of something, too.

Since the publication of the original edition of *Ecstatic Witchcraft* through Llewellyn Worldwide in 2012, I underwent initiation in three other Witchcraft traditions. In May 2013, I was brought into the Anderean Witch House. In September 2016, I underwent Reclaiming initiation, and in July 2018, just before I turned 30, I was initiated into Anderson Feri after seven and a half years of journeying with the lore, myth, technique, and magic of those lineages. These initiations each happened in three different continents, and I experience each one as part of the great and mysterious labyrinth of initiation I stepped into when I entered the Wildwood. It is true that I felt Witchcraft had chosen me. I answered the call. This is core to Ecstatic Witchcraft.

I hope that these words, workings, and Wyrd contained in this book invite, provoke, deepen, and open you. I am so happy that this book has a new life in different languages and in different cultures.

As we say in the Wildwood Tradition, peace, praise, and power to you—and may love, truth, and wisdom reveal beauty in and as all things.

x Fio Gede Parma
January 2023

Introduction

> *"There is the night-flight, the spirit journey, the ability to shapeshift, the power to heal and to harm, and congress with all sorts of spirits, Gods and Goddesses, the dead, and the powers of the Earth. There is the thin edge that needs to be walked between magic and madness, between life and death. There is the boundary that must be leaped or walked or stood upon, always a chancy business at best. There is the going-there and the coming-back-again with lost souls, healing knowledge, gifts for the community, new insights and ancient revelation."*
> —Veronica Cummer, *To Fly By Night:*
> *The Craft of the Hedgewitch*

Anthropologically and culturally speaking, a *Shaman* is an individual endowed with the seemingly supernatural gift to traverse the manifold worlds existing within and around each other simultaneously (as was the late Mircea Eliade's hypothesis). This foundational skill empowers the Shaman to gather cosmic or spiritual information and knowledge, apply it by translating the abstract into practical, forge relationships (allyships) with human and non-human spirit-beings, and further understand the Mysteries of life (as embodied on Earth by the tides and other inherent cycles of nature). Historically speaking, these Shamanic skills are at the heart of all Witchcraft.

The origins of the word and concept Witch is complex and multi-layered. It varied across different landscapes, including "wise one" (*saga*, meaning "Witch" in Latin), "bender/twister of power" (*weik*, a Proto Indo-European term), "seer and knower" (*weid*, another Proto Indo-European term), "singer of sacred songs" (*varð-lokkur*, translating from Old Norse to "warlock"),[5] and "a magical priest/ess" (*weik*, a Proto Indo-European term referring to "one who consecrates with [religio-magic] spirit"). The root of the word *Shaman* lies in the Tungus "saman," which means "one who is excited, moved, or raised."[6] The derivative term now used by anthropologists to categorise a number of medicine-men, traditional healers, wizards, sorcerers, and others is *Shaman*.

The root word *saman* may actually derive from a Tungus word meaning "to know."[7] In fact, the term has traditionally never been a noun; it is applied to the practice itself. These age-old archetypes are akin to the traditional European roles of the village Witch who held herbal healing knowledge and was the keeper of the wisdom of the Earth currents and cosmic alignments, like the myrk-rider and the Hedgewitch, Witches, by their very nature, were and are fringe-dwellers and, by living on the edge, were able to cross the nebulous boundaries separating the realms. Witches are true walkers between the worlds, with one foot in this world and one in the Other.

The Witch, like the Shaman, had helpers: familiar spirits. During the Witch Hysteria in Europe, the general folkloric belief was that Witches' familiar spirits were animal companions. This links with ancient Shamanic, animistic, and totemic beliefs in many cultures. Shamans, like the medicine-men of the Amazon, also work with the plant world, and spirit-allies like peyote (*Lophophora williamsii*) and ayahuasca (*Banisteriopsis caapi*) are considered sacraments by Indigenous Shamans in the Americas. In European lore, we have belladonna (*Atropa belladonna*), wormwood (*Artemisia absinthium*), and fly agaric mushroom (*Amanita muscaria*), all of which are known psychotropics (meaning "turning/altering of the

---

[5] The term "warlock" has often been said to derive from the Old Scottish for "one who breaks oaths," and seemed to be applied to men accused of Witchcraft during persecution because it was thought that men were stronger in all ways than women and, thus, had much more to lose by signing a pact with Satan. However, according to Lady Abigail, as quoted by Storm Faerywolf in his article *A Conjuring of the Male Mysteries in Modern Witchcraft*, the original Old Scottish term *waerloga* means simply "male Witch" or "cunning man." The Old English term of the same spelling does translate as "oath-breaker."

[6] According to Roger Walsh in *The World of Shamanism: New Views of an Ancient Tradition* (Llewellyn, 2007).

[7] In her essay "What the Heck is a Hedgewitch" in Veronica Cummer's *To Fly By Night: The Craft of the Hedgewitch*, Juniper speaks of the word *saman* as translating as "one who knows" (Pendraig, 2010).

soul") or entheogens (meaning "to generate the God within"). In fact, the majority of these plants are listed in old formulae for the infamous "flying ointment." This ointment was one of the major factors in enabling Witches to "fly" to the Sabbats, where, from spirit-beings and a Lord and Lady of the Sabbat, they would be instructed in magical rites and achieve ecstatic states of consciousness through which they obtained mystic insights.[8]

Raven Grimassi (1951–2019), a renowned and sometimes controversial historian of Neo-Paganism and Witchcraft, often divides modern Wicca into two distinct categories: ceremonial Wicca and Shamanic Wicca. It is my belief that ceremonial aspects of Witchcraft and Wicca were developmental and grew out of or responded to inherent Shamanic foundations. "As with much of Europe, ancient cave drawings and artefacts found in Italy reveal primitive ceremonial beliefs related to hunting and the animal kingdom in general. Over the course of many centuries, ancient shamanic-like beliefs evolved into tribal religion, eventually taking the form we now call *La Vecchia Religione*—The Old Religion."[9]

Essentially, the Craft of the Shamanic Witch, as I am writing about it, is a revivalist current which emphasises the underlying mythic and mystic components. This gives life to the ritual and ceremony we use to access these things in the first place. In Shamanic Witchcraft, ritual and ceremony are understood as spiritual technology that enables us to connect and commune with the primal powers of the cosmos. It is important to comprehend this subtle truth, or else we become encumbered by pomp and lose touch with the spirit of the ritual itself. Spontaneous ecstatic communion is the heart of the Craft, not timed and ordered ceremony. Ultimately, the Circle is life, and our invocations call forth the hidden potencies alive within the world(s). The Shamanic Witch embraces the All-in-One and the One-in-All. Hail to the Great Mystery.

This Book's Context and Orientation

Much of this book's content helped to lend framing to the Shamanic Witchcraft apprenticeship I used to teach (see Appendix II). The apprenticeship drew upon a somewhat eclectic (as a descriptive term, not a spiritual identifier) synthesis of ideas, customs, concepts, and traditions contextualised

---

[8] Kenneth Johnson, *Witchcraft and the Shamanic Journey* (Crossed Crow, 2023).

[9] Raven Grimassi, *Hereditary Witchcraft* (Llewellyn, 1999) 10.

by my own personal discipline, deepening, and devotion. The material is influenced by the Wildwood Tradition, Feri understandings, Celtic lore and mythology, and modern interpretations of the Greek Mystery Traditions (specifically the Orphic and Eleusinian). As a Wildwood initiate and priestess, I am also actively and frequently engaging with the Sacred Four (the four Wildwood Divinities) and my other deities and allies, receiving new-old wisdom, lore, and technique directly. It may take me several months (or even years) to fully understand the implications of what I personally receive. Cross-pollination and intimate working with other spirit-workers and Witches have almost always led to uncanny corroboration of what others and I receive via the white thread of spirit communication. Together, as human communities and networks, we redden these practices and this lore once more, helping each other fill in missing pieces.

There are several instances within this book in which I refer to the Feri Tradition explicitly but have only done so if I have felt the insight is necessary. At the publication of the first edition of this book in mid-2012 by Llewellyn Worldwide, I was a year and a half into formal training in the BlueRose Line of Feri with Storm Faerywolf. When I was initiated into Anderson Feri in mid-2018, it was at the hands of two initiates of the Reclaiming Feri lineages. I had also been observing and working with Feri concepts (not techniques) for a few years at that point and had immediately noticed poignant parallels with Wildwood Witchcraft. I also have a family background in animistic and polytheistic spirituality and was exposed from infancy to a tradition which espoused ideas of spiritual technology as magical.

In this book, there are nine chapters which speak on different elements of the Shamanic Craft as I work with it. First, we will be examining the spiritual significance and meaning of Ecstasy in a Shamanic framework. In the second chapter, we will delve into cosmology and the necessity of learning and attuning to the dynamic of the spiral or triple soul complex and how this make-up reflects and embodies cosmic truths. I will share insights into the deeper realities behind casting the Circle and directional-emphasis and orientation; Elemental philosophy will guide us. In Chapter Three, we will investigate drawing down the Gods and possessory work in general: what it means and how it relates to potential peer relationships with the Great Ones. This will help guide us into inquiring about sacred allyships cultivated with the spirits and spirit worlds in Chapter Four, and how to observe, balance, celebrate, and honour our connections and exchanges.

Chapter Five outlines the quintessential Shamanic talent of journeying the realms and how the technique and springboard of trance propels us into accessing a broad range of skillsets integral to the Shamanic Witch. In the sixth chapter, we examine ecstatic spellcraft experiment with unique techniques and methods for our sorcery. Chapter Seven concerns healing and explores channelling what Witches often call the Power for wholeness and renewal, soul retrieval, severing and cleansing of cords and attachments, and water-blessing. In the eighth chapter, we will articulate the divinatory skills of the Witch through the Shamanic lens, along with the associated harnessing of the Sight or Knowing. The Conclusion reviews the journey of the Shamanic Witch and speaks on the Soul-Story and the Mythic life.

As we move through this book, certain implicit and explicit guiding principles will become obvious. The four guiding principles of the Shamanic Craft, as offered in these pages, are:

1. The Magical Worldview of Infinite Possibility
2. Nature is Our Sacred Foundation; Magic is the Essence of Nature; Magic is Our Sacred Charge
3. The Principle of Sacred Equality
4. Total Freedom Equals Total Responsibility

A Note on the Magical Worldview of Infinite Possibility

> *"The internal logic of what Castaneda writes is totally real. I've done many of those things myself and seen other medicine people do them. People indeed walk up walls, walk through gateways; those things are not fiction for native peoples."*
>
> —Arwyn Dreamwalker (Shaman),
> *Drawing Down the Spirits (interviewee)*

Stereotypically and historically, both Witches and Shamans are conceived to be able to enact feats of supernatural strength. Physical flight; shapeshifting; commanding spirits, demons, and deities; oracular knowledge; casting spells and curses; and speaking with the animal and plant worlds are all among our traditional repertoires. Considering my own magical career, I will personally review these apparent skills and seek to illustrate what I have come to call the "Magical Worldview of Infinite Possibility" (MWIP) in this book.

I have witnessed physical levitation; worked with ancient forces to achieve significant tasks, such as affecting the weather, linear time, and space; shifted my energy-body into animal awareness; perceived future, past, and present (from afar) events in amazing clarity; cast spells to great success; and understood and communicated with animals, plants, and other spirit-beings. This is not supernatural. It is within my potential as a living and aware being, and it is within yours. Post-industrial society has divorced us from our innate ability to engage with the limitless realities which are ever-changing and always in flux. The MWIP is a paradigm-shattering paradigm, a paradox of paradoxes.

This experiential paradigm goes hand in hand with the concept of plurality and the idea that multiple realities may exist simultaneously.

The Shamanic Witch is, beyond all else, concerned with pragmatism as contextualised by the MWIP. Therefore, the Shamanic Craft teaches us that we must first be concerned with experience and only after allow this to be belief and, even then, to always question.[10]

If we are able to surrender to infinity, suspending disbelief even for a moment to open to how far-reaching possibility is, we begin to cultivate the confidence within ourselves necessary to trust in the Great Mystery's continual unfolding. We become an active and integral part of the Allness that Is. We remember.

The idea of infinite possibility helps us to unlock ultimate reality, which is never truly ultimate until we are able to understand that the concept of infinity is contained within the All, and that the All is truly beyond itself and the seed of its realisation. A Shamanic Witch honours these truths as primordial and preliminary; without them, how are we able to interact with the primal forces of reality to achieve our goals or further fulfil our ecstasy-driven destinies? It is essential to first consider that magical spirituality isn't hypocritical: it is decidedly overt, sometimes subtle, and often pragmatic.

Magic is an art, a vital force, and an integrated philosophy offering deepening and illumination. It is also a signal to the mind to question. When we are faced with an absolute answer, magic encourages us to revel

---

[10] There is a Feri proverb many initiates remind each other of regularly. We attribute it to the late Grandmaster of the Feri Tradition, Victor Anderson. "Perceive first, believe later."

in that answer's preceding question. Perhaps it has a different answer attached to it, providing an alternate reality and extending into a world not touched on by the "absolute" answer. Perhaps magic is the way in which we relate to our own conceptions of reality and truth? Or perhaps magic allows us to rise above our own self-imposed dilemmas to see the bigger picture and manifold traces of the artist(s)? Magic reminds us of our own art and creativity and restores the brush to our waiting hands. It inspires and answers the question of infinite possibilities. Here is a technology, a dynamic, a paradigm, and a metaphor which escapes all absolutes and paradoxically opens us to truth.

The Mystery in this philosophy is the eternal unknown and the spiralling journey which forever deepens our inherent connections while forging new ones. It is the Grace of Being which we can only intimate in the quiet spaces in between. The magical worldview of infinite possibility is a way to translate the words written down before language ever was. To hear the music of the spheres, though we are bound to silence; to drink of the Deep Well, though there is no depth; to perceive before perception and know before knowledge; and then to stand back and see that all is as it is and will be forever.

May the journey begin!

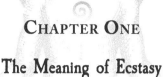

CHAPTER ONE

The Meaning of Ecstasy

"I am consciousness, a thread connecting all living creatures on Earth. I am briar. I am rock, alive and vital. I am cloud, drifting on the high winds of consciousness. I am cattle dog, living on a farm in Tasmania, and I am Great Dane, loving my master. I am hare, running fleet of foot. I am bird, singing on a branch in a garden. Winter is ended, spring is here, and I sing with the joy of life."
—Michael J. Roads, *Journey into Nature*

Mircea Eliade described Shamanism as a technique of ecstasy. The Greeks understood ecstasy as *ekstasis,* which translates to literally "outside standing" or "to stand outside." When the word ecstasy is then contextualised as a magical and spiritual technique, it is clear that the Shaman or Witch experiences ecstasy as standing outside of oneself and only the ego-bound self. Moving beyond the self as experienced in the bounds of society opens us to the idea of self as wild and immanent Divinity. That thing called the "self" is equivalent to that thing called "cosmos." The self is the All-Self.[11] This is true at all times.

As a priestess of the Craft, I am devoted to the service and celebration of the All-Self eternally in its varied and infinite expressions. Each self—each being—is holy and beloved of the Great Mystery, and attaining true ecstasy is our destiny. The concept of the pure will can be understood through this notion. If we are all enlightened, then attuning to and realising our own pure will shall aid us in remembering our wholeness (and holiness). It is our choice to dishonour our Divine origins, but it is also our choice to embrace it.

The Mystery Cults of ancient Europe, such as the Orphics, Pythagoreans, Druids, and Witches, all have their own particular methods of reinforcing

---

[11] See my book *Spirited* (Llewellyn, 195), for more details.

and evoking this sacred reality. The famous Orphic initiatory declaration from the Pætilía Tablet, "I am child of Earth and of Starry Heaven; but my race is of Heaven alone," urges us to embrace our stardom, leading to salvation through memory and awareness of our Divinity here, now, and cosmically. The symbol of the Pythagoreans was the pentagram, an archaic and cross-cultural occult symbol known to contain the Phi ratio explicitly and, thus, to reflect the intelligence of nature and the godhood of human beings in its basic design. Witches of the past and the present have many ways of acknowledging, accepting, and affirming our destiny of ecstasy. In the famous and beloved Charge of the Goddess, attributed to Doreen Valiente (1922–1999), we are taught that the Goddess—specifically Diana in the source text from Charles G. Leland's *Aradia*—will teach us how to unbind and liberate ourselves and to be naked in our rites, to dance, sing, feast, and make love, all in the spirit of ecstasy.

In embracing the naked body, we are, as Witches, making a huge philosophic statement: we declare the body to be Divine and not abhorrent, godly, and not sinful. In fact, the Goddess of the Wise is charging us to do so and, furthermore, to celebrate and praise Her spirit in and through ourselves. Even the simple blessing of *Blessed Be*, which may have been absorbed into Gardnerian Wicca via Christianity, bears deep wisdom. The meaning is congruent with the philosophies and teachings of the Craft: blessed are all things by their very nature. It is our destiny to recognise this simple truth and, in embracing it, to transcend Descartes' "I think therefore I am" self and be freed.

Ecstasy is to be filled with the presence of bliss, but only through love. A vision I had of the Lord Siwa (the Balinese term for Shiva) indicated this to me quite obviously. Siwa is often depicted with a rose at his crown, from which a fountain of pure water or a beam of holy light comes forth. The water or light is bliss and ecstasy, and only through the rose (the gate of love) may we bathe in the presence of the Divine. To love is to know the Mystery, for both are ineffable, and neither can be explained rationally: it is the intimation of the heart. In letting go of the ego's need to control and categorise or filter experiences, we surrender to the pure will, the natural flow of the life force, and thus we return to our destiny to ecstasy. Hence, Witchcraft is truly a world-embracing tradition rather than a world-rejecting one.

Love as Divine Fire

"Whether man or woman, conscious practitioner of the ancient Mysteries or one who simply lives with vitality, a life fully lived is one illuminated by the divine spark within oneself. And that God, who is also mortal, is within each of us. He was within me now; grateful and aroused. I was aware of communion in every part of myself – in body, mind and soul. I had found the God and he was love."

—Phyllis Curott, *The Love Spell*

Love is often touted in New Age philosophies to be synonymous with the being, force, or concept many call "God." As a Witch, I do not relate to the Divine as a plane of neutrality or as an over-arching force of suspension or creation (not overtly, anyway). Rather, the Divine is a shining, a depth within, an intrinsic connection, and the power of presence.

All things are Divine; all things are God. This is the Great Mystery. Love, then (as I experience it), is the feeling or experience of the Divine's Fire (its will to be) in our lives. The Celts called an experience of channelling the Irish *Imbas* or Welsh *Awen*. Both of these words mean a poetic inspiration: "fire in the head."

Fire is an ascending element, with a desire to grow higher and to spread. It burns up Air as it does so and transforms all that passes through it. A candle flame is often enough for one to realise the sacredness of a moment. In fact, the lighting of candles in many spiritual traditions is a solemn and simple method of acknowledging and petitioning the Divine, drawing forth a concentration of that presence or a particular deity. Where the Land meets the Sky meets the Sea, a Fire is lit.

Fire was stolen from the Olympians by Prometheos. A Blue Flame is considered to be the symbol of the Spirit of the Old Ways in Stregheria as put forth by Raven Grimassi; a sign of the presence of the Fey Folk, and, as the well-known Pagan prison chaplain Patrick McCollum once told me, when Earth is taken from a well (Earth and Water), breathed upon, and lit (Air and Fire) a Blue Flame is ignited as the four Elements become one.

Consider the images of the Christ and Mary bearing their flaming hearts in Catholic iconography. Some religions are called fire-worshipping cults because of an emphasis on fire in their rituals, such as Zoroastrianism. The understanding is implicit in many faiths around the world. Fire illumines and transforms through destruction; it enlivens, warms, and impassions. Fire marks the presence of the Divine: love.

Love, by its very nature, is multifaceted, and from a spiritual perspective, it is much more than the love depicted in romantic comedies or tear-jerking movies. Love is frightening, harsh, soul-wrenching, and destructive, and it can simultaneously be empowering, liberating, calming, soothing, and gracious. Love is as love does, and more often than not, as many before me have articulated, love is a verb. When we think of love, as the Tungus-speaking peoples think of their Shamans as an action or something done in the world, we can realise that without our participation within the sacred reality, we may not feel the Divine Presence, the fire in the head, heart, or belly. We must embrace the world, for the world will embrace us in return. The Gods help those who help themselves.

The Rite of Divine Fire

This simple rite will help to open you to the all-pervasive, underlying omnipresence of the Divine. Materials needed:

- A white votive candle
- A rose (whatever colour you prefer)
- Lighter or matches

Breathe into stillness. Light the candle and place the rose before it so that it sits between you and the candle. Gaze peacefully at the rose and candle, absorbing the sight holistically. Don't attempt to impose a vision or instigate a movement away from the here and now. Breathe deeply in, right down into your abdomen, filling your lungs, and sigh vocally. Do this three times. Sit and watch. Observe. Be in the moment. Receive. Breathe.

If you are blind, hold a rose or similar blossom in your hands and imagine into being with a flame. If you cannot access a rose, find something that reminds you of one.

Dionysos and Siwa: Lords of Divine Ecstasy and Surrender to Bliss

Dionysos (Divine one of Nysa)
Siwa (Auspicious One)

I am a devotee of Dionysos. I was born into a family that honours Lord Siwa (*Mahadewa,* meaning "the Great God"). I am not the first (and certainly not the last) example of these two deities being consciously linked.[12]

Dionysos is most often associated in popular culture with some aspects of his Roman form, Bacchus or Bakchos (the wine God, meaning "raving"). However, he is also the spirit of wild ecstasy and abandon, the leader of the frenzied maenads (who carry his thyrsos), and an ancient deity of death and rebirth (initiation) revered by the Orphics.

The following are some of his lesser-known attributes in the form of epithets or Divine titles, which clearly demonstrate his Shamanic nature:

- Agrios (the Wild One)
- Antheos (Blossoming)
- Bromios (He who Roars)
- Bythios (the Deep)
- Khoreutes (the Dancer)
- Dissotokos (Doubly Born)
- Ekstatophoros (Bringer of Ecstasy)
- Eleuthereos (Emancipator)
- Iatros (Healer)
- Lyseos (Liberator)
- Phanes (Illuminator)
- Teletarches (Lord of Initiation)

Dionysos has been called many things in his vast history. His myths of genesis greatly vary, but by looking at the Orphic tradition's Dionysian

---

[12] Please refer to *Gods of Love and Ecstasy: The Traditions of Shiva and Dionysos* by Alain Danielou (Inner Traditions, 1992) for more detail. Many historians and religious comparative researchers feel that Shiva and Dionysos are the same God or derive from a prototypical Lord of the Dance and Ecstasy.

genesis myth, we can understand the meaning of his name Doubly Born (or even, in some cases, thrice-born). Dionysos is born as Zagreos (the Hunter or the Collector of Souls) from the union of Persephone and Zeus, who seizes her as a serpent/drake in the Underworld. Persephone, Lady of the Underworld and Queen of the Dead, carries now the seed of the Potent Sky-Father. The highest God has come together with the deepest Goddess, and from this union of opposites comes the third: the promised child who will break the duality and dissolve the boundaries to bliss. Zagreos is then seen to be angrily pursued by Hera (Queen of Olympos, Lady of Winds, and Old Goddess of Nature) as a Death-Waging Hag (from the Greek *hagnes,* meaning "pure"), and she commands the Titans, the raw and primal forces of nature and pre-Olympian Gods, to tear Zagreos into many pieces. They first trick the young Zagreos into replacing the sceptre and the apple (symbols of sovereignty and wisdom) for the thyrsos (pinecone-tipped wand), a spinning toy, and a mirror. As Zagreos becomes hypnotised by his own reflection, the Titans surround him and undertake the task of destruction with the wild ferocity only Titans can wield. They then stew him in a cauldron (symbol of regeneration), boil, roast, and devour the seven or fourteen pieces of his body (similar to the Osirian myth of dismemberment by his brother Set). However, of course, the allegory is punctuated most clearly by its symbols.

The cauldron is the source of immortality in Pagan myths. Though Apollon, Athene, and/or the Muses (depending on the myth) are sent to gather the pieces of Zagreos and inter them at the centre of the world itself (the *omphalos* or navel at Delphi), the beating heart is entrusted to Semele. Semele is the mortal mother of Dionysos' rebirth, and, once again, Hera's ire is aroused. Hera encourages Semele to implore Zeus to reveal himself in his Divine splendour; though he refuses at first, she continues to yearn for it until Zeus cannot help but to acquiesce to his delicate lover. He appears as lightning, and Semele is reduced to ash.[13]

On the winter solstice, the newly formed Dionysos is sewn from the womb of the now-dead Semele into the thigh of Zeus, who will protect the child until his rebirth at the spring equinox. And thus, can we attest to Dionysos' thrice-born nature: born first from the union of Persephone and Zeus, secondly at the winter solstice when Semele is destroyed and

---

[13] Just as the Titans were by wrath of Zeus after the dismemberment of Zagreos, the human race was said to spring from these ashes and the blood of Zagreos; of "animal" and "divine" heritage.

he must be prematurely extracted, and thirdly when he comes forth from Zeus's thigh at the spring equinox. He is the Dark Lord of the Underworld as the first Zagreos, the Saviour of Spring (and the rebirth/resurrection of life) as he who is reborn at the equinox and the strange eclipse moment in between (the winter solstice), which I have now come to embrace. Much of the seasonal cycle now celebrated by Neo-Pagans the world over can also be found in this ancient Orphic/Olympian-variant myth.

In my personal work with Zagreos, even before I actually looked at literary historical documents and references, he manifests to me as a terrifying Sabbatic lord upon the plains of Thessaly, an area in modern-day Greece known for its Witches and magic. There, he showed me symbols of three triangles intersecting as one, a crooked triangle with the symbol of a solar eclipse in the centre. I felt that this depicted his raw, beating heart, as it was occulted by darkness and then reborn (almost spontaneously) into the light once more. We have here a true bringer of initiation, a Lord of Ecstasy, for the mirror that entrances the young Divine one becomes the catalyst for the entire unfolding of the life-death-rebirth of this God-King.

The mirror, the self-reflection, the revelation of self as Divine: this is the threshold moment that instigates true initiation. Not only does it mirror (pun intended) the many modern Craft rites of initiation, but it also is the classic making of the Shaman. It is for this reason (and many others) that Raven Grimassi claims Dionysos as the original prototype for the Witches' God:

We shall discover...that ancient writings reveal that Dionysos is: born at the winter solstice, dies in the Fall season as a harvest lord figure, dwells in the Underworld, is renewed, appears in seasonal rituals, has a female goddess consort with lunar and underworld aspects, is a Green Man figure, and is a fertility god associated with horned animals such as the bull, goat and stag.[14]

Shiva,[15] on the other hand, is not necessarily considered a horned god, though his apparent representation on the Indus Valley Pashupati Seal from approximately 2350–2000 BCE is definitively a bull-horned figure,

---

[14] Raven Grimassi, *The Witches' Craft: The Roots of Witchcraft and Magical Transformation* (Crossed Crow Books, 2024).

[15] Great information on Shiva in his manifold aspects and related symbols can be found at www.hinduwebsite.com/hinduism/siva.asp

seated in lotus position, surrounded by wild animals, and triple-faced (perhaps the Trimurti). The imagery bears stark resemblance to that of the Cernunnos figure on the famous Gundestrup Cauldron. However, Shiva is a wild god whose key role in Tantric yoga and philosophy proves that he is also a deity of taboos and breaking them, which are powerful techniques to drive one into ecstasy. Meditating or sleeping in a cemetery is a common magical act for many involved in the Tantric arts, and to do so would be absolutely impure in the conventional Hindu outlook.

Although a great majority of the stories associated with the God Shiva concern the holy family (composed of himself, Parvati, and Ganesha),[16] there are others which explain his Divine nature.

Shiva is one of the Trimurti: the three Divine, supreme powers of the Hindu Godhead. Shiva traditionally represents the destroyer aspect, while Brahma is the creator and Vishnu the preserver. One myth tells of Shiva's birth. The powers of creation (Brahma) and preservation (Vishnu) are debating which one is the most powerful. Suddenly, a great pillar of shining light appears before them. It extends into the highest height and the deepest depth. Brahma becomes a goose and flies to the top of the pillar (or tree, as roots and branches are sometimes described), and Vishnu becomes a boar and digs into the Earth, searching for the bottom. However, the two return without ever having discovered the limit to the great pillar. At this moment, Shiva simply walks out of the pillar. They witness this great power, and thus, Shiva becomes destruction and balances the cosmos.

It is not hard to see the Shamanic realities referred to in this myth. The three powers represent the three worlds and perhaps the three selves/souls as well. The great pillar/tree is the World Tree—the Axis

---

[16] The elephant-headed deity's merging of human and elephant occurred because Shiva accidentally cut off his newly-created (from Parvati's dead skin scraped off during bathing) son's head, as Parvati had placed him at the doorway of the palace to deter any unwanted villains from trespassing. Ganesha did not know Shiva, and Shiva did not know Ganesha, and as the son would not stand aside for the father, he severed his head. When Shiva discovered his crime, he traveled North until he came upon an elephant, whose head he severed and replaced for Ganesha's lost head. Ganesha is the first God one prays to in a traditional Hindu *puja* (devotional ritual), as he opens doorways and lifts obstacles. In this way, is he alike to Papa Legba of the Vodou traditions, and Hestia, Hermes, and Hekate of the Greeks.

Mundi—which is also represented sometimes as a mountain, like Mount Meru, sacred to Buddhists, Hindus, and Jains, or Venusberg of German folklore and related to the Witches' Sabbat.

Shiva is often depicted with four arms, four faces, and three eyes. One of his most beloved aspects is as Nataraja—the Lord of the Dance—whose depictions are commonly found on altars of Shivaite Pagans and Hindus. Interestingly, growing up with Siwa, it was much more common to behold images of Siwa in peaceful lotus pose, emanating silent wisdom. I have never really noticed my father hold any other deity above Siwa, although Saraswati is also important to him. He calls her the Goddess of Education.

The way Shiva is traditionally depicted is obviously symbolic of his innate powers, gifts, and areas of influence. Although Shiva is regarded as the deity of destruction (some say a look of his third eye will utterly obliterate), my interactions with the Dancing Lord have been about surrender, freedom, letting go, and becoming at one with the cosmic flow. Destruction of illusion, attachment to ego, and the paradigms of separation facilitate such liberation and awakening, but just as Kali devotees think of Kali Ma as love and compassion overall rather than a death-avenging war Goddess, the Shivaites are similar. Darker aspects of the God's nature might be explored depending on one's inclination, philosophy, or path, but this varies from individual to individual.

Those involved in Tantric pursuits uphold Shiva and Shakti as the two potent forces of the universe. Shakti is power, life force, and what *is*, and Shiva is the blossoming, coming forth, and penetration of this cosmic power so that it becomes sentient, intelligent, and self-aware, and thus affirmed as parallel to the Feri tales of Creation. Tantric rites seek to affirm and celebrate the life force, which often manifests as the human capacity for pleasure, hence the immediate connection of Tantric practice with sacred sexuality. I will leave it to others more versed in the subject to convey the finer points of Tantra. A great starting point, however, is Dr. John Mumford's *Ecstasy through Tantra*. Not only is it an apt book, but it is also an apt title for the purposes of this chapter!

Historically and culturally speaking, both Shiva and Dioynsos are considered wayward deities, outside of the conventional (and approved) ways of thinking and acting, and therefore representing boundaries, barriers, limits, and the destruction and surpassing of these things. As I previously stated, ecstasy is a walking away from the self and into the core of Self itself. This act, this magical and mystical pathway, is innate within the human spiritual and biochemical framework. We are urged to move beyond and to move through our circumstances and to deepen as a result. This is the pathway Witches have either consciously or unconsciously worked with for centuries, if not millennia, along with all mystics, seers, Shamans, and medicine people. It is the reason for our spirit-flight, our trance, and our ability to become vessels and mediums for and speak with the spirits.

The identification of Dionysos with Shiva does not only make historical and cultural sense (although, in practice, these deities are two very distinct beings) but also mythically speaking. Dionysos' journey to the East, initiated by Hera's curse to wander the world in madness, enlightens Dionysos to the process of fermentation, thus introducing the divine liquid of intoxication we now call wine, but he also returns whole. He is no longer completely raving, if you will, and has passed through the barrier of what it means to be compartmentalised as anything by society. He has entered salvation or freedom and has become a saviour as an example to all those who are lost, wandering, and yearning for wholeness. In this way, the practice of ecstasy as a holy technique is a pathway to free us of the shackles that bind us and open us to the marvels of the Mystery.

Shiva, too, urges us to let go of ego, to surrender to the All, and to be at one with the peace instilled. In his Nataraja aspect, Shiva is depicted as standing on a demon/dwarf representing ignorance and ego, poised almost in a graceful warrior stance as a circle of flame surrounds his shining body. To stand on the demon is to prevail over ignorance, and the circle of flame is the circle of transformation; it represents the liminal, the between, the world of the spirits, and our ability to co-exist in a useful and hopefully benevolent way. His posture could very well indicate not only esoteric symbolism but also a yogic stance that could very well lead the mind to such liberation and ecstasy.[17]

One could wax eloquent on the intricacies of Shiva and Dionysos and their contrasts, comparisons, and connections for an eternity. Instead, I wish to conclude this chapter with a ceremony of reverence and contemplation of the Lord Dionysos and the Mahadewa Siwa!

---

[17] See *Ecstatic Trance: New Ritual Body Postures* by Felicitas Goodman (Binkey Kok, 2003).

A Note on the Conjoining of Siwa and Dionysos

Cultural misappropriation is a sore spot for some in the contemporary Pagan community, as there is a tendency in broader New Age philosophies to view all of the world's wisdom as a monolithic box of spiritual treasure from which we can freely take. Initially, I was not actually going to include this little section in this chapter until my acquisitions editor pointed out that Hindus may not necessarily identify as Pagan and that, by working with deities of an Indian/Hindu origin without clarifying the relationship, I might be blurring the boundaries a little too much.

I'm one of those rarer Pagan "converts." I was actually raised in Balinese Hinduism, which possesses a blend of animistic, polytheistic, and monistic theology. My family's tradition is very much steeped in magic and mysticism; spirit possession, divination, healing, ceremony, and prayer are all referred to and practised. However, the Pagan cultures, traditions, myths, and deities of Europe called for me, and I answered. I was aroused by the archetype of the Witch and felt Her essence within my being. Hinduism obviously still permeates my spirituality. In fact, as I type this, there is an altar behind me that both Lakshmi and Ganesha sit upon. Kali and Siwa are both strong influences on me, and I employ Hindu, Vedic, and Tantric mantras at times in my magical work and prayer. For these reasons, I do not think it's odd or inappropriate to work with Siwa and Dionysos together—as long as there is consciousness of their histories with respect and reverence.

Hinduism, like Paganism, is an umbrella term. It is not a monolithic, static religious tradition without diversification or unique expressions. In fact, it is not unheard of to refer to Pagans as the Hindus of the West and Hindus as the Pagans of the East. Hindu traditions have a great deal in common with Celtic cultures and the customs of Western Europe; the parallels are often startlingly clear. There was a burgeoning movement within contemporary Paganism called "Indo-Paganism," which refers to the blending of Eastern and Western principles and practices with meaning, purpose, and passion around the time the first edition of *Ecstatic Witchcraft* was published. I do not identify as an Indo-Pagan, but the merging of the Hindu and Pagan religious and spiritual communities (especially in the US) is an alliance and friendship that I have much hope in.

In saying all of the above, please keep in mind that there are underlying social, political, historical, and spiritual issues which may present either predicaments or an expanded perspective. The key, as always, is to approach all things with profound humility and respect, a seeking to learn and grow with knowledge, and a reverent mirth which enlightens the Gods. For me, the cultural appropriation conversation—which is serious and, unfortunately, often ironically hijacked by white folks—can be quickly summarised. Respect comes from a recognition of cultural context and authority and a living relationship—acknowledging complexity of colonial realities that still exist—with the tradition, teaching, and authority-holders of the culture. Authority implies responsibility to safeguard, honour, and pass things on respectfully.

Hymn to Dionysos

"Come, blessed Dionysos, bull-faced god conceived in fire, Bassareus and Bakchos, many-named master of all. You delight in bloody swords and in the holy Maenads, as you howl throughout Olympos, O roaring and frenzied Bakchos. Armed with thyrsos and wrathful in the extreme, you are honoured by all the gods and by all the men who dwell upon the earth. Come, blessed and leaping god, and bring much joy to all."[18]

Hymn to Siwa/Shiva

"Naagendra haaraaya thriloochanaaya
bhasmaangadhaaraaya maheshwaraaya
Nityaaya shudhdhaaya digambaraaya
tasmai nakaaraaya namahshivaaya."

Translation: "Salutations to Shiva who wears a serpent as a garland, who is three-eyed, whose bare body is covered with ashes, who is forever pure and the very embodiment of sacrifice."[19]

---

[18] Orphic Hymn 45 translated by Athanassakis (*The Orphic Hymns: Text, Translation and Notes,* Society of Biblical Literature, 1988).
[19] Pande, Alka, "Mahashivratri–The Five Elements of Shiva" TimesNowNews. com, 2021.

A Ritual of Reverence and Contemplation

This ritual is a melding of traditional (reconstructed and readapted) Greek blessing rites with an adapted Hindu *puja* to Shiva. The aim of this ritual of reverence and contemplation is to do just that—revere and contemplate—and to allow the movement of self into All Self through devotion.

Materials needed:

For the Dionysos altar (black cloth):
- 1 small ceramic bowl containing water
- 1 white votive candle
- 1 stick of frankincense
- A bunch of purple grapes
- A wine you personally prefer (in a wine glass)
- An image/statue of Dionysos
- A thyrsos (a pinecone-tipped wand, which can be easily made by finding a suitable branch and either super-gluing a pinecone to one of the ends or tying it down with hardy twine)

For the Shiva altar (white cloth):
- 2 statues/images, one of Shiva and one of Ganesha (to open the way)
- Mala prayer beads (worn around the neck to honour Shiva)[20]
- 2 silver vessels (or stainless steel), one containing sandalwood paste and the other to be a receptacle for the five liquids
- 1 tablespoon ghee
- 1 tablespoon dairy milk
- 1 tablespoon coconut oil
- 1 tablespoon water
- 1 tablespoon rose water
- Fresh flowers, coconut, and an assortment of fruit (tropical is best)
- Jasmine incense (stick or cone variety)
- 2 white votive candles (one for Ganesha and one for Shiva)
- Sweets/cakes as offerings for Ganesha

---

[20] Mala prayer beads are a staple of Hindu worship. There are 108 beads, often with a counting bead to keep track. They are often made of sandalwood, which is considered a very holy plant and scent in the East. although the mala beads worn to honour Shiva are generally made of Rudraksha (Rudra-eyed) seeds, a tree native to the Himalayas.

1. Begin by clearing and cleaning the space to be used for the rite in whatever way you see fit, remembering to both clean physically *and* cleanse energetically.
2. Create two altars in the East: one to Dionysos and one to Shiva.
3. On Dionysos' altar, place his image towards the back and set the white votive candle in front of it. In front of the candle, place the bowl of water and balance the stick of frankincense on the bowl. The thyrsos should sit next to the image in the back. Place the glass of wine on one side of the candle and the grapes on the other.
4. On Shiva's altar, place the image/statue towards the back and arrange the mala beads around it. Place the white votive in front of the image. Two silver vessels should sit in front of the white votive, and set the flowers, coconut, and fruits in front of the vessels. The image of Ganesha should be placed to the right of Shiva with the second votive in front of his image. Set the sweets/cakes and the five liquids aside, ready to pour, and place the incense at the very front of the altar.
5. Ground and centre. Gaze at the altars and take in what is displayed, holding and conveying the essence of the two Gods of Ecstasy. Light the candle before Dionysos and call upon the Primal Fire:

"Great Primal Fire, ascend to us with the dawn and rule the sky. Glory of the Sun with burning lustre illumine even the silver Goddess Selene. Ethereal Fire, radiant heat, light-bearer, power of stars, cause now the bloomi ng of the iris and the rose and to the grain be kind. Hear now this prayer of supplication and be thou ever innocent, serene and gentle to this land. Great Primal Fire, I invoke thee!"[21]

6. Light the votive before Ganesha's image and chant the following several times over to invoke his blessings and to open the way for the rite:

"Om Shri Ganeshaya Namah."[22]

Place the sweets/cakes before the image as an offering to Ganesha.

---

[21] English translation of the Orphic Hymn to Primal Fire (I have adapted it slightly, though this is the version I use in my weekly devotions).
[22] Meaning "Om and Salutations to Lord Ganesha."

7. Gaze meditatively at the two flames upon the two shrines and visualize or sense the space encompassed by the joining of these two flames into a sphere of incandescent fire, which purifies the area. Incant the following with impassioned force:

"Hekas, O Hekas, este bebeloi!"[23]

Now, take the frankincense stick and light it from both flames. Then, with intent, plunge it into the bowl of water on Dionysos' altar, saying:

"Kherniptomai![24] *May this water be purified by the sacred flame."*

Carry the water around the space three times in a sunwise (deasil) manner, sprinkling as you go and chanting:

"O Theoi, genoisthe apotropoi kakon![25] *O Gods, turn away evils!"*

Once you have completed the third circumambulation, place the bowl of water, now considered ritually impure (as it has absorbed the miasma/impurities of the mind-state and the place), out of sight and away from the space. The space is now fit and ready to officially welcome in the Gods.

8. Welcome in the two Gods of Ecstasy in your own words.
9. Into one of the silver vessels on Shiva's altar, pour the five holy liquids (ghee, milk, water, oil, and rose water) and declare this offering to him as you gesture in blessing to the flowers, coconut, and other fruits. Anoint yourself and the image of Shiva with sandalwood paste to link in with his power and providence. Finally, light the jasmine incense and white votive in his name.
10. Pick up the glass of wine and recite the following in blessing over it with intention:

"From sun to seed, from seed to vine, from vine to grape, from grape to wine. Kherniptomai in Dionysos' name! Io Io Io Evohe!"[26]

---

[23] Translated literally it means, "Away, O away, you desecrators/profanities!" Pronounce as *heh-kas oh heh-kas es-tay bay-bay-loi.*

[24] Meaning "Purify!" or "Be pure!" Pronounce as *kai-yr-neep-toh-may.*

[25] Pronounced as *Oh thee-oy gen-oys-thee ah-poh-tra-poy kak-on.*

[26] Pronounce as *ee-oh ee-oh ee-oh ee-voh-ay.*

Drink deeply, then sprinkle a little of the wine over the grapes and pour the rest to Dionysos.

11. Holding the thyrsos in hand, recite the Orphic Hymn to Dionysos given previously. Take the mala beads from Shiva's altar and use them to count while you chant 108 "Om Namah Shivaya" mantras. Allow the chanting of the mantra to arouse a soft trance state that will guide you to introspection. After the 108th repetition, close your eyes, bow your head in reverence, and sit in silence for as long as feels natural.

12. When you are ready, open your eyes and again gaze peacefully at the two altars. Repeat the following with intention:

"To the two Gods of Ecstasy and Revelation; to the Great Ones of death, decay, and rebirth into light from chaos; to the Holy Beings of mirth, reverence, and the balance between all things—let there be peace now within me, around me, and let it touch the hearts of all who come into my sphere. I have communed with you for purity, presence, and power. I am purified, present, and powerful. The peace of the lords of the world resides now within me. I am reborn in this moment. IO OM!"

13. Take a moment to return to equilibrium. When ready, begin to unravel and deconstruct the space with respect for the deities and the spirits of place. Leave frankincense to honour them.

CHAPTER TWO

Cosmology and the Spiral Soul

"But the shaman's worlds and levels are more than interconnected; they also interact with one another. Shamans believe that these interactions can be perceived and affected by one who knows how to do so and that the shaman, like a spider at the centre of a cosmic web, can feel and influence distant realms."
—Roger Walsh, M.D., Ph.D, *The World of Shamanism*

As Witches, we look to nature, the great teacher, for Divine inspiration. Nature is the Spirit manifest, God's most perfect expression. Therefore, it is within nature that we will find the secrets, the hidden potencies (the Gods and spirits), and the teachings of life apparent. Humans, too, are part of nature, and recognising and remembering this is essential for our spiritual sanity. As Phyllis Curott so eloquently put it in her *Book of Shadows,* "Standing in the cleansing, empowering surf, I knew that evil is something that arises within human begins when they become disconnected from the natural world."[27]

Witches often weave poetic allegory and metaphor through natural elements in order to ignite consciousness and to receive gnosis. As an auto-chthonic (self-sprouting) tradition, the Old Ways are self-caused within the human dynamic; their origins are within the ether and dream of their own being. Even after centuries without them, those returning to the Pagan traditions of their ancestors are struck with a universal "coming home" feeling. Our traditions, lore, and customs are renewed, and revitalised forms aid practitioners in attuning to age-old forces. However, as Raven Grimassi demonstrates very clearly and successfully in his books,

---

[27] Page 170.

a great deal of modern Witchcraft and Wiccan theological and practical structures derive from periods much earlier than the mid-1900s.[28]

Cosmology is the study of the world(s) and the way it is: the framework of the cosmos, how it manifests organically, and how we perceive or interpret those manifestations. Each and every person possesses a cosmological—if not ontological (meaning "perspective of being")—outlook, though not all are consciously derived or arrived at through personal gnosis, revelation, or communion. It is the nature of Witchcraft as a mystical tradition to ignite consciousness and embrace the world in this ecstatic state, one that invites transcendence from a centre of immanence. We are privy to the ways of cosmology, though; ideally, we understand these perspectives as useful maps and lenses to interact with a living universe, multiverse, or whatever you perceive.

In *By Land, Sky & Sea*, we worked within the paradigm of the Triple Realms as the classic Shamanic representation of the cosmos that has essentially manifested in sacred triplicities. Not only is an external entity—the world—threefold, but the spirit within the body is as well. It is also useful to look at the human spirit as essentially a tripartite division. This concept, at least in the modern Craft traditions, is best conveyed by the various branches of Feri Witchcraft.[29]

Depending on whom you speak to and which line of Feri you are training within, the triple soul has several names. The Three Souls or selves are often identified in the following way:

- Talker, Middle Self, or Breath Soul (Talking Self below)
- Younger Self or Fetch (Shadow Self below)
- Deep/God Self or Holy Daimon (Star Self below)

Although I am a Feri initiate—and was a fresh Feri student at the original writing and publication of this book—my perceptions and experiences of the Three Selves or Souls were and are not entirely governed by Feri insight or lore.

---

[28] Refer to the bibliography for details of these works.

[29] The spelling of Feri/Faerie/Faery changes according to the line and sometimes the individual Witch. Obviously all spellings are valid, but according to Storm Faerywolf (the progenitor of the BlueRose Feri Line), the spelling became "Feri" sometime in the 1990s because Victor Anderson wanted to distinguish his Witchcraft from the Faery taught by R.J. Stewart and other forms of so-called "Faery Wicca."

The Spiral/Triple Soul and the Three Worlds

Personally, I refer to *Talking Self* using the same term, *Younger Self* as "Shadow Self," and *Deep Self* as "Star Self." However, I am apt to change and shift how I speak of the Three Souls. I connect the Three Souls with the Three Worlds of the Shamanic paradigm. Therefore, in my work, *Talking Self* is the agent or companion of land/Middleworld, *Shadow Self* is representative of the sea/Underworld, and *Star Self* is the emissary of the sky/Upperworld. I also place these three selves within the body at what Christopher Penczak calls the "Three Cauldrons." The concept of the Three Cauldrons is said to stem from an Irish teaching called the Cauldron of Posey, and it sits right with me as deeply related to anchorpoints for the Three Souls within the landscape of the body.[30]

The human body has often been portrayed as a symbol of universal intelligence of God or the Divine and the impetus for life, not just within the Three Cauldrons. The best-known historical example of this is Leonardo da Vinci's *Vitruvian Man,* which is a Renaissance image of a muscular, defined male figure spread-eagle over sacred geometry that follows the course and orientation of his body. The pentagram becomes manifest: the sacred star, the God nature within the body, and the immanent consciousness that many of us in the post-modern Pagan culture call "the Goddess." Looking at the body as a map for spiritual reality is an ancient and cross-cultural concept.

The three cauldrons are the Cauldron of the Head, the Cauldron of the Heart, and the Cauldron of the Belly. In many cultures, the "soul" of the individual is said to reside within the head. For example, in my father's Balinese culture, the head of a newborn must not be touched so that the physical (grounding) touch will not interfere with the settling soul. Therefore, for me, the Star Self is anchored in the Cauldron of the Head.

The Cauldron of the Heart represents the interface between the Star Self (Cauldron of the Head) and the Talking Self (Cauldron of the Belly).

---

[30] Penczak mentions that the teaching of the Three Cauldrons derives from a sixteenth century Irish *fili* (mystic-poet) poem called "The Cauldron of Poesy." Another friend of mine also speaks of receiving brief training in the Three Cauldrons for his third degree, but different names were used. I have used the names Penczak refers to them as this was how I first heard of them, and I find them to be apt descriptions.

To me, the heart (which is also the centre of the seven-chakra system and, therefore, the transmuter of vital life force) speaks of the Shadow Self in this mapping because, as a character in one of Charles de Lint's extraordinary Newford books puts it, "the shadow is the guardian of the soul" (Spirits in the Wires).[31] Some may debate why the Shadow Self, as dark as it sounds, should be placed in the Cauldron of the Heart, considering that the heart is of love and the shadow is our repressed, negative nature in mutated form. I also struggled with that when initially linking the Three Cauldrons with the Three Souls and Three Realms. However, as I kept working, a gentle surety seemed to say, "Look harder; there is wisdom here." The harder I looked, the more I pondered, and the more I relaxed into knowing, the more the concept held substance.

I would argue that when we look at the shadow as it is and seek not to simply cast it as a psychological and mechanistic compartment for that which we cannot bear to look at, we find that the shadow is the primal template for the soul and the animal within; the pure, raw, beating heart of life; the yearning to exist. It is desire. Of course, it is our yearnings and desires which are so often judged harshly by a Western society dripping in Christian moralities. However, the shadow is the Guardian at the Gate: he who protects the sanctity of the inner temple (the Divine Self embodied by Star Self). What else is the temple enfolded in and protected by but love? The Shadow Self demonstrates to us that our Child Self (to use another of its manifold names) is innocent. In the Feri tradition, this is expressed as the *Black Heart of Innocence*. That very term poetically encompasses the truth at the heart of the Cauldron of the Heart and the Shadow that sits there.

This, of course, leaves the Talking Self (or Ego) to the Cauldron of the Belly: the grounded rhythms of the manifest world and the daily cycles which inform the way we think, act, and respond. The Belly is the place of fire, heat, transformation, gestation, growth, and fear. It is the centre from which we live and act out based on both internal and external stimuli. In the Wildwood Tradition, when we acknowledge the presence and providence

---

[31] In my mind, this seems to express that all signs point to love and compassion being the seat of the Divine. This is echoed by another sentiment of Phyllis Curott's: "Some say the energy we work with is neither good nor bad, but simply neutral...And yet the encounters I had with raising energy, witnessing a drawing down, working in trance and experiencing visions and epiphanies all convinced me that the energy we worked with was love" (*Book of Shadows*, 214).

of the Three Realms, we gesture down to the earth for Land, up to the heavens for Sky, and, to seal this, we cup our hands together at our chest (heart) for Sea. This not only aligns the Self within the Three Worlds but also the Three Souls at the Three Cauldrons within the body.

In studying the Three Souls of the One Spirit (what I call "Own Holy Self") that dwells within the temple that is each of us, we can begin to garner the wisdom of being. Through metaphor, poetry, ritual, allegory, and symbol, we can look beyond the superficial and connect with the eternal. When we energetically align the Three Souls, as is a daily practice within Feri, Reclaiming, and Wildwood traditions, we are magically remembering who we are so that we may, to use a Church of All Worlds term, *grok* (understand in fullness) life, its Mysteries, and the essence within that makes us who we are. Consciousness—that gives us the very drive and desire to know!

A Witch, with this ignited consciousness or awareness, weaves with the Mysteries and celebrates the sovereignty of Self, which is found when we accept responsibility for our Wyrd and Karma and thereby charge ourselves to service and celebration. Our threads glow in the tapestry, and we become wholly a part of the flow of fate; we become living agents of the life force and are able to communicate and interface within, between, and through. This is the power of the Witch and the Shaman.

The Three Realms Alignment (Three Cauldrons)

This technique is foundational for the work of this book (and, I'd argue, life!). When combined with the Triple/Spiral Soul Alignment (a version of which will be provided later), they help facilitate an external-internal equilibrium.

The Three Realms Alignment draws upon the essence of each realm (Land, Sky, and Sea) in broad expression and condenses and concentrates their potencies into the Three Cauldrons held in the body (at head, heart, and belly). It is also a more powerful way of grounding and centring and becoming the World Tree. There are also methods of aligning the Three Realms without focussing on the Three Cauldrons, but this particular technique draws upon the concept of the Triple Soul Alignment.

The Three Realms Alignment aids in bringing what is outside inside (invocation), and the Triple Soul Alignment has almost the opposite effect: bringing what is inside to the outside (evocation). However, it is neither invocation nor evocation that forms the core of the magical act of either of these techniques; it is alignment and equilibrium.

When we draw in the essences of each realm and concentrate them in the natural energy-receptacles (cauldrons) within our bodies, we come to a pure alignment and a reflection of the external into the internal. We draw upon what is broad, substantial, and conceptual and infuse our beings with the potencies of the cosmos. By doing so, we empower ourselves to reveal and behold the Holy Centre (which exists in all places due to the limitlessness of All) and become the World Tree.

The Three Realms Alignment can be undergone before or after the Triple Soul Alignment. Either way creates an interesting, vivid, and palpable outcome. To align the Three Realms within the Three Cauldrons before aligning the Three Souls creates a pulse-point (inward-outward distillation-expansion) that flows into a primal and ecstatic connection with the potency of Self. To align the Three Souls before aligning the Three Realms within the Three Cauldrons is to create a space where we establish connection to Self before we move out and affect change in the world by becoming the fabric of its being.

Through my practice and teaching of these techniques over the years, they merged into one multi-layered alignment that I have passed for the last decade. This process can be found in detail in my book, *The Witch Belongs to the World: A Spell of Becoming*, as mentioned previously. Returning to this book, however, my heart has been warmed to know that people still practise them as presented here and that they are still relevant and meaningful. They demonstrate as well that we must not confuse the map for the territory, or the concept for the experience. These techniques work, and I am pleased to reintroduce them in printed form.

The Technique

Breathe using the Whole Breath Technique.[32] Cup both hands together below the navel at the belly. Take a deep breath in and open to perceive a cauldron in your belly. Feel its weightiness, its presence, and its receptivity. Breathe out. Take a deep breath in and allow your attention to delve down

---

[32] In brief, there are four groups of four counts in the Whole Breath. It involves breathing in through the nose into the belly for a count of four (or desired length) while visualising light entering the body. This breath is held for a count of four. The exhalation for a count of four comes from the mouth as an audible "Ha!" while the light flows out of the body. Four counts after the exhalation, the light returns through the crown of the head with the next inhalation.

deeply into the Land. Embrace the physical, the dense, and the deep. Breathe out. Take a deep breath in and mentally and energetically draw in the essence of the Land into the Cauldron of Belly. (This may appear green in colour.) Holding onto this breath of power, say aloud:

"Cauldron of Belly—hold Land!"

Cup both hands at the crown of your head and breathe out. Take a deep breath in and open to perceive a cauldron in your head. Feel its weightiness, its presence, and its receptivity. Breathe out. Take a deep breath in and allow your attention to expand outward to soar through Sky, through the celestial spheres, and to embrace the starlight of the deep, dark chasm of space. Breathe out. Take a deep breath in and mentally and energetically draw in the essence of the Sky into the Cauldron of Head. (This may appear violet or purple in colour.) Holding onto this breath of power, say aloud:

"Cauldron of Head—hold Sky!"

Cup both hands at your heart in your chest and breathe out. Take a deep breath in and open to perceive a cauldron in your heart. Feel its weightiness, its presence, and its receptivity. Breathe out. Take a deep breath in and allow your attention to delve and expand out simultaneously, embracing the Sea that encircles you and is heaving and sighing within your being. Feel and see the waves; smell the sea-salt air. Breathe out. Take a deep breath in and mentally and energetically draw in the essence of the Sea into the Cauldron of Heart. (This may appear silver-pink in colour.) Holding onto this breath of power, say aloud:

"Cauldron of Heart—hold Sea!"

If your eyes are closed, open them. With your power hand, trace a shining triquetra of light before you, saying:

"By Land, by Sky, by Sea..."

Hold your hands out as if channelling more light into the symbol and chant:

"By the Ancient Trinity..."

Open your arms to enfold and embrace the triquetra into your body and being. As you physically move your hands back to your heart and absorb the power of this conjured light, say:

"All Three Realms aligned within me."

Hold your hands to the ground. Visualise and feel that roots are delving deeply down into the soil through layers of compacted stone and clods of earth, through veins of mineral, and through pockets of underworld gas and chthonic water before finally drinking in the earth-fire of the molten core of the pulsing planet. Drinking that in, it will rush up through your body, which has become the trunk of an ancient tree, and say aloud with deep resonance:

"I am a Child of Earth…"

Bring your arms up, and spiral and spin your branches and boughs to paint the arc of the Heavens as they journey higher through every layer of atmospheric pressure, raised and aided by breezes and winds. Finally, break through the biosphere of Holy Mother Earth and drink in the silver-white light of the stars. This light races down swiftly, like quicksilver or lightning, into your body and being. Intone:

"…and of starry heaven…"

Bring your hands to cross over at your heart and feel the meeting of the Fire of Earth and the Fire of stars. As your heart pounds in your chest, feel each wave of this cosmic Sea pound the shores of your soul. You will feel enlivened and deeply centred. The opposites, the extremes, have been reconciled within the holy tween place, that force which derives from and is cradled by their love for one another. As the Sky stretches down in infinity to hold and be embraced by the Earth, so is the foaming, cresting Sea the liquid alchemy of their fusion and love. Hold this and say:

"…and the Sea within me knows and remembers."

This Three Realms Alignment with the Three Cauldrons and the becoming of the World Tree is sealed by the chanting of the following:

"I am the World Tree,
For all eternity,
So mote it be!"

The Spiral Soul Alignment

Breathe using the Whole Breath Technique.

Visualise or feel a yellow sphere of light emanating from your chest. This is the body of Talking Self. Feel the name vibrate throughout the yellow light; it strikes a deep reality. Talking Self names, categorises, delineates, communicates in worded language, and provides direct interface between human beings. Without Talking Self, one could not say "I am," differentiate from wholeness or void, or express uniqueness and distinction. Take a deep breath of power in and send it to Talking Self. It will glow with vivid radiance and become brighter and cleaner. Do this twice more.

Visualise or feel a red sphere of light below your navel. This is the body of Shadow Self, also called the Fetch. Feel the name vibrate throughout the red light; it strikes a deep truth. Shadow Self dreams, senses, feels, and communicates in dream language. Shadow Self is the primal ally of the Witch and is our truly primal, animal self. Without Shadow Self, one could not see, touch, taste, hear, smell, or receive impulse, intuition, or instinct. Take a deep breath of power in and send it to Shadow Self. It will glow with vivid radiance and become brighter and cleaner. Do this twice more.

Visualise or feel a blue sphere of light above your head: a blossoming star. This is Star Self. Feel the name vibrate throughout the blue light; it strikes a deep power. Star Self knows, is wise, sees beyond, and is directly connected to the limitless Divine. Without Star Self, we would not be connected to the Divine source in All Things. We would not be able to truly claim our sovereignty of Self and Divine origin (though all parts of Self are equally holy and sacred). Take a deep breath of power in and send it up to Star Self. It will glow with vivid radiance and become brighter and cleaner. On the third breath out, throw your head back and breathe the exhalation and sound of "Ha!" up into Star Self.

Star Self plummets down into the belly and Shadow Self; they rise to meet Talking Self at the Heart Centre (the place of mergence, harmony, and alignment). They will become one: the three primary colours running to mix and meld together. When you feel their holy unity, reflect and say the following aloud:

"My Spiral Soul is now aligned,
Beyond all space, beyond all time;
Within me now the trinity,
Of the Land, the Sky, and Sea.

I now invoke Own Holy Self,
Here and now—So mote it be!"

A Note on Congruence and Contradictions

You may notice that there is not necessarily congruence in anchor points for the realms and souls between the Three Realms Alignment and the Triple/Spiral Soul Alignment. I'd developed the Three Realms Alignment within the Wildwood Tradition, and the Triple Soul Alignment was passed to me by my Feri teachers as quite similar to the one described above, bar the sealing prayer (which I wrote).

In receiving, formalising, and passing on these techniques, I have felt it necessary to retain some form of contradiction to challenge and confront Talking Self, to excite Shadow Self, and to illumine Star Self. We come to realise that the "inconsistencies" are not discrepancies, and that there are many vital and valid pathways and paradigms. These techniques are not set in stone and are open to evolution and adaptation. If one feels drawn to create congruity between the Three Realms Alignment and the Spiral Soul Alignment in terms of the anchor points used, the techniques or their effects would not be compromised. The outcome may provide a different sensation, insight/gnosis, or energetic vibration, but different is often admirable.

I encourage you all to explore, deepen, contradict, challenge, and to walk the Wild/Crooked Way with ignited awareness and deep integrity.

Casting the Circle

Most Witches in this day and age will first learn how to cast a Circle before performing rites and casting spells. Though it is not always considered necessary to do so, especially by non-Wiccan traditions, a Circle is a useful and psychically supportive method of ensuring the Witch's safety and empowering and reinforcing the energy raised within. These are the reasons behind casting a Circle most people hear about. However, the Circle's fundamental principle is largely one of orientation to eternal space and endless time: to here and now.

When we cast the Circle, we are, in fact, tracing the boundaries of the boundless. We are enabling the human mind to comprehend the infinite and thereby gifting the Witch with the ability to create with the living cosmos. As we walk the perceived boundary of the Circle, we perceive light or flame forming a sphere above and below, which directs the "magnetic" principles of magic, the life force, to do just that. As we weave together the beginning and end of the Circle (which in truth has neither), our conscious mind surrenders to the unconscious, and we penetrate the Great Mystery. We—the self—are communicated to the cosmos—the All-Self—that "All that exists, all that was, and all that will be. Here it is…now and forever!"

Beyond the ceremonial aspects of casting a ritual Circle, there lies a mystery which effectively joins the participants with the limitless Divine. When we travel the Circle, we become the Circle, which, in effect, draws forth the very essence of the sacred through to the holy ground we tread. All that is lies here in this moment. The ignited consciousness of the Witch actualises the Eternal Now. The Circle, as a symbol of an underlying sacred reality, effectively communicates the interconnection of all things and, thus, the bigger picture. We are able to transform our consciousness, transcend the ego as limited "I," and dissolve into the All Self. Some Witches—and I would be one of them—would call this "sabbatic." Thus, we are oriented to the universe as a whole and not to a version or piece of it.

As we cast the Circle, we are also reinforcing our experience of the Divine as immanent. We mentally and communally convey that this Circle is cast not to sacralise but to commune with the inherent sanctity of things. If we were attempting to imbue a place or time with a sacred quality, we would be casting squares or triangles (and this is done in some

High Magic orders). As with all things in the magical arts, the symbolism is potent and often universal. The Circle (and the spiral) is the symbol of infinity, rebirth, the womb from which we emerge, and of the ever-renewing cycles of mighty nature.

Between the Worlds…In All the Worlds

"The Circle is cast. I am between the worlds, in all the worlds. What happens between the worlds touches all the worlds. What touches all the worlds changes all the worlds. So mote it be."

The above are the words I use to seal and affirm my Circle during my weekly devotional rituals. They are my adaptation of a similar Reclaiming Circle-casting sealing. I use these words because they embody the attitude I seek to reinforce and manifest consciously day by day. As the Circle empowers the Witch to touch the limitless and enter the time of no-time and the place of no-place, this also extends to the idea of the liminal, or what I like to call "threshold consciousness."

In the Wildwood Tradition, we speak with aspirants about how the tween and twixt places are magically potent and desirable for ritual. For instance, if you stand where the Land meets the Sea meets the Sky (on the beach at the edge of the water), you will be standing in a holy (whole) place charged with the power of the Three Worlds meeting. For this reason, the sabbats, the esbats, dawn, midday, dusk, and midnight (the stations of the sun) are also considered powerful occasions. Ultimately, all places are liminal and between, especially if we consider that, as humans, we tend to be entrenched in dualistic paradigms. Knowing this, however, we can utilise this understanding quite powerfully. Here is that which is cast as mundane; here is that which is cast as magical; here is the Circle in between; all duality dissolve, I bathe in the numinous.

If we are between the worlds, then it only makes sense that we are touching them all, and, therefore, we bring further depth and insight into the preceding section on Casting the Circle. I cast the Circle to temporarily create an affirmed sacred space in which I am between the realms and thus able to contact all simultaneously, or one or two in particular. By entering the tween place, I enter the river of life which surges through the veins of the body of the Goddess, and I become not only one cell of the Greater Being, but I am empowered to move and exist *as* the Greater Being. I actualise the deep potential within myself to be a Creator-Destroyer-Transformer. It is not only possible to create in a linear Point A to Point B fashion when we are within the Circle (and we are at all times; we must merely be conscious of the fact). It is also possible to divine the future, know the past, and understand the present (remember timelessness), traverse the manifold realms, and interact with spirit-beings consciously. This is contextualised as Shamanic when these things are done for the benefit of something more than self as ego: self as necessity, community, and cosmos.

The Elemental Pathways of Sacred Manifestation and Gnosis

"Earth my body, Water my blood, Air my breath and Fire my spirit."
—Author unknown

After the Circle is cast, we generally acknowledge and formally invoke or honour the Elemental powers. This is done separately from an invocation of the Mighty Ones or the Watchers who guard and witness the rite, depending on the tradition. My allies, in this case, are the Elements themselves; without them, I am nothing. Though Spirit both precedes and is the product of the Elements' fusion, as the well-known Pagan chant above illustrates, the Elements are the building blocks of life and thus activate and orient my consciousness.

Let us consider one of the most common ways that modern Witches move through the Elements in the Circle. When we take the general outline of Elemental invocation, starting in the East with Air, and then travelling *deasil* (in the way of the sun) to Fire where the sun is at the midday point (South or North), Water, and then Earth at the midnight point (North or South), we discover a pathway of manifestation from least dense to most dense. When we consider the energetic dynamics behind spellcraft (determination and manifestation), it becomes clear that the Elemental formula empowers such practices. By Air, we first conceive of our desire; by Fire, we impassion ourselves and dare to seize it; by Water, our will is channelled and thus directed; and by Earth, it is made manifest and grounded in the tangible reality. By touching and triggering the highest vibrations of the Elemental planes, we affect the natural process of manifestation, which is initiated by desire. This we know as Witches through the various creation stories we have received and envisioned concerning the Cosmic Goddess who dreamed herself into being, looked upon her reflection, and desired it—thus, all came into being.

If we trace the Circle backwards and unravel it, we begin with Earth and end at Air, where we originally began. When I was travelling in Britain in late 2008, I had an insight through the Wildwood Tradition symbol regarding this Elemental unfolding. The two serpents are always drawn meeting four times with their coils and then meeting and kissing at a fifth point. In one clear moment of gnosis—Divine knowledge—this equated with the fivefold kiss in my mind. Suddenly, the Elemental associations of each point kissed in the rite as we enact it became obvious. If we regard the human being as a geometric or symbolic representation of the Divine, and we hold the head to contain the Divine numen as limitless potential, then we can lift the veil of separation which seeks to brand us as "lowly" or "sinful" and awake to our primordial, innate Godhood. Linking this insight back to the fivefold kiss illuminates the point:[33]

- We kiss the feet and say:

  "Blessed be these feet that dance upon the Earth."

  I associate this with Earth, as the feet stand upon the temple of the Holy Spirit—Earth—the flesh of the Divine.
- We kiss the knees and say:

  "Blessed be these knees that kneel in the river of life."

  I link this point with Water, tracing the Circle backwards to unravel it, as when we kneel, we surrender and flow with the natural rhythms and tides of the world around us.
- We kiss the sex and say:

  "Blessed be this sex that burns brightly with the Fire of creativity."

---

[33] The words here derive from the version of the fivefold kiss I teach to my Shamanic Craft apprentices, derived from personal gnosis through a Wildwood symbol. They relate to the Elemental Pathway of Gnosis: tracing back, from most dense (Earth) to least dense (Air), the Circle of Spirit which contains and comprises the alchemy of the Elements.

I associate this point with Fire, as this is the holy seat of the generative life force. This is the portal to passion and unbridled desire.

- We kiss the breasts and say:

"Blessed be these breasts that draw in the breath of life."

I link this point with Air, as the lungs which take in and expel oxygen to sustain the body's vitality are held here. This is the place in the body in which the Air is literally enshrined.

- We kiss the lips and say:

"Blessed be these lips which sing the songs of Spirit."

I associate this point with Spirit, the fifth Element, because it is through the lips that we correspond and communicate with each other in an enlivened and raw manner. Words are a powerful tool for shaping consciousness by way of shaping our perceptions (and, therefore, our realities), and Spirit is the substance of that consciousness.

By unravelling the Elemental Circle back to its point of origin—Spirit—we are able to transcend the illusion that we are separate and without Divinity, truly able to see and intimate that at the core of our selves lies the hidden potency some call the Holy Guardian Angel, the Buddha, or Goddess. Knowing this sacred truth liberates the soul to soar to heights unconceived by the mind that believes itself to be determined by supernatural forces rather than the creativity that flows through all, within us as well as without. The densest is the most spiritual; the flesh is the Spirit, and the Spirit is the flesh.

East of Where?

When we invoke the Elemental powers, we are telling a story. We are conveying a message of what we hold to be immeasurably sacred, and we are communing with magical laws which will allow us to partake in the sovereignty gifted to all living beings if celebrated.

We have previously established that nothing in existence is without its Elemental support. On a chemical level, Air represents matter in a gaseous state; Fire is the energetic interchange of heat and electricity;

Water is all matter in a liquid state; and Earth represents the physical forms which Spirit becomes. Behind all of this is the Prime Mover: the Spirit, which pervades, informs, and directs all things. This subtle fifth Element embodies the active intelligence of a living cosmos. When we honour the Elements in our Circle, we are retelling the ancient story of creation; we are alluding to the hidden principles which make up life.

Needless to say, the Elements live in all things. (In fact, the Elements *are* all things.) However, it is often true that modern Witches invoke the Elemental powers from the four cardinal directions. Depending on the tradition and the geographical region, the Elemental directional correspondences will be different. Generally speaking, however, the placement is Air in East, Fire in North/South, Water in West, and Earth in South/North (depending on the hemisphere). Why the directional emphasis?

A while ago, I listened to an episode of *Elemental Castings*, T. Thorn Coyle's podcast. In this particular episode, Thorn conducted an interview with Wiccan prison chaplain Patrick McCollum. The interview is quite lengthy, but the two talk about the concept of the immanent Divine and how one of McCollum's early teachers in the Craft took him to a vacant parking lot and asked whether he could see the sacred in this place. At first, he replied that he couldn't, but after thought, reflection, and a word or two of insight from his teacher, he realised that yes, despite the asphalt-covered Earth, everything present had its origins in, was, and is nature. This realisation is one many urban Pagans and Witches come to cherish.

The necessary step after receiving this particular insight is to then consider that humans have a very powerful and often unconscious impact on the world. Through sheer devotion and stubborn will, we are able to manipulate the energetic patterns that imbue the world of form with paradigms it uses to arrange itself. Despite the raw elemental origin of all things, we as a species have twisted and degraded our raw materials, creating a world which rests on the idea that we are separate from nature and that nature is resources. Thus, we are given colonial and consumerist freedom to abuse these resources, destroying and desecrating those things which are essential to our and all livelihoods.

When we cast the Circle to embrace the All and call upon the Elements via the directions, we introspective Witches are then encouraged to look outward to the world of form which we move, eat, and relate in; we celebrate it, restoring its inherent sacred nature to our consciousness.

We invest attention in the outward world as an extension of our own internal identity. Without acknowledging our powerful connections, we forget what it means to be alive.

When we look to the East, the North, the West, and the South, and then return to the Centre, we are saying, "To the East of here is Air, to the North of here is Fire, to the West of here is Water, to the South of here is Earth. Here. Now. Forever I am in the here and now!" We become enlightened to the fact that we are standing *somewhere*, in place. We are alive and conscious in the very centre of all things because the horizon reclines into the infinite, and we are able to look around and be faced with boundlessness, with life as embodied by the Elemental agents of power.

A Shamanic Rite of Casting the Circle and Invoking the Elements

I have decided to include a Shamanic Witchcraft rite of casting the Circle and invoking the Elements for interest's sake and to provide any curious seekers with a potential template. You will need nothing other than yourself as conductor of the rite and offerings for the spirits of place (such as frankincense) unless, of course, you feel drawn to include representations of the Elements or you feel incense and candles would help to arouse the primal senses and create an appropriate atmosphere. It is important to understand that the words mean nothing without emotional understanding, insight, and investment fuelling their expression.

1. Acknowledge the Land you are in and the Peoples here.
2. Align the Spiral Soul and the Three Realms.
3. Touch your hand to the Earth/ground and declare the following with conviction:

> *"Spirits of place, I lay this offering for thee.*
> *May you welcome me as I welcome you."*

Place your offerings.
4. Face the East as the direction of the rising Sun. Hold out your power hand at shoulder level (or point with your index finger if you prefer) and begin to walk deasil whilst envisioning light or sensing power

gathering and concentrating around your sacred space. Intone the following three sentences, one for each of the three rounds:

"I am here. Here is now. Now is forever."

5.   Once you have completed the circumambulations, the following sealing and affirming statement can be made:

"The Circle is cast as it was, as it is, and as it always shall be. I am between the worlds, in all the worlds. What happens between the worlds touches all the worlds. What touches all the worlds changes all the worlds. So mote it be."

6.   Facing East, clap three times loudly. After the third clap, as your hands pull away from each other, vibrate the word "East" through that space. Call forth the spirit of Air with your power hand outstretched to the direction (at shoulder height):

"East of here is Air! Peace, praise,
and power to the Air and Spirits of the East!"

When you speak the word "here," bring your outward-stretching hand to your heart. Upon uttering "peace, praise, and power," open both arms outward as if to embrace and bring both hands to cross over the heart when sealing the invocation. Continue this for North, West, South, and Centre.

7.   Facing North/South,[34] clap three times loudly. After the third clap, as your hands pull away from each other, vibrate the word "North" or "South" through that space. Call forth the spirit of Fire with your power hand outstretched to the direction (pointing straight and upward):

"North/South of here is Fire! Peace, praise,
and power to the Fire and Spirits of the North/South!"

---

[34] If you are in the Northern Hemisphere, deasil refers to a clockwise direction (rather than anti-clockwise for the Southern Hemisphere), and thus the East-North-West-South route becomes East-South-West-North.

8. Facing West, clap three times loudly. After the third clap, as your hands pull away from each other, vibrate the word "West" through that space. Call forth the spirit of Water with your power hand outstretched to the direction (at waist height):

    "West of here is Water! Peace, praise,
    and power to the Water and Spirits of the West!"

9. Facing South/North, clap three times loudly. After the third clap, as your hands pull away from each other, vibrate the word "South" or "North" through that space. Call forth the spirit of Earth with your power hand outstretched to the direction (pointing straight and downward):

    "South/North of here is Earth! Peace, praise,
    and power to the Earth and Spirits of the South/North!"

10. Stand in the Centre of the Circle, facing inward. Clap loudly once and declare the fusion of the Four Elements. Call forth Spirit and open both arms as if to embrace the Centre:

    "In the Centre of Here is Spirit! Peace, praise,
    and power to the Spirit and Spirits of the Centre!"[35]

11. To unravel the Circle after the work/communion, give thanks and bow facing the East and standing in the Centre: farewell Spirit, then Earth, Water, Fire, and Air (turning to face each direction as you do). The following devocations may be used:

    Centre: "Here was Spirit. Here is Spirit. Now and forever, blessed be."
    Earth: "Here was Earth. Here is Earth. Now and forever, blessed be."
    Water: "Here was Water. Here is Water. Now and forever, blessed be."
    Fire: "Here was Fire. Here is Fire. Now and forever, blessed be."
    Air: "Here was Air. Here is Air. Now and forever, blessed be."

---

[35] A further spoken blessing which will accommodate and give reverence to the above, below, and centre direction is a Wildwood Circle-casting seal which states, "As above, so below—to and from us all things flow."

12. To open or release the Circle, simply walk *widdershins* (against the sun) and draw in the power of the Circle through your receptive hand as you make three circumambulations. At your third and final circle, draw in the last of the power and then let it pour out through you into the Earth. Seal this by saying:

> *"Into the Earth for healing. The Circle is open but unbroken.*
> *Merry have we met, merry have we been, merry may we part,*
> *and merry meet again."*

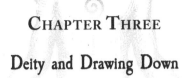

Chapter Three

Deity and Drawing Down

In my first book, *Spirited: Taking Paganism Beyond the Circle*, I devote an entire chapter to exploring the many "theisms" which exist within Paganism in the modern world. These include polytheism, animism, pantheism, monism, henotheism, ditheism (also called *duotheism*), and archetypal psychology. This chapter will discuss the Shamanic understandings of deity as what I have come to call the "hidden potencies" contained within and saturated by concentrated Divine power. This chapter will also delve into the age-old practice of trance possession, also referred to as "drawing down" or "aspecting."[36]

The Gods Amongst Us

In a Shamanic worldview, which possesses the animistic perspective that the world is populated by spirits, the Gods are powerful beings of mythic stature who know explicitly their purposes and are bound to fulfil them. Indeed, these cosmic hidden potencies are so endowed with meaning and devotion that they have become, apparently, greater or transcendent to the lowly humans who serve them. Shamans and Witches (and other aware people) know better.

In *Fifty Years in the Feri Tradition*, Cora Anderson wrote of the Gods, "…it must be understood that the spirits and the Gods do not have

---

[36] Reclaiming Priestess Ravyn Stanfield told me that it is a general "rule" that in the Reclaiming Tradition of Witchcraft the vessel does not fill with the deity's presence/force more than 70%. In this sense, there is still a degree of self-consciousness and determined engagement on the vessel's part. This, then, is what is meant by aspecting: a light form of facilitated drawing down and not full possession.

physical bodies as we do. Although the Gods are much lighter life forms than ourselves, we are all in the same family. We can create much more mana than beings having only etheric bodies. The Gods need us and we need them"[37] (23). This echoes sentiments made by Gerald Gardner to the same effect in his published nonfiction works on Witchcraft.

Traditionally, Witches related to the Gods as potent spirit-beings who are either allies or indifferent; rarely is a deity considered to be particularly antagonistic towards a human being or the human race.[38] Depending on the depth and sincerity of your personal relationship with your own deities, guides, totems, or similar spirits, you may feel the desire or call to dedicate yourself as priestex or devotee to them. More broadly, I have termed the conscious relationships we cultivate with spirit-beings as "allyships," as this word reinforces the mentality that we are working together to achieve a goal and ride fate. It also seems stronger and more intimate than the word "alliance," with its political overtones. The idea of allies cherishes the animistic and pantheistic experiences of the world as alive and intelligent rather than stagnant and inanimate. However, I will explore these concepts in more depth in the next chapter.

When working with the beings we name as deities, it is simply enough to know that we are also Divine and thus no different, except for the subtle allusion that, somehow, the Gods perfectly and explicitly understand their purposes and endeavour to fulfil them to every end. This is part and parcel of flowing with the pure will of nature. The Gods are Hidden Potencies because they have also been called the Mysterious Ones (Reclaiming) and the Mighty Ones (British Traditional). Thus, in creating working relationships with them, we become the Hidden Children because we have released the restrictive and damaging idea that we are somehow lesser.

Many Witches consciously embrace their spiritual pathways as roads towards fully actualising their personal Divinity to become (a) God(dess). This philosophy is echoed in West African-based religions such as Ifa,

---

[37] *Mana* is a Hawaiian word referring to "life force." To me, it is another word for magic.

[38] There are deities in the various world pantheons that are viewed by the general populace to be averse to the harmonious order of the universe, including Set and Satan. However, time and philosophical discernment have both proven that these "evil" Gods are actually powerfully dynamic and an essential component of the organic wellspring we call life. Destruction, death, and decay are necessary processes of release and rebirth.

Lucumi, or Voodoo (also known as Vodou or Vodun), which teach that the *Lwa* (the venerated spirits, or the messengers and mediators of a transcendent Creator) are our beloved dead who have evolved into powerful spirits encapsulating both cosmic and terrestrial orders.

Why are the Gods Important?

I call the Gods the Hidden Potencies because they are themselves embodied and energetic spirit-maps who guide us through specialised ability and inclination. The Gods of Fire may be, by natural evolution, denizens of the creative arts (Brigid), smithcraft (Hephaestos), and volcanoes (Pele). The Gods of healing are also the Gods of solar influence and light (Apollon), hygiene and cleanliness (Hygiea), and the plant-world (Airmid). All things are connected; however, specialised groupings and resonances also naturally occur.

If we consider the Yoruban and Celtic teachings, the Gods are also our ancestors, the beloved dead that we have crowned "deity." We have gifted the immortal lines of procreation and perpetuation with powerfully literal and symbolic leaders and sovereigns. Those spirits which have become our deities draw their power from the cosmos at large and the raw forces in nature, which are the driving catalysts for change and growth. However, it is also true that they have become deities because of potent skill in one form or another. Consider the Tuatha Dé Danann and the mythological cycles of their stories. According to this myth, the people of the Goddess Danu formed the fifth invasion wave of Ireland, adding to the historical overview of the legendary island. The Irish themselves are said to be born of the Children of Mil (also known as the Milesians or the Gaels), who conquered Ireland and created a treaty with the Tuatha Dé Danann to honour their spiritual sovereignty and memory.[39]

The stories of Lugh Lamhadha and Cú Chullain speak of ancestral memories that we have absorbed and passed on in sacred lineage, although these stories—like many Indigenous and cultural mythologies—have been impacted by imperialism and colonialism. There are beliefs amongst various Celts today that the Gaels may be descended from the Tuatha, if not also from other various pre-existing peoples of Ireland (such as the

---

[39] The name "Ireland" itself derives from *Eriu,* one of the three sisters of sovereignty connected to the Tuatha Dé Danann and their tribes.

Firbolg). After all, there are many tales of intermarriage and love affairs between the invading Gaels and the Sidhe folk (the people of the hollow hills, to which the Tuatha Dé Danann retreated and made their homes).

I mention all of this because it is within such myth that we begin to understand there isn't all that much difference between human characters and deities. In fact, there is constant and seemingly mundane prattle and pretence that goes on between the two. The stories also help to align the audiences with the mythic associations of various characters. For instance, Lugh is the many-skilled God because he was able to impress a gathering of his people by announcing to a gatekeeper that he possessed all the skills in one person that the people within the walls attested to individually. Many of those skills were mortal tasks and endeavours but are treated within the story as absolutely vital and on equal footing with so-called supernatural ability. It also has to be understood that the "supernatural" isn't necessarily super or beyond the natural; in fact, in traditional societies, it would be ludicrous to suggest that the Gods were beyond nature because nature is all things, and the Gods are contained within that blessed Mystery.

This begs the question, why are the Gods important? Why do we venerate and honour beings that might not be beyond our own potential? Why do we sacrifice to forces which are not in any way superior to us? The first answer or insight to this question is that Pagan traditions and teachings tend not to view the world as compartmentalised; the dividing lines are often blurred and inconsistent (eternal paradox). Animistic and pantheistic worldviews embrace all things as sacred and consider all things as possessing a numinous force which intimately connects it to the unitive force, engendering and inspiring all things to begin with, or reverences the infinity of things.

There isn't necessarily a definitive beginning, so the Gods would never be considered above or beyond our personal potential, which is absolutely why we venerate and honour them. The Gods are perfectly aligned with their Divine destinies and ultimately know their explicit and implicit purposes within the Web of Life. Thus, to consciously open to one's Will and to live expressing it in every moment is to become God-like. Eventually, this can lead to transcending the illusion of separation and claiming sovereignty of self and, thus, sovereignty of purpose and destiny. The Gods are models and metaphors for us to align and ally with to further work towards actualising our potential and fulfilling our karmic purposes.

In *Spirited*, I speak of how I perceive the Gods through a polytheistic lens. Deities are energetic force-forms built around or deriving from the raw catalytic powers in nature (fire, lightning, storm, earthquake, rain, and so on). This also extends into the conceptual or emotional: transformation, fear, love, anger, radiance, beauty, truth, and more. I tend to be of the opinion that all beliefs, ideas, and opinions are true in the sense that if they are able to marry with and integrate others, they are viable because they expand and open our minds and souls rather than closing or limiting us from experiencing the transcendent. I think of transcendent as immanence extending beyond (panentheism), the indwelling consciousness eternally existing and thus changing. When we are able to transcend and still understand that we are within, we are well on our way to personal Godhood.

The Nature of the Hidden Potencies and Why to Honour Them if We Are Equal

The principle that the Earth is a sacred manifestation (or body, if you will) can only be truly understood when experienced. We have been so conditioned by the paradigm of duality that if you chose to say body and spirit, you would instantly picture a conceptual dichotomy rather than a simple functional difference between a continuum of capacities. All, however, is Divine.

Our deities, the Hidden Potencies, are creative stimuli. (By its own definition, creativity also encompasses destruction). To illustrate the point made here, Demeter is considered a mother or Earth goddess, so she is empowered by a dynamic current beyond her own specificity. She is also that which *she is,* which gives rise to the fact that I am speaking of Demeter now. Mythically derived or not, she is because I am speaking of her and have a knowledge of her beyond myself (or the self which says "I am"). There is "a" spirit within the "I" of Demeter that animates her myth and lends to her presence in the world(s). The spirit is hidden; it is a potency because it has deepened and exists fully on many levels, conscious of the variety of manifestations it adopts to carry out such a function. This hidden potency is magically and spiritually adept, not necessarily through guile (although there are spirits who have taken that road to potency), but because of the origin, process, and continued perpetuation of the living myth of Demeter.

The spirit of Demeter exists unquestionably; philosophically speaking, no one could deny that. It is irrelevant whether we say archetype, demon, illusion, fancy of folk-need, or heroine; Demeter exists because I am speaking of her now with an awareness of her sphere of influence. I know her because she allows herself to be known in the same way that this computer before me allows itself to be known, as does the chair I am sitting on and the faded vase of roses before me. They, too, are potent because they exist, and I know of their presence, and, thus, enters the Principle of Sacred Equality. Truly, the term *god(dess)* or *deity* is a functional or experiential term we give to spirits and things which reveal themselves to us from a "hidden" capacity, having influence, providence, and direct relevance and relationships with our own living souls (potencies).

In this way, we can also understand what is meant by the concept of Lwa and Orisha amongst the traditions which originate from the West African diaspora. This is reflected in how the spirits the Yoruban cultures honour are evolved ("transcended") spirits of ancestral lineage which have potentised through natural processes. They have embraced or flowed into or from a mythic heritage, differentiated, and self-actualised to the point where the Ego is not the Boundary; it is the origin supremely surpassed. It is the seed of a force-field or form that lends itself to presence, providence, and influence on a scale not always personal, often universal, but definitely communal. Therefore, the deities are creative stimuli for the ongoing organic processes of what we call "universe."

This begs the question, why uphold or honour a deity if I am quintessentially equal to them? The answer is clear: why not, if we are all Divinely equal? The honouring of each part of that Divinity is attributed to a yearning for the wholeness of those parts and a reconciliation of difference by the nature of inherent interconnection. You are equal to your mother, though not in every function. However, if you did not honour your mother as mother and love her for her care and compassion, the relationship would soon become severely imbalanced and negatively impact both of you until honour and respect entered the exchange of the relationship (and likewise in the other direction). We are all defined by what we are in relationships with. Our qualities evolve and adapt to what and who enters our sphere of potency: living myth. The fact that Aphrodite, Hermes, Hekate, and Persephone (amongst others) enter my sphere of potency, as I enter theirs' in the name of honour and reverence, is because I identify an indwelling identity which is upheld and enlivened by their presence and relationship. I am who I am, beyond my ego, because of them, and they are uniquely who they are with me through me. To and with anyone else, Aphrodite would not be my Aphrodite, but would still be Aphrodite. Thus is the nature of Spirits, of Potency, Hidden or not.

Deity versus Divine

Many religionists would equate deity with the Divine as an "end-all-be-all" ultimate definition. This limits the spiritualist (as opposed to the religionist) from accepting that they are also Divine or of God. In the Craft, we learn the art of *drawing down* or voluntarily facilitating trance possession (which will be explored shortly). I want to emphasise here that what we call deity is, in fact, simply a small part of the overarching "allness" that is the Divine. Divinity is simply another word for the radiance of all life, for the eternal blessing which is innately connected to Being. Deity or deities are within us and without us; they are archetypal and autonomous beings with self-agendas and accords. The force that many would call God is not so much "deity" as it is another synonym for the unitive force pervading consciousness.[40] This is why we call it a Mystery. Approach the Gods as you would approach another human being—with invested interest in experiencing their unique truths and realities—and the response may astonish, but also empower, you.

Working with the Gods as a Shamanic Witch

The Shamanic Witch perceives all things and beings as possessing personalised intelligence and awareness. As described above, the Gods are worth our time and attention because they represent (and are) eternal potencies which we either aspire towards, honour as great and worthy, or would wish to temporarily borrow to enrich and empower a particular aspect of our own or someone else's life. Following, I will describe the various allyships a Shamanic Witch may have with a deity:

- **Soul Deity:** A term I coined to describe a relationship with a deity with whom we are irrevocably and undeniably interwoven, simply *because.* These are the hardest allyships to explain or rationalise, and I would go so far as to suggest that they are akin to the notion of soulmates within human relationships. Many people who do not use this particular term would identify this kind of relationship as one with their patron deity. However, I believe a Soul Deity extends far

---

[40] Victor Anderson was quoted as saying that originally the word *God* meant "that which is to be reverenced."

beyond the often-utilitarian nature of Divine patronage. A Soul Deity cannot be sought out; it merely happens, and when you know, you know. For me, I do not know where I begin, and Persephone—my Soul Goddess—ends.

- **Patron Deity:** A deity to whom we are allied because of our own unique skills and predispositions. For instance, a poet may be allied with Brigid, a healer with Asklepios, and a dancer with Lord Siwa. A patron deity may reveal themselves to be Soul Deity. For instance, if you are absolutely defined by your poetry (as a metaphorical creative well-spring of all life-experience) or by your healing (as an eternal pursuit to aid in the enhancing of the vitality of wholeness), then chances are the allyship will deepen into something much more intimate. Patron deities are either extremely obvious or elusive, and, as with any kind of spirit-being, there may be more than one, especially if you are devoted to a few things in your life (such as sciences, arts, crafts, professions, and hobbies).

- **Working Deity:** A deity to whom we are allied on purpose. This allyship is often noted as Neo-Paganism's spiritual downfall or proof of the rampant cultural appropriation perpetrated by eclectic practitioners or styles. In truth, cultural appropriation does happen in many traditions and situations, and my advice is to always approach foreign (to you) cultures, customs, deities, and spirits with an attitude of humility, respect, and no expectations. It isn't a crime to pray to or work with a deity that is not of your "people" or culture; this happened often across many eras in the past. However, it is essential to first have reason and resonance if you are to embark on such work with a deity. I implore folks to consider saying, "I will work with Aphrodite," rather than, "I am going to use Aphrodite in this spell," as these are drastically different things. The latter is especially disrespectful to spirit-workers who are in deep connection with these beings. Aphrodite might not like it, either.

- **Power Deity:** A deity to whom we are allied for self-empowerment. A great illustrating example would be Sekhmet for me. She stalked into my Circle in early 2007 after a rather horrendous break-up and, taking over my body, she slashed and tore away at the residual negativity, guilt, and remorse. She renewed my life force and vigour and gave me strong claim over myself. I now count Sekhmet as one of my Gods of Breath, and ever since our first encounter, I have discovered a strong feeling of past-life connection with her and Ubasti. A power deity is akin to the concept of a power animal.

- **Familial Deity:** A deity to whom we are allied because of strong familial bonds; this also goes for "chosen" family, such as strongly connected circles of friends and spiritual families (including but not limited to covens). A familial deity may not necessarily translate as one in which you invest any particular emotional relationship, but because of underlying and enduring connections with particular people, these deities begin to notice and greet us on equal terms. For instance, I would identify Siwa, Ganesha, and Saraswati as familial deities because they are my father's main Gods, and he actively prays to them for my and my family's health and well-being. Energetically, they have become working deities through concerted effort. Other familial deities may simply respect you from afar but never engender other contact.

Again, with any deity (or any being, for that matter), it is important to first familiarise oneself with the associative correspondences on all levels and myths pertaining specifically to the deity. It pays to approach any deity with careful time and consideration so as to honour the exchange and empower it.

It is important to understand that these categorisations of deity-allyships are never so cut and dried, and that tends to go for all things in life, especially when related to the esoteric. For instance, it is quite possible for a familial deity to become a working deity, then a patron, and perhaps eventually a soul deity. In every situation and with every deity, it is important to regard all as individuals with their own unique worth and mythos. Retaining and cultivating an open mind and explorative attitude will ensure a perpetually fertile spirit.

A Note on Formalising an Allyship with Deity

I will not include any particular rituals here as I have found in my own personal experience that when it comes to affirming the allyship (however it is defined, whether it is a working deity or soul deity), the experience is absolutely relative to the deity, feeling, and situation. For instance, when it came time for me to acknowledge my dedication to Hekate, I simply walked outside, sat down, grounded, centred, lit a silver candle, and spoke casually with her. I recall her responding in a very similar, laid-back manner. I did not create or affirm space; I did not utter a delicate prayer or invocation; I simply sat down with her, connected, and communed because that is what felt right. On the other hand, when I first chose to dedicate myself to Persephone's priesthood, I did devise a ritual for the Winter Solstice that year that would formally bring us together in such a union. It was perhaps the first time I employed traditional Greek ritual and language, and I did so to honour the legacy and origins of Persephone. Ultimately, my advice here is to honour the deity and the burgeoning or affirming allyship by researching, communing, and intuiting.

Drawing Down the Gods: Trance Possession

The ability to become a vessel for the spirits, to draw down the Gods into physical incarnation, and to provide the deities a way to viscerally express themselves in forthright presence is known as "trance possession." Many contemporary Pagans use the term "drawing down" or "aspecting" (especially in the Reclaiming Tradition) to refer to a similar experience.

Drawing down the Gods is not necessarily something that is included in the everyday handbook on Witchcraft. Allusions to the Drawing Down of the Moon ceremony, which occurs in British Traditional Witchcraft is, often outlined, but the internal process undergone by the vessel (the priestex who will become the deity) is rarely, if ever, gone into in any detail as it is considered oathbound.

The Spiritual and Shamanic Significance of Trance Possession

The practice of trance possession links us with and reinforces our philosophies of immanence and deity versus or within Divinity. We are able to perceive and interact with the hidden potencies and acquire secret wisdom whilst activating psychic wellsprings of power within. When we draw in the Gods, we are effectively conveying a powerful message to one another: "The Gods are within our reach. We are able to know and bless them, and they are able to know and bless us."

One of my dear friends, Jarrah, said early in our friendship that being able to witness the wonder and reality of the Gods viscerally and vividly allows us to transcend the barriers which inhibit us from understanding the holy truth of interconnection.

In the Introduction to this book, we discussed the magical worldview of infinite possibility and how opening the door to the hidden world(s) inspires initiatory awakenings of immense proportion. We can access and be privy to wonders we would never have dreamed of previously. Infinite possibility becomes a concrete and overt reality rather than a metaphorical subtlety. The difference is that Witches enact their innate ability to reach for the stars and become them rather than limit themselves to stargazing. Life teaches us that awareness *of* is awareness *with,* and thus, even knowing and seeing the stars is enough for many. Perhaps this is the distinction between Witches and non-Witches. Witches embrace infinite possibility as personal destiny rather than a guiding metaphor. Either way, this absolutely relates to the issues of confidence and trust, which allow us to welcome in the deities completely and surrender.

In Shamanic cultures and traditions, the fact that spirits are inclined to express themselves through our bodies and their varied functions is cosmologically accepted. Animism opens the door to perceiving the spirits, and engaging with them is a matter of consciousness, preparedness, skill, and integrity. The spirits respect the same things humans do, as we are all of each other, so the Golden Rule applies here: *do unto others as you would have them do unto you.* Trance possession (or mediumship of any kind) is seen as a gift granted by humility, ecstasy, and sacred contract. As devotees and practitioners of a wisdom path, we are concerned with the accumulation of knowledge for practical and poetic application in any dimension. It should also be noted that though ecstatic bliss is a product of successful trance possession, ecstasy is a vital component to effectively catalyse a possessory experience.

If we consider Vodou once more, we discover that the Lwa are prone to "riding" their devotees like horses. Most rituals within these religions are concerned with such outcomes, and great offerings and sacrifices are made before, during, and after trance possessions to secure the benevolence of the various spirits. I coined the term "allyship" to embody such interrelations between humanity and venerated spirit-beings such as the Gods and the Lwa. Cultivating an allyship is akin to sustaining a celebrated friendship. We must pay time and effort, provide attention to detail, and show open honesty. We are then able to encounter the spirits on both their and our terms and create equal partnerships in which all parties benefit. In fact, it is my experience that the act of ritual itself is an offering which pleases both the spirits and the human participants, as the energy is raised and shared communally, bringing us all to ecstasy.

Anyone who has drawn down will tell you that there are various states of consciousness relating to the depth of the trance and dependent upon the psychic predisposition, preparedness, and experience of the individual undertaking the ceremony. For instance, those who are natural seers are already open to the spirits. (Similarly, it is a common belief that Witches are very easy to hypnotise as we voluntarily open ourselves to such mental and emotional suggestion regularly.) Proper preparation in its many facets is also a necessity. I encourage all of my aspirants and students to either eat very lightly (meaning no meat, refined carbohydrates, or sugars) or to fast for the day of the drawing down (which generally happens after sunset) and, perhaps, for half of the day before as well. I touched on the sacred nature and magical usage of fasting in *By Land, Sky & Sea*, but I encourage anyone interested in the details and dynamics of fasting to read *A Witch's Shadow Magick Compendium* by Raven Digitalis.

Willow Polson references four levels of "drawing down" in her book *The Veil's Edge* in terms of personal consciousness and how it is gradually magnified until full or deep possession is reached. These derive from an essay presented at an annual conference of the Covenant of the Goddess in the US. However, many people, due to a multiplicity of reasons, will never reach (or let themselves reach) full possession. These "grades," if you will, do not form a hierarchy as much as elucidate varying layers of trance states during the act of drawing down deities. These four layers are as follows:

- **Enhancement:** The vessel feels imbued with the energy/mythos of the deity, but not necessarily its visceral energetic presence. The vessel is still very much conscious of self.
- **Inspiration:** The vessel has deepened consciousness so that the presence of the deity may be received. At this time, the deity is connected on an energetic level to the vessel and may direct the body with unique expression and offer wisdom and advice through the vessel. The vessel's understanding of self begins to blur.
- **Integration:** The deity has merged into the vessel, and all acts and words are of a different nature, almost ephemeral or else very unlike the usual character of the vessel. Some would say, in this state, the vessel is "half full" with the deity's presence. The human identity of the vessel begins to dissolve.

- **Possession:** The deity is fully within the vessel, acting and speaking of its own will and accord. Feats of great strength or other "supernatural" acts may occur, such as the raising of winds, the touching of hot coals or incense without harm or physical response, or acrobatic movements. The vessel may have no or little memory of the experience once the deity has departed.

A very useful model I've found when explaining how trance aids in the facilitation of drawing down a deity and the contrasting states of consciousness is one of driving a car. (I don't drive, but I understand the general concept.) Enhancement is when you are behind the wheel, and the deity is sitting and talking with you from the back seat. Inspiration is when you are still sitting behind the wheel, but now the deity is directing you. When you are in integration, you are now sitting in the passenger seat, and the deity has taken the wheel. And when you are in possession, you are either in the back seat or the boot/trunk of the car! However, this model and metaphor is simply a guide to establish some sense of clarity and orientation as we make our way through the Mystery.

Trance Possession as Holy Communion

"Well you see, you don't really believe in the Goddess so much as you experience Her."

—Phyllis Curott, *Book of Shadows*

I believe trance possession to be a Witch's holy communion. When we bring together the lovers of life as underlying, eternal unity, we experience clarity within, and the revelation of One-in-All and All-in-One becomes living fact rather than guiding principle.[41] In the same way, drawing down is a coming together of apparently polar opposites—human and Divine—to achieve epiphany through ecstasy. It allows one to sense self in all things and embrace life as one's fate, karma, or Wyrd and to acknowledge one's own sovereignty. Knowing this, it is hard to mistrust the deities, as they share sacred space and time with us to communicate wisdom and inspiration to the world. It mustn't be forgotten that the

---

[41] I have used the name "Lovers of Life" to avoid the heteronormativity implied by usual perspectives on the Great Rite.

deities also revel in being incarnate discretely in the flesh, of having potential activated and being able to actively express in the world of form the power and potency of the force that informs it.

The holy communion of drawing down concerns the liberation of the deep Star Self into accepting its primal origins. We remember the disparate and lost pieces of our true shining selves and restore it to origin, restoring it to peace and wholeness, ever minding that wholeness is the eternal journey to fulfilment led by primal desire. Within any tradition, holy communion is essentially the founding principle of what religion means to be.[42] When Catholics receive the host, each devotee is truly eating and drinking the body and blood of Christ—the Anointed One—who will redeem and enlighten his believers to the Kingdom of God. On this, Christ declares in the (Gnostic) *Gospel of Thomas*: "Lift the stone and there you will find me. Split the wood and I am there."[43] Drawing down the Gods relinks us with our Divine selves. The all-consuming truth illumines the rich darkness, and we come to the Great Mystery; there is nothing more and nothing less.

Drawing down a deity necessitates the coming forth or blossoming of our own inner Divine self-deity, the God(dess) which dances within the soul and is the ancient, forever spirit flowing with the pure will. This is why it is never too late, because despite the terror we may inflict, the hatred we may sow, or the disaster we may intentionally wreak, it is always possible to claim sovereignty and total freedom from our past.[44]

Though, as the wise say, "Total freedom is total responsibility." Thus, in re-empowering ourselves and rejecting acts of evil, we are *choosing* to be virtuous: "No dualism of 'good and evil' exists in the immortal cosmos. We become virtuous only because we choose to be such." —Kresphontes

The Gods rejoice in this because the difference between forgetting and forgiveness (of and through self) is that we *are* sorry and seek to make amends, to clean and purify the wounds, and to reawaken what was once perhaps a wasteland of our own making into a blissful paradise once more. All of this is mere allegory in the face of the experience of holy communion, in whatever way it manifests. To me, this verifies the claim most Witches

---

[42] If we consider *religio* (the Latin) as referring to a "re-linking" rather than a "binding to/back."

[43] Refer to the Gnostic Society Library for more information.

[44] This is not to say that we can escape the consequences of our actions, or somehow void our karma or absolve "sin" in the way of the doctrine of the confessional leading to forgiveness as in the Roman Catholic Church.

make about our wild spirituality. Ours is an experiential spirituality in which we dive deeply into the Mysteries, and only after returning do we formulate our beliefs (not expectations) on primordial patterns woven into our very being.

Some Cautionary Notes

Please see the Appendices for techniques and processes of aspecting and trance possession. These represent how I have developed and taught these arts since the original publication of this book. However, I'd still like to include some of the original thoughts and perspectives offered in this section.

When I have taught aspecting and possession in workshops and intensives, I am quite considerate and curated about how full possession takes place and how the techniques are worked. Firstly, the reasoning behind this in a workshop scenario is a practical one when dealing with the possibility of working with more than one deity: the beings could conflict in a disastrous way. We often hear accounts of Witches and Pagans calling in several deities at once who all derive from different cultures, people, and pantheons. Often, simply because of energetic unfamiliarity, the spirits clash or don't harmonise, and the ritual deflates or implodes. However, there is also the chance that the aspect of the deity that has entered the space in that particular moment bears a severe personal dislike to another participating spirit.

For instance, it is often joked that calling Kali and the Morrigan into the same space would result in some form of epic explosion. When I reflect on that particular possibility, it does not necessarily feel to me that the oft-anticipated outcome *would* be the reality, considering the deities are resonant in many ways. When we consider the deities beyond their "superficialities" (Kali is also the Compassionate Mother, and the Morrigan is Sovereignty), we may also begin to see that the combination might be a potentially beautiful one. However, I would qualify this by saying that the individual calling in these deities should have a very well-established relationship with both and be able to interface with their presences equally (or close to). Personally, I feel like I must be more careful about the invocation or presence of multiple beings from the same family of Gods of Spirits than I might otherwise, as these beings have mythic and historical tension at times with one another. Other Pagan friends of mine have noted that when certain deities are present in ritual space with them, they personally feel repelled, or the deity vacates the space because of some personal antagonism. Personally, I acknowledge these experiences, as reality is hugely subjective, and respect people's preferences when conducting communal or otherwise public ceremonies. Ultimately, the gods are inherently mysterious, and our human experiences are just that: human. Alone in my devotions and workings, I act in the way that is right and true for my personal path and the allyships that I hold sacred. No one rule will fit everyone; but act with awareness.

Another reason to not have wholesale trance possession experimentation in a big group is that certain individuals are not yet prepared for the experience, both psychically and physically. I know that after I have returned to consciousness, I am told that I have plunged my hands into fire, touched burning coals, pushed burning sticks of incense into my palms and wrists, and when the deity leaves my body, it is generally suddenly, and my body falls to the ground. Over time, my body has conditioned itself to recover almost instantly from these happenings. However, there have been a few occasions where I have been sick for days after or in pain because of a knocked head. Generally speaking, when the deity brings fire or anything hot or burning near my body, either I do not register the pain (during or after), or there are no wounds or markings afterward (unless the deity wishes me to remember; I have two small markings on my left wrist from Epona that did not hurt).

I believe the reasoning for this to be that when the body is elated or deepened in a heavy trance state, which possession or full drawing down beholds, pain is not a necessary factor; just like the Yogis of India, we transcend the body's registration of pain. However, there are some who, in their desire to succeed and prove their worthiness before their community and the Gods, fool themselves into believing that they are indeed possessed or have drawn down and go about committing acts which verify this, and then end up severely harmed because of it. Not only should physical safety be considered, but also the psychic and energetic aspects. There are plenty of effective safeguards, however, that I draw upon in my possessory work (see Appendix III).

A really clear one that I learnt through my involvement with the Reclaiming tradition is to write up a literal contract—with pen and paper—between you and the spirit you will be calling in (or all of the spirits you would do this work with) that includes agreements, boundaries, and prohibitions. This can include things like "you will not pick up sharp objects or touch fire" and "you will not physically touch another living thing in the space unless invited." Be specific. Once the contract is written, charge and bless it with the aid of your allies and spirits, then burn it. When it is ash and no longer burning, rub the ash into the nape of your neck and over your chest. This seals it into all of your skin. You can, over time, renegotiate contracts.

Dealing with the spirits is the ancient Shamanic charge, and as Witches of this vein, we need to excel in this art because to do so is to respect the risk. There is nothing in life worthwhile unless it includes the element of risk. Through skirting the boundaries of risk and sometimes completely surpassing them, we empower ourselves through a dynamic tension that expands, concentrates, and enlivens consciousness to such a point that our potency increases. This ought not be embraced because it is wonderful to be potent on its own but because, when flanked by love and wisdom, potency allows us to better serve and celebrate the life force. It allows us to commit to change that *will* have an effect, deepening the consciousness of Self.

Psychically speaking, damage can occur if one has not committed oneself to the actualization of self-sovereignty through the celebration of personal freedom and the cultivation of self-responsibility. The onus is on the individual to determine the pathway of one's life. Therefore, if one is not grounded and centred, aligned, anchored, autonomous, and able to correctly discern and judge the shifts, changes, and fluxes of energy, then to draw down and effectively surrender is not only impractical, but it could be devastating also. One needs to be grounded and centred so that psychic sustenance is available at all times, and the energy spent on holding the deity can be instantly replaced by connection with the infinite well-springs of life force.[45]

To be aligned (especially with all of your Three Souls) is to create and effect a wholeness that speaks of autonomy, self-respect, and personal attunement to pure will as manifest cosmically (so we are able to meet with the higher vibrations of a discarnate spirit-being, if you will). To be anchored and autonomous is to be held by one's natural inclination to thrive. One's ability to discern and judge the patterns of energy

---

[45] Sometimes this is not the case, and the deity fills you with a presence beyond the need for sustenance.

allows the individual a degree of technical relationship with the magical charge and the ability to enter into the communion on equal footing. Remember, we are of the gods.

Trance possession is generally only undertaken in the presence of others in a ritualistic framework. It can happen spontaneously outside of ceremony but to facilitate it in an inappropriate context is foolhardy. Ensure that there are experienced spirit-workers who understand the dynamics of drawing down and are able to actively support you in such an altered state and catch you if you fall or faint!

The final note of caution I will speak on is one that T. Thorn Coyle and I spoke about when I visited them during my 2010 US journey and tour. We were on the topic of trance possession and how it was integral to our personal paths. Thorn mentioned that, for those who stem from Abrahamic backgrounds (or from post-Christ Western ideologies in general) in which deity is considered absolute, drawing down can become a troublesome pattern leading to unhealthy co-dependency and irrational addictions. For instance, there are some who, on the "omniscient" word of a deity, may commit self-harm or listen to a deity into dangerous situations ("If I say jump…"). A cultivation of self-sovereignty should establish a relationship based on the principle of sacred equality.

When forming allyships with a deity or other spirit-being, it should never be based on subservience; surrender at times, yes, but be subservient never.[46] This then may bring to mind the question: why sacrifice to the Gods or give offerings? My answer to this is that when I am giving sacrifice or making offerings, I am doing so in the heartfelt spirit of gratitude for the manifold gifts deriving from my relationships with the deities and spirits. The majority of the time, the offerings I give to Gods are pledged so that a particular task may be carried out on my behalf by the deity: give and receive. Ultimately, if an allyship with a deity becomes unhealthy and imbalanced because of a need to feel a comforting "absolute" nature of the Divinity, then the sovereign ability to commune viscerally with deity and become vessel for it should not be considered. It would be foolish and dangerous to court the interests of a spirit in such a way when respect for self is the determining factor for all respect in any given situation.

---

[46] I believe the true point of communion between oneself and one's deity is when *all* surrender to Mystery which is shared between the two.

A Note on Gender

> "*...Remember that in the ecstatic state it is very common for male gods to possess females and for female gods to possess males. As a matter of fact, the reversal of male and female roles in a body has long been considered a typical sign of the true ecstatic state.*"
> —Sharon Devlin, as quoted by Margot Adler,
> *"Interview with a Modern Witch," Drawing Down the Moon*

The idea that only a woman may invoke a Goddess and a man a God is ludicrous to me. This is neither ancient nor honest, and it completely vanishes non-binary folks. The cultural attitudes and bigotries which formed and framed the occult teachings within certain Witchcraft traditions were deeply Victorian, misogynistic, white-supremacist, and often incredibly homophobic and transphobic. Due to many of the early public books being written by polarity-focused Wiccans—with uncritiqued talk of masculine and feminine—even the presence of gay people within the Craft was contentious. Polarity viewed through the notion of the binary gender was most often evoked as the argument.

As a queer and non-binary individual, I have never found it difficult to banish gender boundaries and simply accept everyone for who they are, not merely as someone defined by the respective sexual organs which may or may not exist between their legs. This includes the deities. Being who they are, the Gods are able to blur perceived boundaries more often than not. Gods and other spirits may traditionally and culturally express as a gender or not, just as humans can do. In fact, according to the concept of polarity, which certain self-proclaimed "traditionalists" fetishise (and the ideal of balancing these forces of masculine and feminine within), men should be drawing down Goddesses more often, as should women with Gods. However, you will never find me pushing this on anyone, privately or publicly. This is not my frame nor cosmology. What I am attempting to bring to the surface is the inconsistency of various claims within the Pagan community and why it is more liberating and empowering to do as we are called to rather than be constrained by hidebound beliefs which owe more to conservative politics and social bigotry rather than spiritual exploration or truth.

I am honestly very happy to write that in the thirteen years since I first wrote the original manuscript, attitudes in the wider Craft and Pagan worlds around gender and polarity have refined, expanded, and deepened.

Of course, this is due to the fierce and multifarious activism and advocacy of trans- and non-binary people in and outside of these communities. There are several comprehensive resources out there discussing these issues in magical regions.

A Concluding Point

For those who are natural vessels, possessions can occur quite rapidly and without any conscious effort, and there are no methods necessary (although they may help to facilitate more skilful possessions). Indeed, this was the case for much of my life, from ages fifteen to twenty-five. In this case, it is important to ensure that we are confident and willing enough to act and respond from our Sovereignty of Selves so that we may be aware of when and where we are entering into a contract with a spirit to serve as vessel. It is not healthy or desirable to be "used" by a deity or spirit; in fact, this can be very dangerous. This has happened to me on several occasions, though the deities/spirits were by no means malevolent. We must remember and appreciate that the spirits are not necessarily human, and therefore, they do not share our "conventions" or feelings for what is and is not appropriate according to any given context. We are dealing with raw, potent forces and beings which constitute the Living Cosmos. We need to remember to remind them of our human limits, and they will remind us of our fierce and intrinsic Divinity.

CHAPTER FOUR

Spirit Allies

"Moreover, the follower of the Faerie Way does not seek to command such beings, magical sword in one hand, spellbook in the other, like a medieval magician. Cooperation, not compulsion is the watchword."
—Hugh Mynne,
The Faerie Way: A Healing Journey to Other Worlds

I have already used the term "allyship" within this book, but I will go into explicit detail about it in this chapter.

The idea behind an allyship with a spirit-being is rooted in the concept of sacred equality: that all things/beings that exist are inherently equal and empowered to express that fact. If we accept sacred equality as truth, we are then inspired to approach all beings within the All as "worthy." Each and every being is unique, possessing particular stories and skills. I do not call a carpenter for medical advice unless, of course, that carpenter is also somehow a naturopath, doctor, or has medical training of some kind, which, though not impossible, is unlikely. However, individuals are not bound by their professions or what they do for work; there is infinite depth and potential in each and every one of us. Embracing this reality opens us to a plethora of opportunities in rediscovering hidden treasures within each other or forging new connections entirely with others or through the ancient art of evolution: people can and do change.

Humans are spirit-beings too! We are as spiritual and powerful as any other being; knowing and working towards this is what activates our innate ability and nature. Why fear the spirits when we have both spirit and dense physical expression? After all, according to the alchemical formula contained within the Elemental sequence of casting the Circle (discussed in Chapter Two), the densest things can be the most potent. This tends to inspire the thought that because spirits are so-called "discarnate," they are above our own physical laws! This is absolutely true, and so are we if we wish it. Spirit-flight, the Sight or Knowing, spellcraft, drawing down and trance possession, and the very ability to communicate with spirits and share power between us are all evidence of this Shamanic skill. Perhaps this is why, historically and culturally, Witches were (and still are) feared and linked with the faerie folk and other spirits. I won't lie and say there are no reasons to fear a spirit—or a Witch, for that matter—but unless you assault, attack, or offend one, you will have no reason at all.

Witches of all kinds work with spirits; it is a distinguishing factor of our spirituality. Firstly, if a Witch is not deity-focussed (and so many are these days), they will be focussed on working with magical allies of some description. This is the very reason I coined the term "allyship" (over and rather than "alliance"): to emphasise that we are, as Witches, part of a circle of allies working together in harmony to achieve goals, fulfil desires and needs, share knowledge, and nourish wisdom. We serve one another:

> *Reverence and honour cannot be given when one has no understanding of the relationship between the recipient of the gift and the one who offers it. In a true and meaningful exchange, neither one does exclusively the giving or receiving—both mutually participate in the sacred moment. Balance is maintained.*[47]

The image I use is a circle of friends holding hands without a break in the chain rather than the concept of a circle of spirits or forces congregating around a central figure commanding and directing an army. This is not to say that, on various occasions, one spirit (this includes you) may be more to the forefront or centre of the work than the others, but all agreeing to work in unison or synchrony toward achievement and fulfilment leads to profound success. Belonging to a circle of allies with many skills secures this. An example of when the Witch would be in the centre of the circle would be during a spellcasting when the particular desires or needs of the Witch are being worked towards; a deity would be in the centre during a devotional rite. However, all are sharing in the experience and, therefore, affected by it. The central position is taken for utilitarian or practical reasons of focus, potency, and general energy dynamics.

---

[47] Gede Parma, Fio, *Spirited* (Llewellyn, 2009) 132.

Forging an Allyship with a Spirit-Being

Whereas the word "alliance" tends towards the political, the concept or feeling behind the term "allyship" is one of deepening connection and celebration. Honour, integrity, truth, harmony, dedication, friendship, perfect love, and perfect trust are all key elements in the maintenance of an allyship.

Forging an allyship with another spirit-being can often require perseverance. Initially, however, there must be adequate cause for the initiation. This can even be as simple as unknown attraction or endearment towards one another (this is enough for great loves). Whatever the conjoining reason is, once it has been established that there is certainly a connection (for the moment, at least), one can enter into an allyship.

As with working with the gods, there are various levels of relationships shared with the various spirit-beings. Some allyships will be circumstantial and related to locale (for instance, my allyship with various traffic lights); others will be more permanent and based on profession, inclination, or personality. An example of this would be my relationship with the Elementals, particularly the sylphs and the gnomes. I like to sing and do so when I am alone quite often; therefore, I gained the attention of the sylphs from childhood. The gnomes I attracted into my life through the many prosperity spells and charms I have woven for myself and others: they have always been of aid in finding lost objects and in helping to ground and relax me after high-tension situations.

These allyships, while not expressly initiated at any particular time or for any conscious reason, are truly within the realms of the "power-with" attitude/dynamic which Starhawk speaks of as shared power in communal context. All allyships are found within the idea of community, which means "shared unity," and thus, we are all encouraged to look beyond the anthropo-centric and consider what and who else supports us in our continued celebration of existence. This is precisely the reason I do not believe it is accurate to call any a Witch a "solitary," for we are anything but. We are constantly and consistently joined to the whole of the vibrating Web of Wyrd, and our awareness is on enhancing and deepening these connections at all times. In the Wildwood Tradition, we use the term "wanderer" for those of our Fellowship who do not work within the coven structure.

After a certain period of time working and celebrating with a particular spirit-being (or plural), you may enter into a conscious allyship.

The communion to establish such an allyship does not necessarily have to occur within a ceremonial context, unless, of course, you feel that would enhance the experience. The simplest thing one could do is to align the Spiral Soul, open to the spirit-being, and await arrival. Once the spirit-being has arrived, speak openly and honestly with each other, and an allyship will either naturally eventuate or the idea may appear repugnant to the spirit (and perhaps even to you). The latter is highly unlikely, especially if you have been sharing sacred time and space for some time prior. Again, if the allyship has been forged, an offering may be shared to affirm its concrete reality. These offerings, as discussed before, are to reflect the inner Divine nature shining within and in the moment, becoming one and merging.

Sharing Prayer

Prayer is meaningful communication, communion, and collaboration between beings within the cosmos. An allyship exists out of necessity, despite the fact that it may be temporary or completely situational; either way, it naturally occurs due to the shared prayer. A prayer can be a petition in the simplest sense, but the way I experience prayer in a Pagan context—especially as a Witch with ignited consciousness—is as a form of pooling resources to potentiate something specific.

For instance, when I pray for clear, azure-blue skies (with few white, wispy clouds) and star-sprinkled indigo night skies, I visualise this outcome as I would when casting a spell, but I offer the visualisation as a communication of intent and meaning with a spirit-being (or group of them) who I consider to hold sway or skill in manifesting such a situation (sky and weather). Depending on how I am feeling about the situation, I might also spirit-fly into the sky-realm and share counsel with the corresponding spirits. In *The Earth Path*, Starhawk speaks of one of her early Craft teachers saying to make friends with the clouds if she wanted to work the weather. Friends are inclined to help one another, so the connection is a mutually beneficial one of exchange and balance. Again, a successful prayer is not necessarily about the outcome, but it definitely concerns the communication.

A Shamanic Witch may take a leaf out of the prayer book of the ancient Greeks. In ancient Greece, traditional prayer was often simply performed outside or directly in front of a house shrine or altar. It was generally done standing and with arms opened as if to embrace the deity or to offer up/out/down the prayer.[48] I will generally pray in this way, although, at times, I will also pray in the Balinese way: kneeling with both palms pressed together and placed to sit against the crown of the head and pointing to the heavens.

When I pray to the spirits of the sky-realms and the Gods and Goddesses of weather for either rain or clear skies, I begin by (of course) grounding and centring, then opening a channel of communication between Land and Sky. I vibrate the essential (but direct) meaning of my prayer into the ether and await affirmation of reception, which may come as an intuitive understanding/feeling, a strong response within my body, or a clairaudient/clairvoyant response (yes, no, or "we'll see what we can do"). Of course, though I am general about who the spirits I pray to are in my wording, they are specific spirits of skill (weather and sky-wisdom); however, I am also working with *genii loci* (spirits of place). Thus, depending on *where* I would like the effect to directly manifest, the spiritual entities (in particular) may vary, though they are within the same family. This is all essential knowledge if one is to make prayer.

The Beloved Dead

"Ancestors, we call to,
Light the flame remember you,
Through the Veil, across the tides,
We will remember your lives.
All those who are a part,
Of our families and our hearts,
Sail across the sunless sea,
Wheel turning eternally."
—Fio Gede Parma and Hannah of Wildwood

How can one begin to speak of the Beloved Dead, the ancestors who are the very reason we now walk the Earth? During my weekly devotional ritual, after energetic alignments and space preparation and affirmation, I open my hands on either side as if holding the hands of someone on the

---

[48] This depended on to whom one was praying. If the deity is a chthonic/underworld spirit, then the hands and arms are directed downwards.

left and right. Indeed, I am, for on the left is my mother and the people before her and the people to come; on the right is my father and the people before him and the people to come. I then chant the following:

"I stand in the Centre—I am the seed, I am the outcome,
I am the holy Imramma soul-journey of life!"

If we truly reflect upon it, we are the entire sum of our ancestral line and then some. We are who we are, unique and therefore potent, but also the result of the blood, sweat, and tears (quite literally) of our ancestors and the stories they wove. We might not necessarily like our stock, and various members of our family tree may have committed unjust atrocities that we do not agree with or endorse, but we must remember. Remembering in the true sense is reconciling the disparate pieces and fragments of memory and creating a new wholeness from their coming together. In remembering, there is forgiveness, rest, and revelation. We understand that through the tests and trials of time, there is hope. Hope, the last to leave (or the only remaining blessing in) Pandora's box, is the stuff of life. We can only hope because we cannot always know or be completely certain. To hope, trust, and love: these are the blessings of the revelations of the ancestors.

When honouring the Beloved Dead, we work a timeless and powerful magic. We are ensuring their immortality in one way by honouring their names and telling their stories, and we are blessing memory and, therefore, the wholeness of reality by reflecting upon death and the hereafter. At the annual Spiral Dance ritual held by the Bay Area Reclaiming Collective in San Francisco, I experienced a potent honouring of the Beloved Dead.

Around eight to ten Witches, who I will name "death-walkers" for the purposes of this book, walked a constant circle for nearly two hours, speaking aloud the names of the Beloved Dead that had been contributed by the community. They were all of those who had passed through the Veil since the Samhain before. I sat, entranced, with my friend Abel and heeded silently the private calls of desperation, solidarity, hope, and peace. I felt true redemption in that meditation of sonic soothing and even restoration. At the culmination of perhaps twenty or thirty names, all of the death-walkers chanted "what is remembered lives," and the Earth-folk gathered around them reverberated it back. I have a saying: "The song of our ancestors is the laughter of our children." To honour and acknowledge the Beloved Dead, the Ancestors, is to take a spark from that firebrand of hope that kindles the fires of warmth and illumination, which will hold and keep us through the darkness and death.

In the "Legend of the Descent of the Goddess" by Raven Grimassi, he gives the words "and in death we are shown the way to her communion." In *By Land, Sky & Sea*, I speak at length about the importance of embracing death as a threshold to renewed consciousness, to a reawakening of the amazing depth of potential we hold inside. The Beloved Dead are the spiritual allies who are willing and able to aid us in reclaiming these gifts. In fact, studying and reflecting on ancestral heritage will lend many clues as to why, how, and what this potential is.

Here is a ritual of reparation and reconciliation inspired by a part I contributed to a ritual at the inaugural Australian Reclaiming WitchCamp in Victoria. The sacred intention of that particular night's ritual was, "We open our ears to the dreams alive in the land and step through the healing door." It was essentially a ritual in which we created a spell by holding our ancestors' dreams in one hand and the dreams of the land in the other. We then stepped through the healing door into balance and truth by crossing those dreams over our hearts. Before we embarked on sealing this spell, I wove together a spell of my own to charge the four bowls of water in the centre surrounding the altar.

As each of us spoke aloud the names of our ancestors and their dreams, I drew in these threads into one tapestry. As I moved to the centre of the circle with a pulsing, throbbing core of magic between my hands, I sang a variant of the chant that opens this section. The circle answered and joined the song. I sprinkled sacred ochre collected from a stream that traveled directly to the sea into each of the bowls, and as I did, the charge, the spell, became a part of the vibration of that water. Four graces carried those bowls out to the Circle, and each person had the opportunity to wash their hands, not to clean themselves of any perceived past sins of the family, but for healing and wholeness, which only comes with remembering. We firmly wished to root ourselves in the Eternal Now and be cleansed within that undying moment. The following ritual takes its inspiration from that experience.

The Waters of Reparation

You will need:

* A medium-large sized ceramic or glass bowl filled with rain or spring water (large enough for you to dip your hands in)
* Red thread
* Soil from the land you live on

Perform the Three Realms Alignment and the Rite of Divine Fire.

The bowl of water should be placed directly in front of you as you kneel, sit, or stand. The red thread should be on the left of it, and the soil from the land on the right. You may choose to cast the Circle for this rite, but it is not necessary.

As you breathe into the Holy Centre, begin to become distinctly aware of the water sitting before you. Give reverence to the origin of this water and invest sacred presence in the here and now.

Taking the red thread into your left hand, focus inwardly and honour your Ancestors. Perform the following blessing as you hold out both of your hands to either side as if you are holding hands with invisible loved ones (which you are). Say aloud:

> *"My mother (or whatever is true for you) on my left hand and the people before her and the people to come.*
> *My father (or whatever is true for you) on my right hand and the people before him and the people to come."*

Cross your hands over your heart, still holding the red thread.

> *"I stand in the Centre: I am the seed, I am the outcome, I am the holy soul-journey of life. And thus do I call upon my ancestors."*

Visualise and feel the ancient and ever-renewing legacy flowing through you now from both lines that meet to merge in you: the third principle. As you focus on this pulsing power, charge the red thread in the name of your ancestors. Ask yourself, "What were the dreams of my ancestors?"

Place the red thread in the bowl. Take the soil in your right hand and focus outward to the Land and to all that is a part of it (even you). If you are not already outside, walk outside now and sit upon the Earth, at the base of a tree, or where the Land meets the Sky meets the Sea. Breathe into the Holy Centre and listen. Open your ears to truly listen to what the Land is whispering. What does the Land dream of? Try not to ask any questions of and for your own ends; simply yearn and seek to merge with the Land and its presence. When you have received the Land, move back to your bowl of water and recite the following:

"The Land is dreaming…the Land is dreaming…the Land is dreaming! And I have heard."

Pour the soil into the water and cross your hands over your heart. Rock backward and forward as you chant the following until you feel the natural crescendo and release the power into the water:

"By the blessings of my ancestors,
I am made to be here now,
By the sovereignty of Land,
I am given this holy hour.
By the dreams of long ago,
And the dreams that linger on,
I pray that I will reconcile,
What has been and gone."

Throw your hands out to the water and direct the raised power into the bowl. When you are ready, dip your hands into the charged and blessed liquid and wash your hands. As you do this, feel any blockages clear and any negative attachments swiftly dissolve; you are free of anything that would bind you.

Lastly, as you breathe deeply and rhythmically, listen to your Own Holy Self. What are your dreams? Have they been realised, are they unfolding, and how do your dreams transform and renew themselves? What is your dreaming, your living myth? Meditate on this more deeply until you feel that you can make a pledge of reconciliation of Self to Self. State and affirm this aloud as you pour the water directly onto the Earth. The rite is complete.

Animal Totems and Familiars

In the Introduction, I listed several parallel factors that link traditional folkloric beliefs concerning European Witchcraft with Shamanisms the world over. One of the key underlying commonalities is a strong relationship (allyship) with the plant, animal, and mineral worlds, all three of which can be considered to be familiars or totems in the true sense of the word.

A familiar spirit did not always directly connote animal companionship, as is the popular opinion of a Witch's familiar; however, familiar spirits (the apparently demonic spirit-helpers of Witches) sometimes disguised or presented themselves as animals. The animals strongly associated with European Witches have age-old Shamanic links:

- **The Cat:** The concept that black cats are an evil omen is not necessarily a native European belief. Originally, it was a Celtic belief that having a black cat cross one's path was a sign of good luck; the blessings of the old religions become the curses of the new. Cats have long been considered extremely psychic and in-tune creatures and are known for their independence, secrecy, and elusiveness. The cat's medicine is considered to concern independence, psychic insight, wisdom of the night and Otherworld(s), and deftness in grace.

- **The Dog:** "Man's best friend," the dog is the domesticated descendent of ancestral wolves (emissaries of the ancient God of Death, Dark, and Decline). Hounds accompany the Witches' Goddess Diana on her hunt and are therefore directly associated with the Lady of the Moon and of the Mysteries of life and rebirth. In his many works on historical Witchcraft in Europe, Raven Grimassi comments that the presence of hounds (or a stag) depicted with Diana is a symbol of the God in animal-form accompanying her on the hunt which is for and of him. In various traditions of Stregheria, the wolf and the stag are the archaic forms of the Witch God. Dog medicine comprises of loyalty, protection and guardianship, entry to the Underworld (as in Kerberos and the Wolf of Stregheria), and strength of conviction.

- **The Hare/Rabbit:** Both the hare and the rabbit have long been considered manifestations of Witches' familiar spirits in common folklore. The famous self-confessed Scottish Witch, Isobel Gowdie, openly spoke of her Witchcraft to the Scottish authorities and commented that she often changed into the form of a hare when travelling to her Witch gatherings. Another strong association with Witchcraft comes from the lunar connection of hares/rabbits as seen in the Moon. The wisdom of the hare/rabbit concerns fertility, the moon Mysteries, secrecy, swiftness, trickster magic, and humility.

- **The Owl:** Raven Grimassi mentions that the root for the Italian word *strega* (meaning "Witch") is *strix*, which refers to a screech-owl. Marija Gimbutas associates most birds of prey with a Bird Goddess cult that, according to conjecture and several thousand unearthed Bird Goddess artworks, was popular in Old Europe. The owl is a largely nocturnal bird and thus is associated with the Moon and her influence. In the Aegean and Mediterranean regions, the Moon is largely associated with a feminine Divinity (whereas in Northern Europe, it is the Sun that is associated with the feminine), so the owl is again directly associated with the Goddess of the Witches. They are a totem of the Greek Goddesses Athene and Hekate, the latter being the Titan queen connected to all things magical and mystical, and definitely a Queen of the Witches in the true sense of the term. The owl's medicine is of wisdom, second sight, the skill of the hunter (acquisition), and the world of shades and ghosts.

- **The Raven/Crow:** Almost cross-culturally, the raven is considered to be one of the first spirits (if not *the* first). In various Native American cosmologies, the raven is the creator of this world. Similarly, Raven Grimassi records a hereditary Italian folktale in *Hereditary Witchcraft* in which the raven is the creator of the Earth and humanity. (Consider also the plethora of well-known Pagan authors and elders today with the title "raven" in their names somewhere.) The raven and crow are associated with the mighty Morrighan, the Irish Battle-Queen of Death, Sorcery, and Sovereignty. Ravens and crows are messengers of the Otherworld and act as a psychopomp or even a harbinger of death and, therefore, transformation and renewal.

- **The Snake:** The snake and the serpent have an unfortunate associated stigma. Colloquially, the idea that someone is a serpent or a "snake in the grass" means they have ruthless, insidious, and decidedly malevolent behaviour. However, the long history of the snake as a symbol of the old religions is well-established. The snake sheds its skin, so it is thus associated with regeneration, rebirth (life from death), and health. The serpents on Hermes's famed *kerykeion* and the single snake entwining around the rod of Asklepios (blessed son of Apollon, the deified physician) are still seen on the sides of ambulances in

Australia and decorating many international logos concerned with health and healing (including the World Health Organisation). The mighty Celtic Goddess Brigid is also associated with the snake as, on her holy day of Imbolc (the Quickening), the serpent is said to rise again from the land, which is also a euphemism for the waxing strength of the masculine fertility principle. Brigid, too, is a deity of the healing arts. The serpent's medicine is strong and old: wisdom, fertility, renewal, waterways (that lead to the "world-encircling stream," the Ocean), magic and sorcery, healing, and balance.

- **The Goat:** The goat is another dark emblem of Witchcraft. The trial records during the Witch Hysteria often link the goat with the Devil; apparently, it was a popular form for Satan to adopt. The goat is a horned animal and thus is linked with the Horned God and especially with the Greek Pan. The goat is also half of the infamous Baphomet, as depicted by the French magician Éliphas Lévi. Raven Grimassi speaks of several Roman and Italian myths which link the goat with the fertility principle (again connecting with the Horned God). During Lupercalia, which is celebrated around the same time as Imbolc in the Northern Hemisphere, women and men would run naked through the streets as the men whipped them with straps of goat hide (which may have been deer or stag hide at an earlier time). In an Etruscan tale, Juno orders the infertile Sabine women to copulate with goats in order to restore their fecundity, but a priest interprets this as being flagellated with goat hide. The magic of the goat speaks of unbridled fertility and sexuality, the mysteries of the Horned One, dark wisdom, and the strength of Earth.

- **The Stag:** In the Wildwood Tradition, we honour the Stag-Horned God as sovereign of the Light Tide (from Yule to Midsummer). However, the Stag is the promised one who brings and blesses the harvest during the onset of the Dark Tide (from Midsummer to Yule). The God who will become the Stag King is crowned at the Spring Equinox time in our mythos and represents the powers of light, growth, and gain. The stag is a symbol of kingship and the hunt and, again, is associated with the Goddess Diana in her various forms. They are Kern, the Horned One whom Raven Grimassi writes of, and is one aspect of the two-faced God (also known as Janus/Dianus). The stag is the carrier of the souls to the Underworld, the Lord of Death and

Resurrection, as the Gardnerians say, as well as potency and life force overflowing, and the awe-full truth of raw nature.

- **The Frog/Toad:** Another familiar spirit commonly seen accompanying Witches in folkloric depictions is the frog or toad. Though two completely different subsets, the frog and toad are popularly linked when associated with Witchcraft and magic. In many cultures, the frog represents the dew of the heavens and the rising of the sweet waters of the Earth to nourish and sate the parched land. The toad is a healer, a wise one (perhaps a representation of the Old Crone Goddess). Though they may be "ugly," they are fearsome and revered. They are the tide of life contained and gathered in. Frog's medicine is the effervescence and creative fertility of youth; Toad's medicine is the hard-come-by wisdom of rotting, wet things.

Totem Trance Journeys

A note for the revised edition: while the term "totem" is used mindfully and casually by many Indigenous and non-Indigenous persons and communities to this day, it is not a term I have used much (if at all) in the past decade. I appreciate that members of many animistic and spirit-working cultures and traditions throughout Earth today will borrow all kinds of terms passed into the vernacular by anthropology and colonial academia more broadly, such as Indigenous spirit-workers and healers in so-called Brazil and Indonesia utilising the term "Shaman" or "magic" or "Witch doctor." I believe this to be nuanced, organic, specific, or casual, and essentially inescapable. Some First Nations people in so-called Australia might use the term "totem" to communicate a broadly understood idea. Essentially, in this book, I am referring to an animal, plant, or mineral spirit that has a magical or fateful connection to you. I have decided, for the sake of respecting this conversation and to centre complex navigations of cultural appropriation as a Balinese-Australian writer and Witch, to leave the term "totem" in the text.

There are a multitude of totem-finding and totem-meeting trance journeys out there in the world, and the one that follows is neither better nor worse; it is simply another trance journey with one main difference. This trance journey emphasises the connection and communion aspect of the totem-human relationship. It does not assume that you have never met your (or one of your) totem(s), but it provides for those who have yet to do so.

It is recommended, as with most of the exercises and techniques in this book, that you perform the Spiral Soul Alignment, Three Realms Alignment, and Rite of the Divine Fire beforehand. You may either have someone else read the trance journey aloud to you as you trance, or you may wish to record it ahead of time and play it back as you follow.

Breathe deeply and rhythmically. Breathe into your Centre. As you come closer and closer to your Centre, every piece of you, every cell, begins to glow with the radiance of the Divine, and you flow into the limitless light. You become one with it, as you always have been and will continue to be. You realise that the Centre is in All places: you have found the Holy Centre.

There are flickering shadows amassing around you. Before you is a campfire made for you by the one you have come to meet. You wonder at your surroundings. You notice you are in a wild place…how does it appear to you? What plant beings are present? What of the stones, the Earth upon which you sit or stand? Can you smell or hear Water near you? What is the colour of the sky? What are the scents moving through the shifting currents of Air? How do you feel being present in this wild place, far from the ordinary here and there of the mundane world?

As you ponder all of these things and more, you come to again realise that behind all of the thoughts and their attachments, there is something strong, pervasive, and consistent thrumming within and all around you. The heartbeat of nature is your heartbeat, and gradually, the beat becomes definitively audible, and the shadows seem to shake at each pulse.

As the shadows shake and writhe, the Veil ripples, which seems to separate the worlds, and from the other side of the Fire, you see a glimmer of light which just as soon disappears. A silhouette draws itself together, coalesces from the shadows and the rippling air, and a distinct form begins to emerge from that space directly opposite from you. As the form manifests, you suddenly see, in powerful clarity, your totem shining in the illumination of flame and ember!

Your totem draws ever close to the flickering red-yellow flames, and it becomes apparent that you are both here for connection, communion, and counsel. This is the sacred time and space for you to share power, knowledge, wisdom, and insight together. Do this now and indulge in the exchange. (Pause as needed.)

When you feel that you have completed the exchange, music begins to move through the space, and your totem begins to dance and move to the primal rhythm. You find yourself mirroring this movement and as you do, you feel your two essences merging in union. You find that you are becoming more and more akin to your totem, fused and flowing until, quite suddenly, you find yourself looking through the eyes of your totem and staring across the dancing Fire into what seems to be a mirror, for the reflection is exact, distinct, and non-human! You embrace this transformation, this sharing of skin and shape, of form and frame. You have not become your totem; you have simply drawn so close that you are sharing the same time and space and are able to borrow of its faculties and experience. If you feel inclined, allow yourself time to explore the fruitful possibilities of this new mode of meaning and expression of existence. (Pause as needed.)

As the dark dome of night begins to lighten at a distant edge and unearthly hues of wandering light seem to creep over the horizon, you find yourself in your familiar form once more, on the same side of the Fire that you first approached. You nod, thank, and honour your totem and your sacred allyship, and you recall your breathing, deep and rhythmic, until that focus saturates every piece of your being.

You are breathing…in…and out…in…and out. You are breathing… long…and deep…long…and deep. You remember your physicality in the here and now, of the place that you are, that surrounds you and fixes you by law of time and space. And yet, as you open your eyes and become aware of this world once more, you know that if you wish or yearn to move through the Veil once more to explore infinity, you simply need to find the ripple and slip through it.

Breathe. Centre. Ground. Be here and now.

The Difference Between a Familiar and a Totem

The Anglicised word *totem* derives from an Ojibwe root, *ode*, and the word *doodem*, referring to anything related to heart and kinship. Totem tends to refer to an over-arching spirit-ally (animal, plant, or mineral) protecting and blessing a particular group of people (such as a tribe, clan, or family). This particular ally may actually embody or exist as the mythic ancestor and protector of the group. A familiar, on the other hand, is a personal spirit-helper who, according to popular English-speaking interpretations, tends to appear in animal form most of the time and may occasionally derive its magical potency from being a living, sentient, incarnate animal. Since the New Age movement, the word *totem* has come to mean, for those exploring newer or appropriated variants of age-old spiritual philosophy and tradition, a spirit-ally directly invested in aiding, inspiring, and guiding a particular individual.

The Witch's familiar is closer to a Spiritualist spirit guide and plays the part of a protector, mentor, initiator (sometimes), and friend on equal footing who shares interest, time, and space with the Witch. Many modern Witches consider their pets familiars if or when the Witch begins to notice their continued presence at or attraction to magical rites. A familiar spirit may or may not express as a living animal.

While totems may be a clan guide or ancestral inspiration and wisdom passed on through oral teachings and celebrations, standing as an embodiment of the mythic strength of a people, a totem may also act as an individual's spiritual ally in the energetic pattern of animal, plant, or mineral in the contemporary sense. A familiar is a personal guardian, guide, and friend with invested interest in an individual (and vice versa), and, in some ways, this can be synonymous with a totem who may turn up in moments of danger to save a member of that totem clan or group. The origins of the word "familiar" lie with "familial" or "family" (some may also say "servant" from Latin *famulus*); see my book *The Witch Belongs to the World* and Lee Morgan's *A Deed without a Name* for more on familiar spirits.

I can attest to familiar spirits relating to the ancestors, as often, after a particularly arduous or intense power-raising, I will find that, as I am grounding and equalising my energy with that of my surroundings, a multitude of etheric hands (which I sometimes see and sometimes feel) stroking my aura. I have always identified these spirit-hands with my family-familiar spirits. This has a special meaning to me now, considering an auric-cleansing technique Ravyn Stanfield (a Reclaiming and Feri priestess) performed on me had immediate parallels.

Ultimately, it seems, as with the casual usage of a variety of terms within the greater Pagan or even magical community, the words *totem* and *familiar* may occasionally appear to mean the same thing and, at other times, represent variant concepts. For the purposes of this book, *totem* will mean "a non-human spirit ally who is intrinsically a part of you and your ancestral threads," and a *familiar* spirit may or may not be human (who is no longer alive) or be ancestral. Again, it's a fine line.

The Importance of Spirits of Place

It is quite natural for a Witch (or anyone) to enter a new house, building, park, or region in general and to receive a "reading" on the feeling or energy of the site. This is generally considered to constitute the "vibes" of the place, and the reading maps out the overall energetic blueprint or imprint of the location. However, my experience with reading so-called vibes tends to fall into a different category of interpretation, and more and more Witches are beginning to (or do) feel this way.

Spirits of place come by many cultural names in both Pagan and non-Pagan traditions. The Roman term was *genius loci,* while the Irish might simply say "faerie" or "Tuatha" (depending on their mythological frame or time period); the ancient Greeks might point to "nymphs," or the English of the eighteenth and nineteenth centuries might reference "sprites." Either way, in this particular usage as spirits of place, these entities are embodied potencies of the land or area and are implicitly tied to place.

Spirits of place carry the vital charge of the land, and the term is indeed an umbrella term which may apply to a host of unique and specific spirits, but just as the natives of West Village in Manhattan (New York City) retain and vibrate a specific charge (though each person is an individual), so do the spirits of place.

I feel that an illustrating example is needed here to truly flesh out the concept and reality of spirits of place:

From late August 2010 to early January 2011, I traveled through the West Country of England, Ireland, the US, and Canada. For some of this time, I was the guest guide for the sacred sites tour—*Dragon's Eye Tours*—created and facilitated by Wiccan priestess Christine Casey. I also traveled through the States promoting the new release of my book, *By Land, Sky & Sea.* I spoke of grounding and centring as an appropriate and effective technique of grounding one's energies in new land and introducing oneself, and communing with the spirits of place. By the same token, the giving of offerings is a highly sacrosanct practice and traditionally expresses the principle of sacred exchange (balance). Thus, as I traveled through the Northern Hemisphere and came to new lands, new places, and new spirits and guardians, I would spend sacred time connecting and communing. I would breathe deeply in, deeply out, send out roots and branches, become the mighty World Tree, and then speak aloud my greetings and benedictions to the spirits of place. I would then bless offerings in their name(s) and leave them by a tree, stone, river, or windowsill (any place that called me).

On my last night in New York City, my friend Dylan and I decided to explore Inwood Forest Park, where I was staying nearby. I had previously walked the various forest trails and spoken with the very awake and very active spirits. It was only after circling and meditating in the place for a week that I came upon a boulder bearing a plaque which explained that the site I stood upon was the legendary meeting place of the Dutch colonialists and the Lenape Indians: the site of the infamous and deceitful exchange of Manhattan Island for beads. I was also told that the surrounding forest was virgin; this, to me, explained the intensity of the presences I felt there.

That night, Dylan and I were walking the dog of the women who were hosting me, and we decided to walk into the forest. As we entered the shadows, I noticed a figure wearing white step aside from the path, only metres in front of us, and standing still in the line of trees, unmoving, waiting. I felt a strange intensity and asked Dylan if he, too, could see the figure. Dylan at first replied that he couldn't, but then he began to make out a man he described as wearing white warrior garb. We both agreed that to walk forward might invite hostility, so we backtracked and walked away. While neither of us felt in danger, we did feel a deep and penetrating stare upon our backs.

I had intended to leave offerings in thanks to the spirits of New York City for welcoming me to their land at the famous boulder, so before walking away completely from the forest, we paused by the boulder, lit incense, and made prayers of thanks to the spirits of place. As we walked farther away, I could make out several silhouettes of white-clothed, tall figures pacing back and forth at the very edge of the dark forest. These I took to be the warrior spirits of the Lenape, or perhaps something even older, woven into the very fabric of that untouched forest.

This example illustrates several important points concerning encounters and relationships with the spirits of any given place (though all will be significantly different). Spirits of place will not always necessarily be gentle, welcoming, or caring for human concerns. In fact, when I first ventured into the Inwood Forest to hold my devotional circle for the week, I ended up being absolutely drenched by a spontaneous downpour. It was the fastest circle I ever cast and ever opened. Once I emerged from the woods, the rain stopped, and I could only laugh. Despite the fact that I always acknowledge the spirits of place in all of my rituals and devotional circles, I felt that I was "chased out" because I had not given enough time or care to the offerings given. The next day, I returned to give more offerings of frankincense and myrrh, which were definitely well-received. Even the most spirit-aware and respectful Witches may unintentionally cause offence to the spirits.

The second point is to listen to your instincts and intuition regarding how to act and behave when the spirits of place make contact with you. I can't be absolutely sure, but I definitely feel that if Dylan and I had proceeded into the forest along that path that night, we would have been barred and perhaps even forcefully pushed out. I know of this occurring to several Witches in Australia when experiencing Indigenous sacred sites. Conversely, if you feel genuinely welcomed and elated by the spiritual communication, then by all means, proceed if the proper protocol is followed.

Point number three: the importance of making, blessing, and giving offerings. The offerings must be of worth: either the money spent on them must be reasonable, or appropriate thought and intent must have been imbued into the offerings themselves (will this offering serve or please the spirit[s]? Why and how?). For instance, it is not enough to simply pick up a rock on one's way to a ritual, gathering, or devotional and hand it over as a Divine offering unless, of course, that rock struck you there and then as the correct item to offer. This may be because it resembles a symbol connected with the deity or spirit (such as an inverted triangle for Persephone or Demeter), bears a colour connected with the deity or spirit, or perhaps there is no particular external sign of correspondence, and it simply felt right.

The key is simply that the offering itself should represent the spark of Divinity related to the deity or spirit to you and will, therefore, be of the essence of the spirit. The offering of the gift is like a returning of essence to essence: filling out the wholeness and sustaining the vital charge of the spirit. In this way, Gerald Gardner was speaking truth when he spoke of the Old Gods needing our help and attention just as much as we require theirs.

Spirits of place retain and facilitate the flow of the vital charge of a locale; they are the emissaries of the living land and embody the Divinities of tree, stone, leaf, stream, river, log, hill, and flower. They are also the potencies of skyscrapers, ships, skate parks, and alleys. As mentioned previously, this is perhaps why the genius loci are said to be synonymous with faeries, nymphs, and sprites, depending on the mythological context and the etymological usage of the word. However, popular and cultural uses of words do not always follow the linear path of etymology. Often, a people or group will create their own meanings for words, even if those words have ancient lineages. The spirits of any given place do not necessarily require what we think of as placation, not in the sense that the *buta kala* (the chaotic "demon" spirits of Bali which are sated with offerings of blood or alcohol previous to carrying out Balinese ceremonies) do. Spirits of place do require one's respect, attention, and favour. The following ritual acknowledgement can be used as a template for any spirits of place offering.

Ritual of Acknowledgement

Stand where you feel the power of the place is naturally pooling. This site may be marked by an overt or thoroughly symbolic embodiment, such as a tree or stone. Ground and centre in the way that is familiar and potent to you (or use the Three Realms Alignment). Hold the offering(s) and charge and bless them in the name of the spirits of place. When you feel that the offering(s) are full and overflowing with vitality, lay them down and gesture physically to them while stating aloud the following declaration/blessing:

> *"Spirits of place, I lay this offering for you. May you welcome me as I welcome you. Blessed be."*

Now, either carry out the work or ritual you came to do or turn and leave the site. It is traditional advice to not turn and look back; simply walk away with a silent understanding in your heart that you have perpetuated the balance of the cosmos and, as such, have sustained and celebrated the life force we Witches call magic.

Walking with the Spirits

I have defined Witchcraft as an Ecstasy-driven, Earth-based, Mystery tradition, and I have called it a sacred discipline, where *discipline* translates as intent, purpose, rhythm, and the conscious cultivation of these things in one's life. Discipline can also translate as my dear friend Laura's definition: "Discipline is the pattern which arises from the soul when reflecting on the Divinity in the world."

I have also declared my belief that one cannot be a Witch alone, for that would be anathema to all of our philosophies and our sacred truths. Nothing, and no one, is alone. A Witch is empowered not through or by external agency but by the innate connections we share with the multiplicity of Spirit's expressions that exist in the cosmos we call Great Mystery. We share and celebrate the vitality that flows through and animates each of us as alive and thus sacred. We are each a potency that is not only hidden but also seeks expression.

The Gods are Hidden Potencies because their expression is not won by self-actualisation alone but the sheer and overwhelming desire to enmesh influence in the fabric of Being and be of use and of relevance. Often, the Gods are born of myriad meeting roads, along which the light, wind, rain, and warmth are carried so that the original seed may be nurtured and brought forth from darkness into light. The birth of the Gods is a timeless act that precedes thought. Each of us must find that same origin within and bring forth the Divine seed which our chosen or fated spiritual disciplines will nurture, nourish, and provide sustenance to grow and thrive. When we walk with the spirits, we sing to each other the song of here and now: the Circle is cast, I am ready, I am living, breathing, and death will only renew me. I choose to walk with you so that we may help and heal each other in celebration of the life force we share.

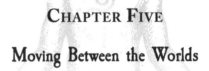

CHAPTER FIVE

Moving Between the Worlds

"Those shamans who did travel to them [other worlds] often had to reckon with an elaborate geography in each. Sometimes their spirit-flight involved moving up or down onto these other cosmic levels, and sometimes sideways into alternative worlds upon the terrestrial plane."
—Ronald Hutton, *Shamans*

As I breathed in the land and opened my mind to the sky above, I felt a ripple to my right but a strong and ancient yet vital presence over my left shoulder. I felt that the Veil had lifted in response to my communion with the spirits of place, and so I shifted my consciousness and slipped through the Veil to the tween where I made a sacrifice to the old wood spirit and Ibis of the Brisbane City Botanic Gardens.

Mircea Eliade called the ability to move between the worlds the pre-eminently shamanic technique and postulated that this was achieved through ecstatic trance states. As ecstasy translates to dissolving the egoic barrier and liberating one's consciousness from separation to interconnection, the skill behind moving between the worlds is, of course, dependent on both mental discipline and a strong acceptance of the magical world-view of infinite possibility.

Consider for a moment the cross-cultural perception of the Shamanic Three Worlds. The Upperworld, Middleworld, and Underworld are all connected by the World Tree, World Mountain, or Cosmic Pillar (Axis Mundi). As I tend to resonate best with the World Tree symbolism, I will refer to the Axis Mundi by that title throughout. To effectively travel and move between the worlds is to know the World Tree as the centre, not only of the cosmos but of self-as-cosmos. If one can embrace

the centre within and see the Divine reality that declares the boundlessness of the living cosmos, then we can affirm the World Tree within and
accept personal destiny to be "Shamanic," accessing the manifold realms
and attaining wisdom and gnosis. As the saying that I was told comes
from Vodou goes, "all are born of magic," and thus, it is destined that we
should be able to directly intimate the methods which make best use of
that primal and undying connection.

Following is a glimpse of how I personally interact with and view the
Shamanic cosmology.

The Sun (the capacity for the emanation of light or Existence-
Knowing-Itself) represents enlightened cosmic consciousness,
Grandmother Weaver, God herself, and Chaos birthing differentiation
(and thus dynamic contrast), causing reflection of "other" and potential
to be and thrive in being. Nature, at least from the perspective of this
planet and this solar system, has shown us that our own Sun alludes to
the circular motion causing the interplay of day and night, which just
so happens to emphasize the four cardinal directions. The Sun rises in
the East, is at its zenith in the North/South, sets in the West, and passes
through our midnight South/North only to commit once more to the
dawn and renew its familiar cycle. We know, of course, that this is because
of our planet's gradual twenty-four-hourly revolution (or thereabouts)
and the 365.25 days of orbit around the Sun annually and our axis tilt.
However, the metaphor strengthens the underlying message that cycles
and seasons illumine and inspire our being.

Cosmologically speaking, the four corners of the world are illustrated
by the Sun and grounded in the Middleworld of Land, as it is only
possible to conceive of directions if we are standing in One Place and
looking out from that "unmoving" centre. Only then can we adequately
and poetically say, from here is East, from here is North, from here is
West, and from here is South, standing in the Centre where they meet.
The four basic Elements of life may be felt in these four directions. The
fact that there is a World Tree joining the Three Realms and that there is
a Sun, source of light to illumine, means that a shadow will be cast if the
light is obstructed by the World Tree. This "shadow" is what is known as
the Veil, which allows us to understand, for all intents and purposes, that
there is a nebulous "separation" between the realms, which only exists to
tell us that we are passing between the realms.

The Underworld exists beneath and within the roots of the mighty World Tree. Coiled within the roots is a dark serpent of the Earth, and this serpent is guarded by the Three Sisters of Wyrd, the keepers of the Well of Memory, which they only grant access to those who are of noble heart. These Three Sisters are known by many titles, including the *Norns* (Norse), the *Moreae* (Greek), the *Fates* (Roman), and the *Wyrd Sisters* (Anglo-Saxon). There are always three, or at least numbers divisible by three (like the nine priestesses of Avalon or the famed nine Muses or faerie maidens), and for some, they represent the cycle of life embodied by humanity, or in this case, the primordial feminine: the young one, the mother or mistress, and the ancient crone.

The sacred triplicity of the Fate Goddess as honoured by Witches is undoubtedly ancient, attested by myth and lore. The Well of Memory is often coupled with a Well or River of Forgetfulness. We are said to lose memory of past existences (as our souls are recycled) by drinking from this well. However, the Orphics of ancient Greece avoided the River Lethe (Forgetfulness) in the Underworld and went instead to drink from the Lake of Memory so that their consciousness remained eternal and gnosis of the Divine self would carry on. I believe that we are able to make that choice personally and that, in truth, there is no difference between either of the rivers or wells, as they derive from the same primal waters. It is only if we accept that our essences end upon physical death that we inevitably drown ourselves in the River of Forgetfulness, or at least that would be so within this cosmology. Again, it is by the ways of nature that we can even fathom eternal life, and all things in nature are recycled, reborn, renewed, and restored.

The Upperworld is reached by ascending the World Tree and opening to the glory of the star-lit realms of light. Those who scale the Tree to bathe in the sweetness of celestial light increase in vibration, and because of this, the Gods and spirits can be met on equal footing, and visions unfold. It is also true that the vibration within the Underworld is in necessary contrast to that of the Middleworld (and those within) so "other" experiences are more able to occur in the realm below also. The Upperworld reminds us of the limitlessness of light, so we are able to conceive of beyond and are opened—split open, in fact—to the eternity of things. It is in the Upperworld that we can truly claim the sovereignty of self as Divine and everlasting, but only by returning to the Middleworld do we ground this simple truth and enact being, which instigates the power to move between the worlds and attain wisdom in the first place. The Underworld helps us to understand this forever truth. And what is up is down, and down is up.

The Tree's branches and roots mirror each other, as if to say there is neither up nor down, only what is. The Tree's mystery, and thus the Mystery of All, is whispered in the mutability of things and the constant reflection of the powerful truths underlying the potencies which allow us to open and embrace the Divine Spirit. The conduit between the above and the below is the determining and qualifying factor related to the merging of the worlds: their interconnectivity. The role of the Shamanic Witch is to enact within themselves the reality and providence of the World Tree so that the power of the Gods is gifted and we deepen to the point of boundlessness. Only from the perspective or presence of infinity can we truly understand and cherish the Allness that we require within the Circle to be able to access the potencies that enact the creativity of the world(s).

In *By Land, Sky & Sea*, I wrote about the technique I find most effective for spirit-flight, trance, vision-journeys, and Oracular Seership, which are all relative to one fundamental principle: that the self is All-Self; Atman and Brahman; microcosm and macrocosm; and as above, so below. What is contained within the Greater Being is, in essence, synonymous with the substance that is "I" or my Own Holy Self. The "I" dwells within us all and is not necessarily related to what we call ego. The "I" is simply the product of reflection, sentience, and awareness. The "I" factor allows us independent and contrasting consciousness so that we may effectively experience and create evolving memory. The paradox is that while we don't exist fundamentally, *essentially*, we do. We are identifiable as the wholeness of immanence, but separated out and distinct to allow for the realisation in the first place that even pondering "God," the Divine, and Spirit directly infers that these concepts are naturally ingrained in our deep selves. We are of the Earth and the starry heavens, but we all come from the realm of stars, as the Orphics knew and modern physics would agree.

In this chapter, I will speak on techniques of trance as portals to the Otherworld. I will also speak on the Veil and on how to find and work with it, and on the multiple "roads" we may walk to explore the cosmic geography.

Trance as Foundation

I have often said that the foundation of all magical work is breath. If one can breathe with power, then one can weave with magical power (life force) and indeed wholly and truly enter into and become it. This enacts the ability to cast spells; draw down the spirits; divine the past, present, and future; and, yes, to move between the worlds.

In *By Land, Sky & Sea*, I briefly touched on the dynamics and principles behind trance and its significance to Shamanic Witchcraft. However, this significance must not be understated. I spoke of trance as Self becoming intoxicated with the All-Self (the essential truth, as detailed previously). However, trance, in its basic utilitarian sense, can also simply refer to an altered state of consciousness.

When discussing the definition of Witchcraft and qualifying the "Ecstasy-driven" component, there are some who have suggested that forms of Wiccan Witchcraft do not rest heavily on trance. However, these positions may derive from the same paradigm, which informs the belief that one does not necessarily have to practise magic to be a Wiccan. I sincerely believe and experience the casting of the Circle, which is both a construct and concept of Wiccan technique, as an inherently magical one. Also, to cast the Circle (in whatever way and with whatever focus) is a gradual deepening of a state of consciousness that is highly conducive to magical ritual. It is also a traditional Wiccan hallmark to raise power in the Circle, to divine and cast spells, and to draw down the God or the Goddess; these are all magical acts. I state this because trance lies at the heart of all of our work in various forms of Witchcraft; it is indeed our foundation, and it begins with breath. If one can breathe, then one can trance.

In Chapter Three, I spoke of the personal predisposition to certain states of consciousness when approaching trance possession. To highlight this, I wish to make it clear that there are some human beings naturally oriented to deeper trance states and others who might not be able to handle the depth or intensity. However, neither is better nor more sacred than the other. Another thought to consider is something that Ravyn Stanfield articulated to the teaching team at the inaugural Reclaiming WitchCamp in Australia. In response to concerns expressed relating to aspecting or drawing down and levels of trance, Ravyn said, "Our bodies are made for this." While I still maintain that there is such a thing as dangerous territory (not necessarily to be avoided) in our spirituality,

I believe Ravyn is correct in this assertion. We are incarnate, body is spirit, all is spiritual, and we are infinitely designed for the capacity of magical undertaking. Trance is part and parcel of a well-trained human being. Again, if you can breathe, you can trance.

The Veil and How to Work with It

The Veil is another one of those amorphic or easily brushed-over concepts within the magical and Shamanic Crafts. However, when exploring trance, it is a necessity to consider the Veil and its implications.

As I illustrated before, within my personal perspective on Shamanic cosmology, the Veil is the shadow caused by the Tree obstructing the light of the Sun (the "coming forth" of Divinity). Therefore, the shadow forms the edges of the periphery: it is as the subconscious. The Veil is the glimmer, or what I like to call the "ripple," that we feel when we are close to the Otherworld. This is not a specifically geographically situated location but a state of consciousness which invites such transition. There are sacred sites in this world that have been specially designed and engineered to evoke certain states of mind within visitors. These sites are often astronomically aligned and draw upon magnetic currents within the Earth, like Stonehenge or Avebury. Some of these sites are also naturally occurring within the landscape and are often known power places in which two or more ley lines (also known as "dragon lines" by some) cross and converge, such as Glastonbury Tor. It is at these geographical locations that the Veil is constantly rippling. However, the Veil's ripple is only a breath away.

The Veil's Ripple

The anecdote that I used to open this chapter was set a month before my handfasting in the Botanic Gardens in which it was held. I spoke with the spirits of place in that area to arrange for a rain-free occasion, and, beautifully, this was the case. As I breathed into my Centre and began to merge with the land, I did, in fact, feel the "ripple" and knew instinctively that this was an indication of the shifting of the edges of realms. Mentally and energetically, I grasped the edges of the wandering threads and swiftly slipped through the Veil and through the worlds. I found this

95

exercise did not require a great deal of effort, but it did require a concerted and conscious effect on my behalf.

Much of the dynamics of our energetic-magical work relies upon the confidence and skill of the Witch or spirit-worker. This is different from arrogance, in which one believes they possess absolute capability and can do no wrong.

A Technique for Finding the Veil and Moving Through It

Breathe to your Centre.

Breathe to the Holy Centre (one and the same).

Align with this forever truth.

Concentrate on your auric field. When you are aware of its permeable boundaries, mentally and energetically fill the aura with your presence and then expand it until it will go no further. Your energetic vibration should now be heightened.

Breathe and wait in patience and alertness.

You may feel the ripple without having to call the Veil, but if that is not the case, mentally call out to the Veil, the Shadow, and fill yourself with desire for this to be so. Soon, you will feel the ripple. When you do, mentally and energetically take hold of the Veil and swiftly and surely slip through into the Other. It is quite difficult to adequately describe how this will feel. However, it is one of those "take the risk and leap" scenarios. Even if you do not feel certain that you have "taken hold" of the Veil, intuit your way through the process. Do this several times until you can feel the shift, even if it is barely momentary. Slipping through the Veil is like cupping water in your hands; there is a trick to doing it.

What to Do When You Are on the Other Side

The "Other" is considered the non-ordinary reality of Michael Harner's Core Shamanism.[49] I find the term *non-ordinary* descriptive in the sense that it implies "that which is not included within accepted consensual reality." The overculture decrees, through apparent consensus, that certain aspects of what Witches might call the Great Mystery are deemed appropriate

---

[49] I have never studied "Core Shamanism" as put forward by Michael Harner. In fact, what I know of Harner and Core Shamanism only comes from secondary sources.

and, therefore, substantially and objectively "real." However, when we truly study this attitude, it is revealed to be hugely subjective and less objective than originally thought (though, again, neither is testimony to what is true, authentic, or real). For all intents and purposes, the Other is just as real as consensual reality, if not intensely more so.

When one has achieved the transition from "this" side to the Other (the Veil creates the illusion of separation, though, of course, it is simply a shadow), we are able to draw upon the depth of the wellspring of our potentiality. We are free and open because we have essentially allowed our minds to embrace more-than and that which is beyond, as a transition seems to have occurred. This altering or deepening of consciousness is associated with trance, and thus, we have attained the prime Shamanic and ecstatic skill: to move between the worlds. What are we to accomplish with this act, however? What is the significance of this ability?

I have often said that the Shamanic skill is less about the moving between the worlds (or shifting paradigms, as the case may be) and more about the absorption of otherworldly information and the transformation and distillation of such knowledge into practical remedy or advice here and now. Instead of referring to the ambiguous Shaman and hunt scenario, I'd like to offer examples from my own Shamanic services and cunning charges.[50]

This first example will speak on the apparent movement of my consciousness from one realm to another and then back again with renewed or newly acquired understanding.

Five months into my original Feri training, my teacher directed me to travel into the Air Realm, or what he called the Air Temple. We did this by walking down the golden road that is also part of becoming one with the Crossroads (a technique of opening to the tween and coming to the Holy Centre) and moving through a portal inscribed with the alchemical sigil for Air. Since that first induction (as I had never overtly worked with "inner temples" of the Elements), I independently explored the power and providence of Air at my own pace. I connected and communed with the associated Guardian, and alongside me was a form of

---

[50] I use the term "cunning charge" to refer to the fact that I am a working Witch. People come to me seeking help with love, finance, protection, property (selling and buying), finding lost objects, healing, divination, and some (usually Witches and Pagans) request me as a vessel for a deity or spirit. I charge for the majority of these services.

the Feri Blue God, as I had discovered he enjoyed the psychopomp role. On one particular visit to the Air Temple, the Guardian of the realm took my hand and flew me up to a crevice within a cliff face. There, he passed on an incantation which seemed to derive from both Latin and Hebrew. The incantation aided me in riding the wind with great ease! I was also shown a particular symbol, again resembling Hebrew characters, and it seemed to resonate with the power of Air. I brought back pieces of abstract information, knowledge, and symbology from this Other realm that had practical uses nonetheless.

This second anecdote refers to the notion that, in fact, the Other saturates "this side" and that there is, indeed, no difference between the two. Many contemporary fantasy stories commenting on the Faerie realms and the like often speak on the idea that the Faerie world and the realms of humanity move further and further apart. However, this has nothing to do with any energetic "placement" or "movement" of these planes/worlds but of the overwhelming paradigm in Western cultures, which declares Faerie to be fake. Faerie is still very much here and now; we simply have to accept that fact and shift our perception. When we have attained confidence (which is different from belief) in this assertion, we are able to truly embrace our own innate capacity to move between the realms.

I am often called upon by friends and family (and this definitely includes coven siblings) to identify spirits or energies within homes and commune with or banish them. In this case, one of my then-coven siblings invited me over to check on a perceived spirit residing within her house, where they lived with two other Wildwood Witches. I had been told that running could be heard at night from room to room when all were in bed and that the spirit had blown air directly in this Witch's ears. I sat in the centre of the house and breathed into silence and Centre. I then simply called out to the potential resident spirit, and he appeared cycling on an old penny-farthing bicycle. He had intense green eyes, long, choppy blonde hair, and a blue tailcoat with a red undergarment. He was a Faerie. He told me his name was Jack and that he had been attracted to the house because of the Faerie altar that had been built in the backyard by the Witches and by the primal energy of a recent Bacchic rite.

After this initial meeting, I moved downstairs to sit and talk with my friends. In the empty chair directly opposite me appeared Jack, smiling broadly, eyes gleaming. I told them Jack was present, and the housemates began to ask questions through me but directed at Jack. Jack found this most hilarious and decided to give what I thought were sardonic answers in return. For instance, they wanted to know if their offerings of chocolate and wine were satisfying. In response, Jack requested three drops of no-pulp orange juice in white wine. I couldn't help but laugh. As with many of the Faerie people I have met, Jack could not be said to abide by any human sense of convention. He conveyed to me that he worked on an equal-opportunity give-receive basis and that he would bless the house if offerings were constant and consistent. This is congruent with Faerie lore and with my interactions with a variety of spirits. All of this information was simple for me to access and the only key to acquiring it was the confidence in my skill to do just that (and, of course, breath and trance).

Trance Journeys

Below, you will find trance journeys which aid in the exploration of the major realms and regions of the Shamanic cosmos as discussed in this book. This style of trance journey is open and will hopefully provide an effective springboard from which to delve more deeply into the mythos and teachings of each realm or feature. I encourage the personalisation of experience and the invitation to reception, or, rather, the idea that these encounters and interactions are profoundly authentic, so elements of surprise and unfolding will unravel without self-determined volition. Remember that if the text below says "see" or "visualise," please insert whichever sense or perceptions are most relevant to your experience. These days, I almost always say "sense, feel, notice, or perceive" when leading trance journeys or magical workings. When we close our eyes (or not) and journey inward, we must remember the lesson of the Spiral Soul. When we feel we are drawing inward, we are simultaneously moving outward, and conversely, when we journey out, we are moving into the Holy Centre. With this in mind, journey well!

The World Tree

The World Tree, or the Tree of Life, is the axis that represents the wholeness of the Three Worlds. It is the Centre and the circumference, the matrix and the keeper. The World Tree is our ladder of ascent, our spiral staircase into shadow, and our doorway to the four directions. The World

Tree is where we come to meet at the Crossroads and celebrate our ancient and ever-renewing Craft.

> *Breathe deeply and rhythmically. Come to the Holy Centre. Embrace the forever truth, that Self is All-Self. You dissolve into the boundless, the limitless infinity of the living cosmos. Breathe deeply and rhythmically.*
>
> *You awaken to yourself, standing before a titanic tree, spiralling and spinning into eternity. You cannot perceive the beginning or the end of this tree. As you look upwards, you see the boughs and branches pierce the Veil of the heavens, and the light of the Sun and Moon moves like an endless wheel in a continuous arc above. You look downward through the tangled mass of roots and glimpse secret streams of glistening water that seem to travel in undulating patterns until they disappear at the lips of what looks like an ancient well. You hear the hissing of serpents and the breath of dragons. You hear the distant call of an eagle, and you crane your head to perceive the limitless, coalescing light of the arc of the Sky. An eagle, a majestic bird of prey, traces the symbol for infinity directly above you. You become gradually aware that you are now standing right next to the World Tree, and its girth is imperceptible. Under the shade of the Tree, the Veil of night falls upon you, and you sense rippling in every corner. "Corner of what?" This thought echoes through your clear yet alert mind.*
>
> *"The Four Corners of the World." This answer ripples back through the Ether, shimmering at the edge of darkness. Suddenly, four roads appear, creating a convergence at the Tree: a mighty Crossroads.*

Prayer

> *"World Tree, Tree of Life, I am born of your Holy Centre, I stand at your mighty Crossroads, and I am enlivened by the here and now. World Tree, Tree of Life, I am your Own Holy Child. I am the World Tree, for all eternity, so mote it be."*

The Power of the Directions

The four cardinal directions represent the spatial awareness of the Land, the manifest, the incarnate, and the corporeal. To be able to conceive of the directions means that we have a point of reference anchored in space and time, and this, of course, helps to reinforce that we are indeed in some place. By honouring the directions, we potentise that place to become the convergence of the four directions, and thus the mighty Crossroads, that world tween the worlds. This is further heightened by the fact that the three other directions are also present. The Great Above and the Great Below are present because here we are, standing at the World Tree, branches spiralling upward into radiance and roots delving downward into the Well. The Centre, the seventh direction that each of us brings and activates—the true reference point of the unfolding of the directions—is the gift of being and the ignited awareness that comes with acknowledging and celebrating this earnest fact. Everywhere is a Centre, or, in fact, the Holy Centre.

By walking into each direction, along each of the roads, we open to the pathways of manifestation and gnosis, depending on which way we walk and with which intention. To walk the motion of the Sun, to mimic the light's arc and movement, is to ally oneself with the waxing tide: growth, expansion, and creativity. To walk against the Sun, to contradict its passage, is to ally oneself with the waning tide: decline, contraction, and destruction. Both are necessary for the Shamanic Witch. To walk with the Sun is to walk into light; to walk against the Sun is to walk into shadow and darkness. We disappear beyond the Veil (the Shadow), which is caused by the Tree obstructing the continuum of light. This, by pure will, is attested by the ways of nature. One must decide whether walking into the East (or any direction) is the initiation of a cycle or whether it is a journey of intent, focus, and investment in one direction for a time and its associated magics and mysteries.

If we also associate the directions with Elements (which we will for the purposes of this book), then each direction beholds certain powers and providence. If I choose to walk down the Road to the West (often aligned with Water), then I may either work some deep, oceanic love spell or begin a cycle of banishing an element in my life associated with Water if I were to walk against the Sun, or drawing in an element of Water if I moved deasil. Of course, there is much more to it than this.

I spoke before of the pathways of gnosis and manifestation in relation to the directions and the Tree. It would be easy to assume that for these pathways to be the case, one would have to move to the direction associated with Air and then travel to Fire, Water, and Earth (manifestation) or move from the direction of Earth to Water, Fire, and then Air (gnosis). Remember, of course, that these formulae only exist because Spirit (the predecessor and the "product," the fifth that makes the four into one) underlies these processes. However, we can also effectively place Spirit in the Centre at the position of the World Tree itself; the Great Above and the Great Below are extensions of this quintessence held from different perspectives. To effectively craft these pathways while moving between the worlds is not necessarily about placement or correspondence; it is, however, about orientation and attitude.

Orientation from the Holy Centre (Spirit), acknowledging the Great Above and the Great Below (which hold us), and then moving to the East, we witness the rising of the sun and open to the Element of Air (clarity of intent and distillation of thought). We bow, give thanks, and gracefully move deasil to the North (Fire: impassioned intent and activation of energy), witnessing the peak of the light, giving thanks, and moving again with the Sun to the West (Water: channelled intent and flowing energy) and giving thanks. We dance with the Sun beyond what appears to be their last final resting place for the Tide of Light and come to the South (Earth: grounding of intent and planting of energetic seeds) and give thanks.

However, the cycle is not complete. We must walk full circuit, returning to the Eastern point and then the Holy Centre, acknowledging Above and Below (as above, so below), giving and receiving the magical charge which has been clarified, impassioned, channelled, and grounded by the Elements. By Spirit, the fifth, the quintessence, we come to truly honour and realise (in the literal sense) our intent and accept it for ourselves, owning the charge and becoming actively responsible for our magic.

To walk the pathway of gnosis would be to again begin in the Holy Centre and walk outward to the South (Earth: physicality), then to the West (Water: emotional landscape held by the senses), to the North (Astral: the star-fire of the spirit), then to the East (Air, the mental sphere, conceptualisation, and inspiration). To complete this pathway, you would walk the complete circuit, returning to South and then to the Centre, acknowledge Above and Below (this time with the emphasis of "as without, so within"). This way, you have ignited the spark of the Spirit, of Own Holy Self, and accepted and embraced it. Thus, it is possible not only to activate either pathway within the external world but also when you are moving between the worlds and in what some may view as the "internal planes."

Following, I will briefly speak of the powers and providence of each direction or "road."

- **The Road to the East:** Walk this road to soar with the Element of Air and its associated qualities of thought, clarity, communication, resonance, intellect, and music.

- **The Road to the North/South:** Walk this road to dance with the Element of Fire and its associated qualities of light, passion, courage, sexuality, and transformation.
- **The Road to the West:** Walk this road to flow with the Element of Water and its associated qualities of love, cleansing, depth, intuition, and death.
- **The Road to the South/North:** Walk this road to delve into the Element of Earth and its associated qualities of grounding, prosperity, sensuality, fecundity, rest, and renewal.
- **The Road to the Sky:** The Realm of the Sky—and thus the road to it—is one of expansion, knowledge brought to wisdom, visions, deity, and freedom. We may scale the Tree with hand and foot, but it is far simpler to call upon the Emissary of the Heavens: the Great Bird.

Upon the Great Bird: the Mount of the Gods

Before embarking on this journey, it is important to first place oneself at the World Tree and come to the Holy Centre. Go through the World Tree trance journey.

Look up and witness the celestial interplay of light and darkness. Perceive the star-fire, just as you feel the coolness of the breath of deep space. As you wonder at the possibilities, you hear the faint echo of a bird's call. You glance up and see this Great Bird tracing infinity patterns across the arc of the Sky. The Mount of the Gods continues to echo its call out through the Three Worlds, and this call quickens your heartbeat. Your throbbing heart yearns to ascend, climbing higher—fly! You feel ancient wings unfurl and unfold from the beating crest of your crimson heart, and at this, the Great Bird looks down upon you; though the Bird is high and far above you, you notice the graceful crane of its head and the startling clarity of its eyes. A soundless, wordless call emanates from deep within you, and the Great Bird hearkens and spirals downward to land directly before you. Extend your arms in a gesture of reverence and embrace. Remember to breathe. [51]

---

[51] The Great Bird of the Sky can be the Muan Bird of the Mayans, the Garuda of the Hindu traditions, the Eagle of many Native American tribes, and perhaps even the Phoenix of Regeneration. The Great Bird is *your* Great Bird.

Counsel/Council with the Starry Ones

*To ascend into the Sky opens one to the possibility of counsel and com-
munication with the gods. I have often pondered why the deities or
gods are said to reside in the Sky. My feeling is that, again, this is not a
geographical (or hierarchical) inclination so much as a cosmological and
mythic one. The Sky is not simply the atmospheric layers of gas and light
that encircle our planet but the outward and upward (from our land-
locked point of reference) expansion of reality. The Sky is essentially the
symbolic manifestation of what we nominally call "space" (both literally
and symbolically).*

*To say the gods dwell in the heavens or in the Sky is not to negate
chthonic or oceanic spirits and deities (or earth and forest spirits
either), but to acknowledge the higher energetic vibration through
which the gods express themselves. To travel to the Sky is to raise one's
vibration to meet with the vibration of the gods, which enables one
to share counsel or council with the Starry Ones. This also does not
mean that the gods do not "descend" to share their counsel with us
(hence drawing "down").*

*The Great Bird bows to you in response to your gesture of reverence
and embrace, and you bow to seal the exchange of honour. Cast your
senses out to surround both you and the Great Bird. What is the feeling?
Ask silently, "Are you to be my mount?" How does the Great Bird respond
to this, energetically or apparently?*

*If you can determine the response is positive, you walk towards the
Bird and mount it. The Bird unfolds its gracious, expansive wings, and a
swift, clean draught of wind moves through the manifold celestial feathers.
The Great Bird takes flight, and your body leans forward as your hands
and forearms fold around the Bird's neck. You notice, as the wind rushes
past and you climb in altitude, that there seems to be one star brighter
than the rest at the apex of the heavens, crowning the World Tree.
As you soar higher and higher upon the Mount of the Gods, the azure
blue sky melts and melds into the dark chasm of space filled with the
campfires of heaven.*

*It is here that that bright star seems to eclipse the swollen darkness
with its diamond-white light. You draw nearer and nearer and find that
the white light of the star unfolds, becoming a shimmering white plain.
Then you land and demount the Great Bird, turning to give thanks and
staring directly into the jet-black eyes of your ally in the Sky. You turn to*

face what seems to be an altar rising from the shifting diamond-white light; it swirls like mist and coalesces to form columns of light in a circle surrounding the altar. You enter the temple and make a silent prayer to the Starry Ones, the hidden potencies, the gods and goddesses, and you listen, wait, and watch....

When you have finished your counsel with the gods, you give deep thanks and reverence and turn to walk back to your Mount, the Great Bird. You do not look back at the temple or the altar and simply settle onto your ally, leaning in with a firm grasp as you are transported safely and swiftly back down to Land beside the towering World Tree. You give thanks and reverence to the Great Bird and watch as it returns home, Sky-bound.

The Road to the Underworld

The road to the Underworld can take us one of two major highways: literally downward to visit the Sisters of Wyrd/Fate who guard the Well of Memory, or across the Sunless Sea to the Isle of Apples. Of course, there are multiple by-ways and paths "off the beaten track."

Within the Celtic cosmology of Land, Sky, and Sea, it is Sea that is parallel with or synonymous to the Underworld. Briefly, again, the reasoning is that in the Celtic cultures, the great Atlantic Ocean was to the West, and as the sun set over the immortal horizon, it disappeared across the sunless sea through the mist and claimed the throne of the Underworld. We often expect the "underworld" to be dark, obscure, and gloomy, but it may be our current paradigm of the Christian Hell that shapes this perception for us. We must remember that to many ancient and mystical cultures and societies, it was believed that there were stars or fields of light under the soil, and this is the power that the seeds drew their great strength and potency to bring forth crops and abundance or fertility. The Underworld/Sea is, in fact, a place of prosperity, riches, renewal, rest, and revivification. Its companion is Shadow Self (or Fetch), and thus, we are also moving through the "subconscious": the bridge between the conscious Talking Self and the Star Self, the realm of Dreams.

We walk upon the heaving white waves of the cresting Sea and find ourselves dancing through dream-swollen mists. The Other is all around. Here it is, the true space between Land and Sky. We meet the past, present, and future and the infinite possibilities that swirl endlessly around our Wyrd.

The Well of Memory and the Sisters of Wyrd

The Well of Memory was discussed in *By Land, Sky & Sea*, and I relayed the powerful, transformational story of a dear friend of mine and his journey through and with death to remembering. Memory is not simply a recollection of past events; it is the reflection of the Weaver, God herself, within the vibration of the Web and the unfolding of her Holy Being. Memory is the Divine mirror to the thoughts, actions, and weavings of Own Holy Self. Memory is neither etheric nor entirely substantial; it is the breath in between and, as such, is a gift of the Sea, the Underworld. It is upon reflection and in hindsight that we begin to perceive the "bigger picture."

This trance journey intends for an encounter with the Sisters of Wyrd or the Keepers of Fate. Whatever names or faces they show to you are the right ones, and you will derive the insight and wisdom needed.

Before embarking on this journey, it is important to first place oneself at the World Tree and come to the Holy Centre. Go through the World Tree trance journey.

You stand before the World Tree and listen to the deep, chthonic pulse of Water against stone. You yearn to travel the Road to the Underworld. Nostalgia overwhelms your being, and you glide towards the Great Tree. In your mind, an image of a perfect door forms, and as you near the Tree, you find that this exact image becomes the portal through which you must enter the Tree. When you reach the door in the Tree, you find that a key is required to unlock the door. Your hands come to your throat, and you find a key on a thread around your neck. This key is yours and yours alone, and it slides neatly into the keyhole, turns, and the door yields open.

Before you, an ancient and shadow-swept spiral staircase twists and turns. The stairs disappear around a corner, and your first foot forward is followed swiftly by your second. As each step down becomes broader and lower, you find that it becomes a gradual meditation of deepening. You sink more deeply into the rhythm and repetition of the descent. You are so involved and enraptured by this process that you are almost shocked when you see a warm, flickering light in the distance. It grows brighter and more filled with a radiant warmth, and soon, you find yourself at the edge of a wide and open cavern.

As you step inward into what feels like a warm-wet womb, you notice a cauldron in the centre of the cavern. The cauldron's base disappears straight into the soft earth beneath it; it seems to become a well. Three figures surround the cauldron-well. They are draped in grey robes and emanate a feeling of timelessness. As you take a further step into the cavern, the sound piques their interest, and they glance up at you. Their faces are hidden by translucent veils, and yet you notice their bright, deep eyes, constantly watering at the edges as if tears of overwhelming memories are welling up inside. They open their arms collectively and call you into their embrace.

You drift over to the Sisters as if wading through a dream, and you find that you are kneeling now, surrounded by the Wyrd Ones, as they create a circle around you with their bodies and beings. Hands held, they begin to resonate a low chant, wordless yet ancient. You peer over the edge of the cauldron's lip. What do you see?

To the Isle of Apples Across the Sunless Sea

You perceive a massing of shadow on the surface of the water, and you are drawn further in, your eyes coming to a clearer focus to behold the Mystery of shadow dancing with Water. The low chant becomes a high-vibrating shriek, almost bloodcurdling, and you hear the massing and writhing voices of beloved dead and ancestors from long ago. A desirous force moves you to lean further into the cauldron until your nose and lips touch the velvet tension of the water's surface…you fall—you fall!

There is no splash or cold-wrapped shivering body, for you are in a boat sailing across a silver-shining Sea. You are sailing upon calm waters, weaving through wave after wave of blessed serenity.

Suddenly, the scent of fresh-blooming apples washes over you, overwhelming and intoxicating your senses. Faintly, you perceive a mass of land rising from the cresting waves in the distance. As a strong current of wind fills the sails above you, you glide swiftly to the shores of this soulful island. In your mind, you name this place the Isle of Apples for the strong scent of this fruit.

Above you, a silver Sun and a golden Moon dance together and kiss sweetly. You walk across diamond-white sand and move to higher ground into thickly treed forest. A Wildwood. There are twisted trees and tangled flowers, stones dreaming in the emerald hue of the sacred place, and herbs slithering like cunning serpents through the enraptured undergrowth. Tree-boughs heavy-laden with apples appear at every bend, and you find yourself standing at the entrance to a perfect apple grove.

Your heart seems to grow silent, reverent of the stillness and solitude of this place. There is a cauldron in the centre of this grove too, and an old woman guards the liquid-flaming crucible. She gestures openly to you with one finger, and her dark, intense stare transfixes your spirit. You move, as if in a trance, to the cauldron in the centre of the apple grove. The nearer you come to the cauldron, the younger the woman becomes until she appears as a playful and potent being. She is holding a wooden ladle and offers you a drink from the steaming broth she is stirring and keeping. You lean into drink but she pulls the ladle away from you and laughs. The apple trees surrounding you begin to vibrate, shake, and seem to laugh in return. An apple drops from one of the branches of one of the nine trees and rolls to your feet. The young girl giggles and stares down towards the apple. You know and hear her thoughts.

You pick up the bright red apple, knowing that this is a gift, a blessing, from this Otherworldly place across the Sunless Sea. You look up once more and smile at the golden Moon and silver Sun. You look back across the cauldron, and in the young one's place is a full-bellied woman: a Mistress. She holds the ladle out to you again, and as you lean in to drink, holding the apple in your left hand and channelling blazing intent from your right, a veil of black space folds around you. There is no looking; there is nowhere to look until you seem to be floating in the cool breath of the primordial seas, and you gaze up at what seems to be three Moons high in the heavens. These three Moons bear timeless faces, and fluttering breezes shift the silken robes they wear...robes? Faces? The Three Sisters of Wyrd, of Fate living and knowing itself, peer down upon you. You are kneeling in the waters of the cauldron.

You stand and step out of the cauldron, and the Sisters hold out a white robe for you. You dress and breathe in the sweetness of the cavern: sage, rosemary, peppermint, mugwort, and thyme have been burning, their smell strong. You look down at your left hand and see that you are still firmly grasping the apple the woman gifted you. You hold it up to the flickering flame of the cauldron, and the Sisters kneel and bow their heads to the Mighty One, to the secret within. You know what you must do. The robe that you are wearing is fitted with a cord belt, and hanging in a pouch is a blade. You unsheathe it, and it glimmers in the firelight.

With the blade in your right hand, you slice the apple in half crosswise. The star!

You find yourself at the topmost of the World Tree, hands free and open to the winds of change to the changing course of Fate. Your star shines radiantly above you, resting upon your crown. You whisper this holy prayer as you look down upon the patterns of the undulating Land: "Who is this flower above me?"

You sing this holy prayer as you cradle the bright star upon your crown: "And what is the work of this God?"

You chant this holy prayer as your hands fold upon the secret of your heart and the red-flesh apple that reminds you: "I would know myself in all my parts."

CHAPTER SIX

Ecstatic Spellcraft

"You must envision it to experience it. Summon it with every dancing molecule of your body, with every vesper, every wish and prayer, every uttered breath. Do not believe –know!"
—Phyllis Curott, *The Love Spell*

Those who have read my book *Spirited* will be familiar with what I call "successful spellcraft," which consists of tried and true methods and metaphysical laws that govern the energetic realms and assure the Witch of success in their magical endeavours. In this chapter, I will be introducing a technique of Shamanic spellcraft called "ecstatic spellcraft," which awakens the primal senses and inspires the spirit to embrace its destiny to manifest.

As Witches, our spells do not define who we are, but it is important to understand our spells as psychic imprints, which can be effectively traced back to their point of origin (the caster, the dreamer, or we who desire). When we cast a spell, we are making affirmed choices and devoting ourselves to seeing out the course until direct manifestation. At times, this may be as straightforward as requiring extra cash and obtaining it through spellcraft within a matter of days or casting out energetic nets to draw in love or a well-suited lover and waiting a full solar cycle until the fulfilment of the charge.

During that year, the spell will teach the Witch about the true nature of self-love and how when we stop looking, love finds us. Spellcraft is much more than it seems and is hardly a superficial or selfish act unless it is approached in that manner. For instance, most of the spells I cast are for others' benefit. They range from selling property to evoking happiness and strength. I have also found that a spell is no discrete thing, and in retrospect, once the "floodgates" are opened, they can rarely, if ever, be closed and will continue to take effect and express in a variety of ways.

Ecstatic spellcraft utilises trance states in order to propel the Witch's innate life force into an intensified spiral of power. This kind of spellcraft is generally performed on one's own; however, the presence of others will not necessarily detract from the raw energy being raised. Dance, songs, and chants, columns of incense smoke, and the rhythmic pulse underlying effective ritual will aid in the efficacy of such workings. Following, I will examine different aspects of ecstatic spellcraft and provide an effective method through which to implement the sacred practice.

Spellcraft as Empowerment and Liberation

"She who fain
Would learn all sorcery yet has not won
Its deepest secrets, them my mother will
Teach her, in truth all things as yet unknown.
And ye shall all be freed from slavery,
And so ye shall be free in everything..."
                              —*Aradia: Gospel of the Witches*[52]

In early 2010, I ran a series of workshops entitled *The Spirited Life: Walking the Talk of the Witch*. One part of the workshop involved the discussion of magic as psychology, philosophy, art and science, and life force. After the preliminary discussion, I would then lead the group in a psyball-creation exercise, in which we created energetic vessels for needs, desires, or wishes and, at the intuited time, we each released them into the cosmos (or ourselves or another physical container) so that they would come to manifest in the natural order of things. Afterwards, during the debrief, I would ask everyone how they felt about being able to successfully, with the power innate within, create change and bring renewal or end to various aspects within their lives. The answers were

---

[52] Leland, Charles Godfrey, Mario Pazzaglini, and Dina Pazzaglini (trans.). *Aradia, or the Gospel of the Witches: A New Translation*. Phoenix Publishing, 1998, pp. 140–141.

generally similar: "I feel empowered, natural, alive, a part of all existence, and inextricably connected. I feel that it is my destiny to manifest."

When we can truly embrace the destiny within all of us to co-create with the cosmic forces that also flow through us, we awaken to the deep source of primal power that reminds us constantly that we are Divine and walk as Gods amongst Gods.

The practice of spellcraft is not merely for the attainment of "things," it is also medicine: we are able to definitively choose our own paths and, therefore, be an active and conscious part of the All of Creativity. When I hear that spellcraft is akin to prayer, I tend to shudder inwardly; this is simply not my experience and, therefore, not my belief. Spellcraft and its associated magical methodologies are concerned with affirming a choice and wilfully manifesting to attain desire, fulfil necessity, and effect change. Spellcraft is acknowledging, accepting, and affirming the sacred principle or charge of the Witches: magic.

Spellcraft provides a context for our empowerment and liberation as human beings because it is a sorcerous pathway.

Sorcery

The idea of "sorcery" in the contemporary Craft traditions is sometimes met with derision or scepticism, even insularly. Sorcery seems to negate the idea that Witchcraft is a religious tradition. Raven Grimassi often speaks of a distinction between *Stregheria* (the Old Religion, "of the Witches") and *Stregoneria* (sorcery). Grimassi places an emphasis on Aradia, her Mother Diana, and the Horned Consort. While magic and spellcraft are integral (or part and parcel) of the Witches' religion, the emphasis seems to be on the Mystery tradition as interwoven into the theology.

My first Feri teacher, Storm Faerywolf (founder of the BlueRose line of Feri), expressed to me it is not the fault of the Traditional Craft that it has become associated with religion and mystery traditions and that the entwined strands of spirituality and sorcery can be called the "Crooked Path" or what I also like to call the "Wild Way." I would also add to this that all things are Spirit; therefore, all is implicitly spiritual.

In some of the foundational texts of the modern Witchcraft revival as catalysed by Gerald Gardner, we find an interesting notion that, somehow, Witches (or what Gardner classes as the "Clandestine Priesthood of the Wica") were opposed to working magicians and so-called sorcerers.

This is not only ahistorical, but also blatantly reductive and dichotomous. If anything, the cunning people of those times and places—England in the sixteenth and seventeenth centuries, for instance—who were often paid or traded with for their services were fiercely opposed to so-called malevolent Witches, who were considered a bane in those societies. Sorcery, however, belongs to those cunning people, Witches, spirit workers, and service magicians of many kinds. It is also true, as scholars such as Emma Wilby and Owen Davies discuss thoroughly in their books, that the line between a cunning person or a Witch and one accused of evil sorcery by neighbours or the powers that be is very thin indeed.

The very word *sorcery* has its roots in Old French and Medieval Latin, and it is applied to both Witches and wizards by French speakers. As is usual for Witches, it also has a connection to the uncanny capacity to work with fate. Fate for Witches may be the way we conceive of the Providence or Great Mystery that endlessly creates, transforms, and destroys all things, of which we are a part. Sorcery is the ability to remember and draw power from this intrinsic Divinity, sovereignty, and agency and work wonders with it. We are weavers with Grandmother Weaver, as Wildwood Witches might say, and we are potentially active fates, as my beloved Lee Morgan would say.

To be sorcerous is to be grounded in the here and now and to endeavour to enhance the fullness of one's quality of life. The road would then divert, which is where the analogy of the Crooked Path or Wild Way can come into play. We can continue on the path of focussing only (or largely) on the mundane, physical, and directly immediate plane, or we could *also* delve into the centre of the here and now and come to find the intense power of Divinity that resonates within it and align or devote to it. Truly, however, if one cannot or does not respect this Divinity (however we choose to relate to it), the power will not work for us. There is great merit in both religion and what we normally class as "magic," but what I would call sorcery.

To be sorcerous is to endeavour to be of aid, not only to oneself, but to one's human and non-human community (though you may specialise in one or the other) and, eventually, to the greater cosmos. These gradients have names in the ancient Greek traditions: *thaumaturgy* (sorcery and "practical" magic) and *theurgy* (magic and ritual for communion with the God[s] and with the Immanent Divine).

This all resonates with the original Charge of the Goddess, or, rather, the Aradian charge from Diana (Queen of the Witches) to her Divine daughter, Aradia. In this text, first published in the late nineteenth century, we discover that in adhering to *La Vecchia Religione*—literally "the Old Religion"—a Witch attains to certain gifts or powers. The following is a slightly modernised version by Raven Grimassi:

> *"To bring success in love.*
> *To bless and consecrate (and to banish and curse).*
> *To speak with spirits.*
> *To know of hidden things.*
> *To call forth spirits.*
> *To know the Voice of the Wind.*
> *To possess the knowledge of transformation.*
> *To possess the knowledge of divination.*
> *To know and understand secret signs.*
> *To cure disease.*
> *To bring forth beauty.*
> *To have influence over wild beasts."*[53]

Spellcraft as Determination to Manifest: Through the Elements

I have mentioned the Elemental Pathways of both manifestation and gnosis throughout this book, and in this section, I will readdress how and why they are connected to the concept of and execution of spellcraft.

If spellcraft is underlined by the determination to manifest, then the Pathway of Manifestation is the obvious formula to achieve this.

Air: Clarity of Intent and Distillation of Thought

Ask yourself:

What is my intent? Why is this my intent? How will I specify my intent? Is my intent relevant to my context or circumstance? How will my intent help to empower and liberate my pure will? How will my intent help to enhance and deepen my living myth?

---

[53] Raven Grimassi, *Italian Witchcraft* (Llewellyn, 2000) 299–300.

Fire: Impassioned Intent and Activation of Energy

Do:

Excite your senses. Titillate your visual, olfactory, aural, oral, and tactile senses! Raise the body (and therefore spirit) to a state of arousal, provocation, and/or ecstasy; move into or through extremities. If you begin to tire of the rhythm or repetition of your method of raising power, ensure that you break through this barrier. Be sure, however, that you tread the fine line between compulsion and exertion safely.

Water: Channelled Intent and Flowing Energy

Feel:

The tide of magical power (vital life force) is heaving and sighing. Know the breaking point and open your consciousness to intuit the moment of climax and, thus, release. Feel absolute conviction towards your goal and flow in that pure stream of ecstasy that has lifted your own vibration!

Earth: Grounding of Intent and Planting of Energetic Seeds

Know:

The intent has traveled towards its completion and has become a seed of itself to be nourished within the Cauldron of Spirit (the dark cauldron of nature). The seeds have been planted, and it is advised that privacy, mystery, and reverence be held for the spell seed as it begins to grow, imbued by a greatly focussed power.

A Note on "Order"

During a workshop I held in Canberra (Australian Capital Territory), I presented this concept of what I have sometimes referred to as the formulae hidden within the Elemental pathways. A friend of mine added that to effectively cast a spell or work towards the fulfilment of an end, one might not necessarily start with Air and the clarification of intent; one might be impassioned (Fire) by a cause first and then seek to work magically, which I completely agree with. However, I am referring more to a "mechanism" than the unfolding dynamic of how one journeys towards casting a spell or how motivation or impetus develops and arises. I maintain that, in order to cast a successful spell, one must centre into clarity of intent and then move from that point into impassioning, channelling, and grounding it. However, one can be motivated and inspired by any part of this Elemental equation to create change in the first place.

Elemental Pathway of Manifestation: A Spell

You need absolutely nothing external for this working.

Breathe into your Centre.

As you breathe deeply and rhythmically, begin to draw down cosmic light and let it pool at your crown. It amplifies as the vibration intensifies, and you feel the word "Spirit" resonate through your being. You begin to feel heightened and truly connected to the All, to infinite possibility.

As you breathe deeply and rhythmically and you draw this cosmic light of Spirit down through your crown, your head, it condenses into a seed of pulsing light. It hovers at the gateway of your lips, and as your breath cycles, it begins to glow and radiate, and you clarify your intention. You create a visualisation or a strong sensation or knowing—a target to build upon—of the outcome as you desire it and not the process of how it will develop. The word "Air" vibrates through your being, and as it does, it draws this visualisation into your chest, in which your primal heart is pounding ceaselessly and creating a meter for the power which is raising to a point and about to dance in the Fire.

As you breathe deeply and rhythmically and you draw this Spirit seed into your sex, the Fire of generation glows brightly. The flames in this ancient crucible dance with the vigour of passion and the courage of daring! The visualisation no longer needs to be held by the head or mind. It is now taken into the flame and transformed into a thriving, lived experience. You feel it in every piece of you, and the word "Fire" races through your being.

As you breathe deeply and rhythmically, this power becomes channelled to a point and swoops through your being, bringing you to your knees (perhaps physically, but definitively symbolically). The word "Water" wells up inside of your swollen soulfulness; pieces and pieces of desire, longing, ferocious need, and yearning to change and transform (yourself or a situation) begin to weave together and melt into a river that rushes toward a sea.

As you breathe deeply and rhythmically, this holy river of power comes to a broad delta and empties into a sea which becomes a cauldron: the dark cauldron of nature. The Spirit seed, which has been carried by this momentum of energy, this force, this writhing, excited power, is now dropped into the moist darkness of this cauldron, and the word "Earth" moans from its belly (the centre and circumference). Now, you remember your feet and how they are rooted upon the ground and drawn down irrevocably by the force of gravity, calling all things to become fixed. And so shall your spell be fixed!

This technique is anchored by the same points that the Fivefold Blessing works with. In its reverse order, it becomes the pathway of manifestation as discussed (from least dense to densest). The Spirit seed (or seed of light) has come from Spirit, has been clarified and distilled by Air in the chest, impassioned and activated by Fire in the sex, channelled by Water at the knees, and grounded and planted by Earth in the feet. What is subtly implied, of course, is that the dark cauldron of nature in which the seed has been planted is, in fact, the cosmic matrix, and therefore, we return to Spirit. This continuous cycle will affect the ether and impregnate it with the "thought-form" expressed by the seed; it will arrange itself to reflect it. This action triggers the process whereby the essential creation becomes embodied within the immediacy of the flesh and the direct here and now. So is the spell cast and so is the outcome necessitated.

The Law of Three, Karma, and Spellcraft

"I am the owner of my karma.
I inherit my karma.
I am born of my karma.
I am related to my karma.
I live supported by my karma.
Whatever karma I create, whether good or evil, that I shall inherit."
—The Buddha, *Anguttara Nikaya V. 57—Upajjhatthana Sutta*[54]

The capacity of spellcraft to instruct in the ways of the Witch is infinite. Forever is the Witch learning the cosmic laws (the ways of nature) through

---

[54] Bhikkhu, Thanissaro (trans.), The Buddha, *Anguttara Nikaya V. 57—Upajjhatthana Sutta*, 1997.

the true Law of Three: a law that, in my mind at least, does not represent any kind of ancient Pagan morality or ethical code of conduct.

When we point—the way we might think of a Witch holding out their pointer finger to cast a spell —three fingers point back at us. I have a rhyme to illustrate this point:

> *"As I point, three fingers point back at me.*
> *Their names are Is, Was, and Shall Be."*

Everything I do affects the Wyrd, and the Wyrd affects me: the ever-emergent, unfolding dynamic fate threads of all things. As a Witch, I am one of the Wyrd Ones (just like those Weird Sisters of Shakespeare's famous Scottish play), and my work is to sorcerously weave with the Wyrd, co-creating desired patterns. This is the Threefold Law I am most poetically intrigued by: the notion that what I am doing is woven of the momentum of the past, my response to that which is, and the possibilities of what might become. Of course, on some level, all of this will then affect me as well. Consequences, in this case, are desired: the whole point of magic is to make something happen, to change something into another.

We often speak of the Threefold Law in terms of aversion. Most beginner's texts on modern-day Witchcraft explain that our "ethics" stem from a desire to avert the wrath of the Threefold Law. Conversely, many authors seem to suggest that the only reason to do good is because, according to the Law of Three, we will incur three times the good we originally sent out. This, as Phyllis Curott so astutely points out in her *Book of Shadows,* is not ethics. In many ways, however, it is certainly morality—or rather, a rule on what not to do to avoid suffering. In this way, karma is not the Law of Three.

Karma translates literally as "action." Action implies reaction, and all reactions bear consequence. As Witches, we are taught to be masters of our own destinies and, therefore, to accept the consequences of our every action, to fully accept and embrace our karma. To reject one's karma is to run from one's shadow, and this we know to be utterly foolish. The way of the shadow is the way of the Witch, and certainly of the Shaman (and thus especially the Shamanic Witch). If we reject or repress our karma, we negate the consequences (though we can never escape them), and we never learn.

An instance of the rejection of karma and negation of consequences would be a malicious murderer who deludes himself by confessing his sins to a Catholic priest and then continues to inflict harm. If we never learn, we never grow, and we can never deepen, evolve, or transform. Or, when such transitions do take place, they happen *to* us and not with our agency; we are unconscious of the power presented to us, and thus we are truly dead. Or, if the power takes us anyway, we see only evil and turn from the wisdom that could be ours if only we understood the ways of nature and of the cosmos. This is the true message of the Tower card in the traditional tarot. The Tower represents the true Shamanic initiation, regardless of whether it is consciously cultivated or shockingly revealed.

When we cast a spell, we are decisively and definitively aligning to a certain choice. Spells are always cast at the crossroads (either literally or metaphorically), meaning we decide the path we will take moving forward; the spell reveals the choice we must make in order to invoke, banish, or empower whatever it is we are working toward. Allow me to illustrate this concept:

You decide to cast a money spell because you need and want a steadier flow of financial income in your life. You are working diligently in all aspects of my life to open as many doors to such a possibility as you can, and now, as a Witch, you make the affirmed choice to energetically and powerfully restore or bring prosperity to and in your life. The spell you cast will effectively open the floodgate to what it is you desire. It is backed by a powerful need and a powerful wanting (therefore, a lack and a void that needs and will be filled). You align yourself with the powers of prosperity; you potentise the spellcasting through the technique of ritual and call upon various spirits to aid in aspect (such as Zeus for success and restoration to sovereignty or Hermes for commercial instinct and flow). You vow to yourself that you are worthy of success, so you will exhibit all outward and inward signs that you are the right candidate for financial prosperity from this moment on. You unleash the power. The gate opens. You receive. You are grateful and give thanks. You have made the choice.

The ritual of the spellcasting gave that choice impetus and integrity in all the worlds (assuming you understood the dynamics of energetics correctly and align to all the worlds), so the spell will work; there is no way it cannot. You have simply given your spirit lease to venture down the path that will allow both energies—your own and that of your prosperity—to meet in the middle. You have called to yourself a particular destiny and mirrored it within your being. The spell has revealed the aspect of fate that could have been and now, because you decided it to be so, is.

Spells instruct us in the ways of the Witch, both philosophically and energetically. The reality is that all things are connected because the Self that is me (bound by the ego which declares "I am I") was able to create discrete certainty out of infinite possibility. Choice is the determining factor, and the Craft teaches us that total freedom equals total responsibility. Ethically, I have learned to revere the Law of Three because my actions will bear reactions, and those reactions give birth to consequences I am responsible for. I cultivate the quality of my life out of desire, yearning, and need.

The Goddess Who is All Guides Our Magic

The Goddess who is All, who birthed Self from Self, came into Being (into what was, is, and always will be) because of desire! She yearned to feel, to know, to touch, and to be…she needed this, for whatever reason, and thus the Eye of the Goddess opened, and there has forever been intelligence and consciousness in the worlds. That thing we call God and the awareness that life has for itself was birthed itself because of choice. Affirmation of Self beyond ego!

"I am," she said, and all other "I"s were born within that one. All spells that are cast give birth to new "I"s (or Eyes). However, because they come from original intent stemming from "you," the effects and the karma that ensues will be your karma, so the true nature of sorcery, magic, and spellcasting becomes realized within the Witch.

We are able to steer our personal course through the tidal rivers of the blood in the body of God. These rivers are infinite and the current is ever-changing, the tides accustomed to inner rhythms. We may choose to follow whatever river, row into new territory, alight on land, and nourish ourselves for a spell (literally), or continue to the ocean and subsume consciousness in the holy milk of All. Spellcraft is more than a basic methodology which allows us to secure what it is we desire or need; it is also a way to become truly real in a world often reduced to superficiality.

We take it upon ourselves to create destiny and walk with fate (not against or away from); we restore self-sovereignty and regain the wholeness that is the agency of Spirit. We effectively become the gods we are. In that moment of spellcasting, we are utilizing the basic elements of life to forge new realities from an ocean of infinite chance and possibility.

We are saying "this shall be" and ordaining it so, establishing concrete foundations for change, growth, transformation, and rebirth. Therefore, spellcasting is both a powerful and a dangerous art. As with all things worthwhile, there is always an element of risk.

What Spells Reveal About the Nature of Things

Spells also teach us about the nature of things and the Aspects: of what it means to love, to be prosperous; feel protected, safe, and secure; glow with beauty; and attract wonder!

Let me speak of love....

In late 2008, I journeyed for nine weeks through the UK, Ireland, and Greece with two beloved Wildwood Witches. We came together one afternoon in a small, forested area in an Oxfordshire village and cast our destinies with three apples, calling for Love. We envisioned what we personally desired, raised the mighty power, and released it, allowing it freedom to manifest our wills. We each felt the pull in the next few months of what was to come, as all Witches do once they have affirmed their decisions and chosen to work toward them with magical impetus.

When I returned to Australia, it was a week before our festival of Beltaine (October 31 or thereabouts in the Southern Hemisphere). I felt my wonder-voyage was punctuated by this holy day. Then, my ex-boyfriend happened to be visiting from Japan, where he moved after we broke up in early 2007. We decided to see each other in absolutely platonic circumstances for the first time in nearly two years. A few weeks later, I met and started dating a very attractive dancer. That was short-lived, and yet every card pulled, every song sang, and every wind-blown spoke of love coming for me.

I cried out to Aphrodite and both she and Freya came. They taught me that before I could truly draw true and powerful love into my life, I needed to claim the sovereignty of my Self: I needed to fall in love with me, to pluck the apple that was mine—and mine alone—to eat. Over the next few months, I worked with the Grail, the receptivity and deep poetry of my own Being, and my own capacity to accept, receive, and be open to the Mystery. One balmy January evening, as I walked home from a friend's house, Aphrodite appeared before me: "...Aphrodite came with a sword and told me I was ready and I know I am...but either way it's my journey. She poured the blessed waters of her/my grail over me and then I prayed for blessings."[55]

The Golden Goddess smiled as she held the cup above my head. I could hear the Divine water inside of it—the water of my self-love—splashing around, brimming and ready to overflow. Her eyes shone with clear and ethereal radiance, her laughter echoing through my soul. She upturned the holy cup and down flowed the water of my love, and into the depth of me did it run. There was a secret in her smile as she shimmered into the air.

The new moon came in the month of April. The inner court of the Coven of the Wildwood meditated in each direction and with each Element and banished or resolved those things which we felt hindered or blocked our soul-growth.

"We passed negative feelings concerning ourselves/lives into elemental objects aligned with these emotions and released and accepted empowerment instead. With each one we only glowed more as we went around the Circle...Air was my inspiration/growth/words/writing; Fire was my lack of embracing my sensual/sexual nature; Water was my sense of flow and sacrifice; and Earth was my criticisms of others' health choices. I watched my fire candle burn down and become two flames as the wick had split in two, and then the chalice tipped and the water spilt onto me. Love is coming..."[56]

At a healing weekend a week and a half later, my dear friend Becky read my cards. She saw that a particular individual would be coming into my life: a dark-haired foreigner. Indeed, two weeks later, while out dancing spontaneously, my eyes locked on a dark-haired, handsome face. He watched me from across the room as I danced happily and without a care. I waited, leaving it to fate and his own choice: if he wanted to talk to me, he would. It all flowed. Then, from behind, I felt his hand brush against me and his fingers wrapped around mine. We danced. We also ended up falling in love and being handfasted.

Through one spell—one affirmed choice, one empowered intention—I shifted the course of my fate or enhanced and deepened it. Not

---

[55] Journal entry from my Book of Shadows, Wednesday, 28 of January, 2009, waxing moon.

[56] Journal entry from my Book of Shadows, Wednesday, 1 of April, 2009, waxing moon.

only does a spell have the propensity to manifest our desires, fulfil our needs, and catalyse necessary changes, spells cast successfully also, by their very nature, summon our Wyrd. That which becomes, becomes us. Through sovereignty of Self, we have aligned Own Holy Self, and we potentise the hidden potency; we are innately gifted with Divine creativity. It is our birthright.

The Shamanic Spellcasting

The spellcasting ritual below provides a framework for Ecstatic Spellcraft. This particular method, like much of what I am offering within this book, organically evolved through my cultivated practice, exploration of lore and mythos, and intimate interaction with the spirits. Hekate, in particular, aided in my reception of this technique; the Great Goddess hinted to me that the four directions also have another function within sorcerous arts. Not only do they provide us with powerful and resonant orientation to sacred cosmology, but they are also gateways to the potencies that are magic, that is, life force. When we unlock the gates and open to the flow of magical power, we become imbued with the holy spark of creativity, which meets with our own hidden potency and is ignited.

 Ecstatic Spellcraft is just that—ecstatic—and it requires indulgence. I am not hinting at external substances or agencies; I am speaking of the attitude one brings to the process, treating the experience of the spell as one to be entirely present within. When I cast spells, I become them: I become the realised potentiality of what I am seeking to draw in, banish, or transform. Whether I am working for myself or another, I am ultimately working for the greater good, and not in the moralistic sense.

The Greater Good

"Do good because it is good to do so."

—Unknown

I must first make it obvious that I am not speaking necessarily of good versus evil (at least, not in the dualistic way). I am speaking of *the Good* that Plato touched on and Plotinus affirmed. Most simply, *goodness* or *the Good* is the grace of the Divine expressed. It is the flow that derives from the realised pure will as it journeys through life. Sometimes, "bad" things will happen as part of this flow, but they are not "evil." They offer us opportunity to strengthen, deepen, renew, and learn; often, they are mirror reflections or alternate, converse reactions to an overall trend or cause. The "good" things also do this in different ways.

We define good and bad in rather absolute ways in modern Western society. In the Shamanic Craft, and in most Witchcraft and Paganisms, the black-and-white philosophy holds no water; however, this tends to be the paradigm of the overculture. Often, a Pagan might cite the rainbow analogy (and I have done this in the past) to broaden the perspective beyond simply "black-and-white." However, this might be too simple an explanation. Yes, there is indeed an entire spectrum of colour that could codify or represent a variety of "ethical" shades of moral fibre, but in all truth, what is moral about nature? Ethics seem to be a distinctly human endeavour. What is "moral" or "ethical" about a hawk sinking its piercingly sharp talons into an unsuspecting field mouse? What is ethical about a tsunami that destroys a coastal village or annual floods which spread disease and kill thousands of defenceless, poverty-stricken people? Yet ethics *is* decidedly present whenever humans are involved.

When a hawk kills a field mouse, it is because the hawk has stalked, hunted, and skilfully manoeuvred a descent and swoop, which success-fully targeted and obtained the field mouse. We would call this survival of the fittest in Darwin's terminology (although this may be a reductive oversimplification). Nature holds harmony, and ecosystems have evolved to thrive on an integrated and holistic pattern involving several hundred or thousand species, which all rely on one another in an interlinked chain. It is not nature, however, which created the hundreds upon thousands of impoverished people who swarm the regions vulnerable to monsoonal flooding in Bangladesh.

It was and is human interference: economic manipulation, colonial imposition and dispossession, cultural caste attitudes (directing stratified human value), overpopulation, ignorance due to poor education (again resting upon society, government, and economy), and environmental degradation influenced by all of these factors and their side effects. When humans decided to shift from nomadic, small family, and clan lifestyles and situate themselves permanently, farming and irrigating the land, impacting it directly and continuously, the natural balance began to suffer. It would be extremely difficult to turn back the clock on this; we must now innovate and invite new ways of living and sustaining our human cultures within the broader matrix of natural balance.

Ancient Indigenous cultures in so-called Australia received and passed on clan and kinship laws and lore, which directed the people on how to live with the land with minimal impact and great wisdom. Laws govern how many eggs one can take from a bird's nest, how many fish one can spear from a river, and when and how one can travel in certain areas. Many of their traditional processes, like fire-farming, also drastically altered the landscape over thousands of years, but the intention of techniques like fire-farming was both to flush out game for food and survival and to preserve and sustain the integrity of the bushland (many of the plant species benefit greatly from the heat and flame).

Fire-farming allowed for thick old growth to die and for the germination of particular seeds in the now rich, active soil. Today, settler-colonial Australis mostly ignore Aboriginal knowledge. Modern humans of Western empires often ignore the nomadic and tribal instincts that birthed the spirituality of the Shaman and understanding of the land as living, vital, and necessary. How do we resurrect the ethical systems which aid humanity to add to the harmony and synergy of nature?

How does any of the above impact a Witch's ethics when it comes to the empowered choices we propel into momentum by casting a spell or committing to sorcerous intent? We must come to realise that ethics is only applicable to the bigger picture (from the human perspective) when we align with the rest of nature: its equilibrium. We are not divorced from nature, and neither are our lives and all that involves (prosperity, love, security, hearth and home, family, work, and so on). When we ask that something is done "for the greater good," we are actually asking, "How will this choice or action add to my life's balance, fullness, and equilibrium? How will I (as a person and associated circumstance, like quality of life) be enhanced, deepened, realised, and defined by this?"

I maintain that the only "ultimate" ethic a Witch (or anyone) can live by is that "total freedom equals total responsibility." There are no specific moral imperatives to be ever-loving, compassionate, peaceful, unaffected, or unattached, for example; there is only the understanding that to actualise true sovereignty of Self (and that is all we can ever hope to be sovereign "over"), we must make ourselves worthy of that deep potentiality. We must be entirely accountable and responsible. The only way to achieve this is to work for ignited awareness and to reinforce this every day of our lives. This is the journey of the Witch.

The Technique

Meditate upon the Elemental Pathway of Manifestation; reflect and ask yourself the questions posed and become grounded in your intent.

This spellcasting requires one spirit-ally who can act as a Gate-Keeper. In my case, this is often Hekate, but for others, it may be Hermes, Papa Legba, Ganesha, or whoever you or your tradition works with in this capacity. This may also be mutable within your own practice. For instance, if Hekate does not stand at the Gates for me, then I would most likely ask Hermes or perhaps my fetch-mate. However, it is to Hekate that I go to first in this endeavour, especially as related to spellcraft and sorcery.

This technique does not require specific items and provides an open framework for the individual to personalise, adapt, and fill out as they see fit. Personally, I work with minimal materials when casting spells (sometimes none), but depending on the circumstance, I might employ the agency of plant or stone allies, candles, or pouches and bags. Due to my cunning charge, I leave the mode of the spell up to the individual's preferences. If you need or desire something tactile, then I will create a necklace, bracelet, charm bag, or something similar. However, in many cases, I will be working for someone physically distanced from me who is unable to physically retrieve anything from me in the timeframe.

While these physical items can indeed help the process psychologically or metaphysically (and often both simultaneously), an effectively casted spell with power does not have to rely on a tactile reminder to manifest unless, of course, the power is released into one. This then becomes the link of the spell and must be burnt (like a candle), kept on the person (such as a charm, amulet, or talisman), or released to the Elements (into a waterway, the wind, burnt, or buried in the Earth) in some form, and often only after the spell has worked and results have been seen.

The Meaning of the Words

"I unlock the gates of magic,
I untie the ties of time,
I surrender to all space,
Invoking power with this rhyme!"

The initiating incantation I wrote for Shamanic spellcasting illustrates how one should approach the act and with what emphases in mind.

I Unlock the Gates of Magic

The gates of magic can be visualised or anchored at the directions, whether you focus on the four cardinal directions or the six/seven spoken of in Feri. They are the swirling vortices of ancient, ever-renewing power (whether you consider that mana, qi, prana, or magic) that surges from the "corners" of the cosmos when we come to our Holy Centre. This power makes all things possible.

In the technique offered below, the directions would have already been acknowledged and honoured before this incantation or prayer is made. Therefore, we are reiterating and reaffirming their power but also placing our trust in one of our invoked allies: the Gate-Keeper. The Gate-Keeper fulfils the role of standing guard at these open portals and watching over the merging of worlds, facilitating the flow. As the other realms become one with our own and infinite possibility is ignited, we are able to truly plant our energetic seeds in the Aether, in the Spirit, and in the realm of the highest vibration. This will enact the metaphysical laws of manifestation as has been discussed.

The gates also represent what we are barred from: the barriers to seizing power and making change. Thus, unlocking and opening the gates of magic is the beginning and stirring of power within the Witch.

I Untie the Ties of Time

Another reiteration of what Circle-casting has established, both energetically and cosmologically, for the working. This works to ensure that the linear A-B movement of time (or illusion thereof) is superseded and that, in touching the flow of all, we effectively become the flow of all and, thus, the active agency of the will of Fate.

I Surrender to All Space

As with untying the "ties of time," this phrase reaffirms the sacred orientation to "space outside of space and time outside of time." To "surrender" to this is to allow oneself to be saturated by the very nature of all space, which equals spacelessness; it would be just as accurate to say, "I surrender to all spacelessness." By doing this, we come to the here and now, the tween, the All in One-One in All, and cultivate the poetic, philosophical, and fundamental truths of the Circle.

Invoking Power with this Rhyme

Perhaps one of the most important points. Rhyme comes from the Greek *rhei,* meaning "to flow." Rhei also gives us rhythm, and rhythm (which can be channelled by rhyme) allows for the powerful flow of magic to be raised, directed, amplified, and released. On a practical note, rhythm provides a framework through which we may enter a trance state safely and lay aside the calculations of Talking Self (whom we already engaged through the Elemental reflections) to delve into the indulgences of Shadow Self, and thereby connect and commune with Star Self, who will aid us in planting the seed of our intent in the vibrating Ether.

When I cast a spell, it is ecstatic because I become entirely entranced by the process. I revel and riot between the worlds where the power surges and flows free because I can be the totality of my being and step into my Own Holy Self. I activate my hidden potency, and it becomes a living potency. I self-actualise; I become God(dess). I often ask to be left alone when I undergo a working because I am aware of how I transform, and this can frighten others at times. It is akin to a kind of possession, yet what I am filled with is myself in condensed and concentrated form. I have not only opened the gates of magic at the corners of the cosmos, but I have opened gateways within myself to enormous potential; I have dissolved into time and surrendered to space and, therefore, have placed myself firmly in the here and now, touching all. I invoke the power with rhyme and rhythm and draw to a point. I am Witch!

The Ritual

Breathe. Align both the Three Realms and the Three Souls (or reverse order, depending on your feeling). Cast the Circle and honour the directions. Make your prayer/invocation to your Gate-Keeper, and then incant the following aloud, making the appropriate offerings or gestures:

> *"I unlock the gates of magic,*
> *I untie the ties of time,*
> *I surrender to all space,*
> *Invoking power with this rhyme!"*

State the purpose—your intent—clearly, perhaps using the following formula as you instigate the visualisation and allow it to subsume your consciousness:

> *"By Air, my intent (state intention aloud) is clarified;*
> *By Fire, my intent (state intention aloud) is impassioned;*
> *By Water, my intent (state intention aloud) is channelled;*
> *By Earth, my intent (state intention aloud) is grounded;*
> *In the name of Spirit, my intent is given to magic!"*

Begin to raise the power in whichever way you wish or feel is appropriate for the endeavour. I will generally clap, stamp my feet rhythmically, or dance free form within the Circle. Rocking, sexual intercourse, masturbation, drumming, and other rhythmic movements are also options. I will also chant the following to aid:

> *"I raise the power, I raise the power;*
> *I raise it well, I raise it well;*
> *In this hour, in this hour;*
> *For this spell, for this spell!"*

Continue rhythmically until the energy begins to crescendo, then climax, and you intuit the moment to release (releasing not only the energy, but the visualisation, the attachment, and so on). At this point, it is important to be swollen with the knowledge that the spell will and has worked and for the greater good; it is complete, it is done. Fall to the ground, collapse in a heap, and, depending, on how overwhelmed you feel, one or both of the following can be done to ensure psychic equilibrium is restored.

1. If saliva has built up in your mouth, spit it onto the ground. Wet the forefinger of your power hand with the spittle, anoint your forehead with it, and say,

    "Power in me, with me, for me."

2. Resonate the phrase "stone of the Earth" through your body and being. This effectively restores the balance to the body, the equilibrium to the spirit, and the sanity of the mind. I say *sanity* because, in true Shamanic spellcraft, one becomes frenzied with the power.

Post-Spell

Often, the first thing we learn about spellcasting in the Craft is that we must never think upon our spells in the aftermath. I disagree. I believe we should not dwell upon them or become anxious about when and how the outcome will manifest. The best analogy I have heard was that casting a spell is like planting a seed; if you continuously dig up the seed to see if it is growing, chances are it will not grow. If you do think upon your spell, consider your thoughts to be like the water and sunlight a seed requires to germinate and grow. Ensure that your thoughts add to and enhance the possibilities of manifestation rather than bar, hinder, or debilitate.

Another important consideration is what I call the spell's seal. In many mystical and magical cultures, Divination occurs to ensure that offerings and sacrifices have been well-received by the Gods or spirits. Through many years of casting spells (for both others and me), I have noticed that in the following few hours (and sometimes instantly), a synchronous seal will present itself as to whether the spell was effective or not. Examples I have experienced include the opening of Aphrodite's legs after a love spell for a friend, a police car driving past the moment I exited a business

I helped to bless and protect, and receiving too much change back after a prosperity spell. These were obvious signs (or seals) to me that the spell had been successful, so any anxiety concerning the spell's forthcoming results was put to rest. Generally speaking, if the spell is ineffective, one will feel very strongly incomplete, disappointed, or even ill, depending on the nature of the working, during the working, or immediately after. Either attempt the working again or meditate on or Divine the reason as to why the spell may have failed.

The Success of Spellcraft

I am of the opinion and experience that spellcraft works ninety percent of the time. There are generally only two reasons a spell or working fails:

1. The will was not aligned with the working, or the spell failed because of a lack of focus or diligence on the part of the caster.
2. A greater will opposed the will of the Witch or another spirit or force denied you access to the desired outcome.

The remedy to the first point is to simply try again and ensure that one is completely present within the working and flowing with the magical current. Purifications and alignment techniques, such as further Spiral Soul and Three Realms workings, will aid with this. If materials are used or allies invoked, then all must be vibrating together; the materials should be charged to the task and the allies awoken and enhanced to the charge. Also, check cosmic or celestial conditions (such as the phase of the Moon, day of the week, astrological sign, or planetary hour), as these may make a difference. However, I generally maintain that if the need or desire is strong, so shall be the working, no matter what day or phase of the Moon.

The remedy for the second point is further meditation and Divination. It could be that a deity or spirit you are allied with resents what you are working for or that it may be against a binding, *geis*, or vow you are forgetting or attempting to circumnavigate. In this case, counsel with the spirit(s) will either clear the problem or at least enlighten you to it. If the will that is stronger is another human being's (such as another spirit-worker, Witch, or Shaman), if you believe strongly in the endeavour, you may perform a banishing on the influence and a protection from it or enter into battle. An example of when not to enter battle would be the following:

One of my uncles in Bali once told my mother and me about an instance in which one Balian (a type of Balinese Shaman) was working against rain for the smooth-running of a ceremony; simultaneously, another Balian a few villages over was doing the same thing for another ceremony. The Balian with the stronger will won out, and it rained in the other village. The rain clouds were present in the atmosphere—they weren't going to simply evanesce—so they moved over a few villages and emptied their bounty on the other village.

A situation in which it might be appropriate to "enter into battle" would be if someone had a personal vendetta against you and was simply attempting to thwart your every action. If this was persistent and effective, one might strike back with a banishing and protection (as mentioned previously) or a binding or curse. The latter should never be entered into lightly, but their use is contextual, and in remembering the ethic of total freedom equals total responsibility, we are charged to act upon our volition as we each personally determine appropriate.

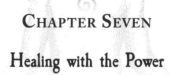

CHAPTER SEVEN

Healing with the Power

"Healing rituals transform the inner world of participants, especially patients. Rituals change experience and expectations, nourish a sense of relationship and support, and encourage reconciliation with the spirits and the sacred. These subjective experiences mediate and evoke objective effects on the body and its disease."
—Roger Walsh, M.D., Ph.D, *The World of Shamanism*

The healing art passed to me through my Balinese family has, for the most part, been a subtle one, though it has still been hugely important in our family's tradition.[57] My late grandmother was a well-known healer in her community, and my late grandfather had a powerful gift with massage: he could almost instantly entrance those he massaged, or else they would fall into a deep sleep. He did this for me countless times. My father has often asked for me to heal him but has also offered it informally to friends and family as "passing or giving power." *Sakti* is the Balinese word for power; it derives from the Sanskrit *shakti* for the wellspring of vitality that we identify as feminine and as the originator and the holder of all things, the partner to Shiva.

The healing which I personally practise would be considered "pranic." However, just like my gift of palmistry, I have never had formal training in any particular modality, nor do I wish to at this stage, though it has been offered to me freely several times. I find my methods are both potent and successful. I have healed headaches, migraines, cramps, stopped the

---

[57] This is not to negate my mother's family, which has a strong and long history of healing. In fact, all of my mother's sisters are or were either nurses or teachers. I have also mentioned my great-great-aunt, Sister Elizabeth Kenny, in my previous books.

flow of blood, and have generally restored the vital force on many occasions. I do this by simply grounding and centring, building up my auric field, accessing a flow of power from heaven through Earth, and wilfully directing and channelling this force into the individual. As I do this, I simply let the light do its work naturally, or I facilitate the healing outcome through visualisation and energetic sensing.

I also employ Shamanic ritual and spirit possession as techniques of healing. These are the arts I will outline within this chapter.

The Laying on of Hands

The title to this section might be misleading, but it embodies a broader concept. To become a conduit for healing power or light and to let it flow through you and from you, directed by your hands, is an age-old and effective technique. Just as in the art of Reiki (to which I have never been attuned), your hands may either be placed directly on the physical body of the patient or placed on or in the aura.

The laying on of hands is an art that knows no religious bounds and appears in many traditions. I already mentioned that my father passes power or *sakti* through his hands (as did his father); in *By Land, Sky & Sea,* I speak about "pressure touch," a simple variant of this kind of energetic healing work. Depending on the situation and the individual, physical touch may actually be more beneficial; in other cases, the reverse is desirable or necessary (such as for those who have been raped or physically assaulted). What pressure touch enables is the stimulation of the senses and thus the vital flow of life force, which restores the energetic integrity on every level and reconnects self to Self.

The Energetic Bodies and Centres

The Aura

The aura is the energetic field of vital force which emanates from the spirit-core of our body and being. It is that part of us which can be seen as the "Shining One" (a term of T. Thorn Coyle's), which equates to our Talking Self, as its golden hue surrounds us with a protective layer and provides us with a telepathic modality of interface. The aura is said to be the body of the Talking Self, as the "etheric or second skin" that many seers will perceive parallels with the "Sticky One" (also a term of T. Thorn Coyle's *Morningstar*), or our Shadow Self. Shadow Self is also called Sticky One because the energy of this soul is the etheric or psychic mark we leave on everything we encounter; it *sticks*. For this reason, the healer must shield and protect themselves before attempting to heal another; one must be able to enter into the patient's auric field and remain unaffected by the energetic manifestations of the illness.

If we are visually oriented and can see the colour(s) of the aura, then we will be able to translate directly what emotional or psychic state the body is in. However, if one does not see in the psychic way, it is still possible to interpret the aura through other senses. One might simply feel the aura and its colours and know the state or states, for example. A general correspondence chart of colours in the aura might read:

- **Light Blue:** Calm, peaceful, healthy, and balanced
- **Dark Blue:** Serene, tranquil, deep peace, and spiritually rich (or issues relating to sleep and dreams)
- **Purple/Violet:** Psychic, attuned, and open
- **Orange:** Magnetised, vibrant, vital, and attractive (in the dynamic sense)
- **Yellow:** Clear thought and swift intellect
- **Gold:** Spiritually charged and blessed
- **Silver:** Lunar influence, dreams, and mentality (or issues relating to mental health)
- **Pink:** Loving and loved, emotionally supported, and healing
- **Red:** Impassioned and sexually charged (issues relating to the blood and stress)
- **Green:** Healing and health, growth, grounding, and connection (or issues relating to convalescence)
- **Black:** Blockage and disease (or serious illness or imbalance in the body), some say great power
- **Grey:** Weakness and ambiguity (may become ill soon if not addressed)
- **Brown:** Grounded in body

Of course, it must be understood that the colours are relative and that they may change meaning if found in particular regions around the body. For instance, if I saw someone whose belly area was saturated by brown and black, I might ask if they were suffering from constipation because of the combination of brown being body-static or grounded and black implying disruption or blockage. If I saw pink surrounded by red around the heart centre with black spikes interspersed and green and silver haloing the head, I might suggest that this individual is healing from a broken relationship and that, while the thoughts are clearing and the dreamscape is providing relief, the emotional realm is still suffering from momentary lapses (which is, of course, entirely natural after a break-up!).

The aura can give us a variety of clues and hints on exactly what parts of the Self we need to address in a healing session. During a psychic whole-health consultation, the aura is the first thing I check even before the patient openly discusses their problems; both to demonstrate the authenticity of my skills (and to test myself) and therefore earn trust from the patient, and also to energetically orient myself. Often, the healing begins before the hands are laid, so to speak.

The Chakras

It might not immediately make sense as to why I am referring to the chakras in this book, considering we are working with the Three Realms energetically, the Three Cauldrons, and the Three Souls. Why, then, would I challenge the triplicity by introducing a seven-fold energetic system? I have already spoken on congruence and contradiction, and this is one of the reasons I am speaking on the chakras now (but that is a peripheral reason). Truly, I am including a section on the chakras here because they may be essential knowledge to a healer. While I am aware there is always the risk I might decontextualize the system from its origin in Hindu or Indian traditions, I have worked with the chakra system extensively, and I was born into the Hindu religion. We each possess the seven chakras. For the sake of parallels, one can associate the seven chakras with the Three Cauldrons if the distinctions are maintained and respected:

- **Cauldron of the Belly:** Root, Sacral, and Solar Plexus
- **Cauldron of the Head:** Crown, Third Eye, and Throat
- **Cauldron of the Heart:** Heart

The Difference Between Aligning the Chakras and the Three Realms/ Cauldrons/ Souls

The Three Realms are broad cosmic concepts and realities, and we align to them within our own sphere; we actualise the Holy Centre. The Three Souls are private and personal for everyone; we all have three of our own souls that are as unique as we are. When we align the Spiral Soul, we connect and commune with Own Holy Self. When we cleanse, balance, and align the seven major chakras (in the order of Root, Sacral, Solar Plexus, Heart, Throat, Third Eye, and Crown), we are literally doing just that and connecting with what I like to call the "rainbow ladder" (or, in Sanskrit, *sushumna*) that ascends and descends through the body, allowing the vital life force to flow steadily through us. The seven chakras, which are physically and psychically anchored in locations of the body that contain the major endocrine glands, represent the places in which the life force naturally concentrates. These chakras must be cleansed and balanced within themselves so that neither extremity nor dullness is retained within them.

When we open each chakra (Sanskrit for "wheel") or energy-centre, we open not a part of our soul/s but one of our psychic organs, and we direct cleansing and balancing power in hopes that the natural response will be to align with the Rainbow Ladder and to therefore open the physical body (that is the direct expression of the Spirit) to Health.

Each chakra is also connected with different aspects of our humanity:

- **Root (Red):** Security, foundation, and survival
- **Sacral (Orange):** Sexuality, sensuality, and intimacy
- **Solar Plexus (Yellow):** Self-esteem, self-honour, and power
- **Heart (Green):** Compassion, understanding, and love. The Central Chakra and the transmuter of life force.
- **Throat (Azure Blue):** Communication and expression
- **Third Eye (Indigo):** Insight, knowledge, and thought
- **Crown (Violet/White):** Connection, wisdom, and opening

If particular magic aligning with any of the energies of the chakras is needed, one could work with that centre in meditation or trance and direct power from that place for spellwork. For example, to heighten one's psychic senses, it is a great idea to concentrate one's awareness at the Third Eye and to cleanse, balance, and align it within itself, then open it to receive universal information.

Working with the Spirits: Techniques for Deity/Ally Aid (Channelling Through the Force of Another)

When conducting a healing in the Shamanic Craft, it is often the case that a deity or other spirit-being will be called for assistance or even as the prime catalyst of the working. For instance, I will sometimes call to Brigid or my ancestors (particularly my father's mother, though she has very much passed her power on to me) for aid in healing. Other times, I will simply "plug in," so to speak, to bring forth the healing light and provide the channel for it to flow into the recipient. When working with an ally, however, the effects of the healing are often more immediate, tangible, and potent.

To call upon a spirit-ally to aid in healing is a simple thing. Simply call out, either aloud or within, to the spirit(s) and make it known why you are asking for their presence and aid. When I call to Brigid, I might say:

> *"O Holy Brigid, Triple Goddess of Healing, Poetry, and Blacksmiths,*
> *I call to you as Healer now. I call to the Gentle White Cow and the*
> *Green Vital Land; I call to the Healing Flame and the Deep Well.*
> *Céad míle fáilte!"*[58]

When Brigid comes, I feel her overshadow me from behind, and her hands merge with mine. In this way, together, we channel the flow of the vital force synergistically, and I benefit from the Goddess's vast experience. I can simply let go, surrender, and let the Goddess work. Of course, my physical presence and conscious facilitation provide the framework of intent for the healing and lend to the overall efficacy.

In working with spirits, the boundary between possession and less-intense forms of aid can be blurry. I will often feel as if the deity is "half-sitting" in me, and while I do not necessarily forget any details of the event, I will definitely feel altered and held in liminal space. This may

---

[58] This is an Irish Gaelic phrase which means "a hundred, thousand welcomes." It is pronounced *"cay-d meel-ah fuhl-cha."*

happen spontaneously during a working (healing or not), in which case the spirit will most likely be one of my allies, or it may occur during a very strong working in which I have consciously called for the presence or influence of a spirit. This may be because I was a natural vessel or "horse." I also believe that this state should not be attempted in the context of a working that is not actively possessory; it is not a desirable or necessary state to achieve success in magical workings. Unless it is something that happens naturally to you and does not produce negative side-effects, I would warn against it.

As mentioned before, your familiar spirits or totems may also aid in the work of healing by performing a number of "house-cleaning" tasks:

• Ensuring that you are kept energetically equalised and psychically protected
• Brushing off psychic debris or any attachments from etheric contact
• Guarding against malevolent spirits who may be involved in the cause of illness
• Adding to and enhancing the power you are channelling for healing

If you are conscious of and acknowledge your familiar and totemic spirits, it is quite possible that their aid will be automatic; however, it does not hurt to invite it openly. In the case of familiar spirits (as they work in the periphery), as with any ward, you may set up, assign, and delegate specific tasks. Make sure that your tone is not commanding or oppressive but kind and conciliatory. (This is just good manners, plain and simple.) Emphasise that you are working together as cells within a body, contributing to a wholeness greater than the sum of the parts. This is the aim of true, deep magic.

The Restoration of Wholeness

One of the powerful implications of the art of healing is that health is obtainable. In fact, it is just around the corner; we must simply take the brave step into the darkness and seize it of our own volition. When I was studying Western Herbal Medicine in college, we were often told by our naturopathic lecturers that the patients we might see in any natural health clinic would be expected to take the healing into their own hands. It would be our job as natural health therapists to facilitate and aid in the opening to healing and health rather than disempower or disengage an individual from the organic process.

In contrast, many people find it preferable to lay the healing in the hands of doctors who will (generally) hand over a drug to mask the symptoms; veiled medical terms will be used, and there is never a sense of equality or dialogue. The healing process is not facilitated so much as held in total by the doctor; in some circumstances, this is both necessary and desirable, but in other situations, it is disempowering, weakening, and ultimately very dangerous.

To emphasise the art of healing as the restoration of wholeness (remembering the word is directly parallel to "holiness") is to give credence to our deepest natures. We are always whole all of the time, but we often forget and need to remember. In other circumstances, we become so off-centre and off-balance that the wholeness blurs, and we lose our foundation and footing. We fall and we begin to fear, eroding our self-esteem, self-honour, and power from within, and we begin to become deceived by the illusion that all is lost. Nothing can be truly lost that is truly yours. We are born from wholeness, with wholeness, and to wholeness we shall go. Our journey is to ride the shifting tides of this current and make ourselves worthy of this most excellent gift the Self gives to Self!

In our individuation, we are innately connected, and in our connection, we have sprung from the body of being. In being, we are alive, and in living, we are present. (A constant and ever-present gift!) These affirmations are eternal truths that are with us continuously. Borrow from them, make them your own, sing them loudly and proudly, and we will each ignite the wholeness that we are. In knowing this, we learn to nourish it; in nourishing, we deepen; and in deepening, we embrace the dark cauldron of nature.

Whole Self–Whole Earth

In December 2009, the esteemed Parliament of the World's Religions (POWR) was held for a week in Melbourne, Australia. I was blessed to be a speaker and presenter at the POWR, and on Wednesday morning, I presented a spiritual observance entitled "Whole Self–Whole Earth." The premise of this observance was to highlight the basic theology and cosmology of contemporary Paganism in its broadest sense: that the Earth is holy, that the cosmos are alive, and that we are reflections of this truth. If we are whole within Self, then the Earth, too, can become whole. This is akin to the principle of peace that the current Dalai Lama of Tibetan Buddhism engenders: that inner peace begets world peace.

> *"We grounded and centred in a prolonged fashion, focussing especially on the groundedness and connection with Earth and cosmos. Whole in ourselves—n our place. I spoke about interconnection—of cosmic/ internal reflection; As Above, So Below; As Within, So Without. We cast Circle: 'From hand to hand...' Greeted Elements through song: 'Earth my body...' And the Great Mystery.*
>
> *We raised that power and asserted our inner wholeness as we each came forth from the Chasm and claimed the rite/right to be! We turned to our neighbours and affirmed 'You are whole,' taking that into our hearts, we then channelled and directed the power into the tween place. We spiralled, singing, 'Mother I feel you under my feet...' We raised, released, and grounded. We let that healing wholeness be absorbed by our Holy Living Mother. We unravelled the space and returned."*[59]

To cultivate living relationship with the Earth and cosmos is to have this reflected in Self. This is part of the restoration of wholeness because it is not a wholeness that is discretely yours and apart from others. The wholeness is an organic, unfolding web of interconnection, which is not only a boundless circle to an ever-deepening centre, but also an infinite spiral.

The Rite of Self-Blessing

The following self-blessing can be used as an affirmation, prayer, or ritual in order to instil this sacred awareness of wholeness/holiness in Self.

This ritual can be performed daily or absorbed into your discipline or rhythm however you see fit. It can also be called upon as a preparatory technique for intense energetic or trance work, such as drawing down. It may also be used at the culmination of rituals as another way to represent the Great Rite (also known as *Hieros Gamos* or *Sacred Marriage*) without emphasising external or gendered polarities, as the Third or Middle

---

[59] From my Book of Shadows, Wednesday, 9 December 2009, waning moon.

Way of the Shaman. For the deepest effect, perform the Three Realms Alignment and/or the Spiral Soul Alignment before this blessing.

You may choose to use a chalice filled with water or an athame (sword) or to simply gesture them.

Breathe into your Centre. Ground. Cast the Circle if you like (but it is not necessary).

As you breathe deeply and rhythmically (kneeling, sitting, or standing), gaze at the chalice filled with liquid and say:

> *"I am the cup;*
> *I am the wine of life."*

Visualise or feel cleansing light moving from your heart-centre (Own Holy Self, the place that is between and reconciles opposition or duality and the meeting place of the Three Souls) and into the chalice.

Stand and take the athame (draw it from the Earth as Arthur drew Excalibur from the Stone) and draw a circle around the chalice and yourself in the air, saying:

> *"I am the sword;*
> *I am the Circle."*

Bring the athame down into the chalice and feel the charge of union; the underlying wholeness is remembered.

Pick up the cup and say:

> *"I drink deeply of the wellspring of my Mystery;*
> *From the Earth, I draw my life force.*
> *Water is life, unbound and free;*
> *Water—this water—will cleanse and bless me!"*

Drink all of the liquid. Feel as if you are being washed clean and pure as the liquid moves through you.

Seal the rite by intoning:

> *"I am the beloved of the Goddess, the Gods, and my Own Holy Self.*
> *My Divine Mystery is revealed and beheld. I am my own blessing.*
> *So mote it be."*

A Shamanic Craft Healing

In the Shamanic Craft here, a healing is a consciously created sacred time and space in which the restoration or honouring of innate wholeness is directed by a healer. Shamans and Witches have always been healers, and we are empowered to heal because we embrace the sanctity of the life force, and by our most sacred principle of magic, we are able to harness the vital flow for benevolence and well-being. When we speak of healing, we imply the desire for health on as many levels as possible.

My own understanding of health and healing as an able-bodied person with the associated privilege in an intensely ableist society has increased dramatically over the past years. Healing and health will look and feel different for each person, and there is no such thing as a standard for optimal health that covers everyone. Shamanic Witchcraft absolutely honours this and works with spirit helpers and allies on behalf of the Triple Soul of the person being worked on. Witch magic and healing can also be wielded to assist people in navigating unjust medical and societal systems that disenfranchise and disable people. May healing magic be thought of as an act of exploring an intensively interrelational web of connections in order to benefit us all.

Health and healing, in the context of the Shamanic Craft discussed in this book, also ensure that we are honouring our implicit connections and interdependence with all things in Life. When I heal, I sometimes weave in the Feri Star Goddess prayer, as it reinforces to me the reality of sacred exchange and purity of flow: that, by their very nature, all things are born to die and be reborn.[60] This is the truth of immortality, and so to heal is to also bring awareness to the forces of being which hold the limitlessness of life.

The preceding sections form the foundation and (dare I say it) steps for my usual way of conducting a healing.

1. Ground and Centre (such as Three Realms Alignment or Spiral Soul Alignment)
2. Work through/with the aura

---

[60] The "standard" Anderson Feri Star Goddess prayer is "Holy Mother, in you we live, move, and have our being. From you all things emerge, and unto you all things return."

3. Open, cleanse, balance, and align the chakras (or work specifically with the cauldrons in a similar fashion)
4. Call upon the aid of allies
5. Channel the light of healing
6. Restore and remember wholeness
7. Water-blessing (Rite of self-blessing or *Kala*)

These steps unfold to a space of relaxation, remembering, and revivification for the patient. As I outline each of the steps, I will also add finer details and deconstruct the inherent meaning or purpose behind the act.

Ground and Centre

This step is quite self-explanatory: both the healer and the patient ground and centre. This can be done as a facilitated exercise simultaneously, or, depending on the personal inclinations of the patient, the patient can simply lie down (or sit comfortably in a chair) and breathe deeply, cycling their breath, as the healer centres privately.

This step is, of course, essential. At this point, you might also wish to set up a temporary shield against psychic debris or attachment. This can be done quite simply through either calling upon one's familiar spirits to draw in light and cocoon it around the body or setting specific wards (of flame, of light, of web, or similar) at particular locations around the body.

Work Through/With the Aura

At this point, the auric field is "lifted" to a higher vibration in order to open the patient to the light of healing (which is both cosmic and Earthly; consider it starlight, knowing also that there is a star within the Earth). The way in which I approach this is to quickly clear the aura of any peripheral energetic distractions by sweeping my hands with intent across the surface of the body a few inches above the physical boundaries and flicking the debris off to be absorbed into the ground with a prayer to the Earth Mother for "recycling." I then hold my hands at the centre point (either around the solar plexus or belly region) of the body, and with simple will applied, heighten the auric vibration. The sensation of a blooming flower settles within me as I do this, which could be visualised as the auric energies elevate and open.

Open, Cleanse, Balance, and Align the Chakras

Make direct and empowered conjurations to the chakras, beginning at the base chakra (the Red Root) and continuing up the rainbow ladder. Hold your power hand over the area of the body (in the case of the root chakra, the region would be located at the genitalia if the patient is lying face-up) and begin to make deasil circles as you visualise the sphere of light opening like a flower and spinning like the sun. As you do this, begin to connect with the light and channel it through to aid in the cleansing and balancing of each chakra. The conjuration I make is the same for every chakra, and I simply replace the name and colour:

"Red wheel of light—Root Chakra—open like a flower and spin the sun! Cleanse, balance, and align within yourself!"

However, for each chakra upwards, I will add:

"...Connect and align with the lower (however many chakras) of (list the colours below, such as orange and red if it was the Solar Plexus Chakra)."

Therefore, as I facilitate a gradual progression upwards through the system, the patient is aware that we are not just working with the chakras in isolation but as organs within the energy-bodies that connect and work as a whole greater than the sum of its parts.

As I work to open, cleanse, balance, and align, I also visualise that each chakra becomes brighter, more vivid, and visceral as I channel light. I make a special point of also connecting the Root Chakra through a red cord of light to the very centre of the Earth. When I reach the Crown Chakra, I tap the head very quickly and lightly with the first two fingers of my power hand and perceive a great rushing of light from the heavens into the patient.

What this serves to do is establish a direct and empowered link to the light for the patient and consolidate the connection to that power within the healer. I will then move my hands downwards over the patient's body to distribute the light throughout. At this point, I also ask the patient to take that light where they feel it is most needed, intuitively or logically.

Call upon the Aid of Allies

As I explained briefly, a healing (or any working) can become much more powerful and successful if one is working in concert with an ally or two or more. The connection between the healer and the ally should be a firm one, and the invitation or acknowledgement of the ally's presence and power can be either an inward or verbal declaration, depending on the nature of the healing and the patient. You can revisit the example provided with Brigid.

Channel the Light of Healing

The light I am speaking of (almost vaguely so) is not of any particular current, as far as I can tell. I am not attuned to Reiki in any form and am by no means an expert, but I have been told that what I am working with is very similar. It has been mentioned to me that we are all innately and intrinsically connected to this force anyway because *Reiki* means and is "universal life force." We all partake in this force because it is universal, and therefore, we all have personal access to it at all times. (Therefore, I find the point of expertise moot.) Those who are attuned in the specific energetic disciplines of healing are endowed with particular lineages and esoteric techniques, lore, and knowledge which create a particular shape or form within the healer.[61] The power/light/energy moulds to that vessel, and a particular shared experience may unfold.

The light I work with is something I also think of as universal but is particularly aligned with the stars, or, rather, that convalescing liquid, diamond-like flame which emerges forth from the campfires of the angels. It is alive, potent, and serpentine, like water and fire married.

To channel this light after having opened the patient to the current is to breathe with the intent of drawing down the light and bringing it up from the Earth. Feel how it meets, mixes, mingles, and marries together in the Heart Centre, then flows down your arms and out your hands like rivers returning to the sea. This light is intelligent and is deeply aware of where it is needed, so as you breathe, affirm yourself as vessel for its force and simply go with the flow of light. You may psychically become

---

[61] Lineages build up psychic momentum and thus become currents or connect us with currents.

aware of regions in the body that require the light and direct it that way; in my experience, this is quite organic. The light penetrates to the very sub-atomic dark space within the cells, and there it pools, saturates, and vibrates. The healing is part and parcel of the channelling.

Restore and Remember Wholeness

After the channelling of the light, I brush away any remaining debris or attachments, flick them to the ground, and ensure that they are banished and recycled by drawing banishing (Earth) pentagrams over the ground and invoking the aid of the Mother:

> *"Great Mother, I pray that this energy will be recycled by you and cleansed, balanced, and aligned within itself."*

I then move my hands very swiftly from crown to foot over the patient's body through the charged aura and gently bring down the aura to almost skin-level so that, from there, it will become its natural shape and fullness again. To bring the aura to the skin also serves to reconnect the patient with physicality and to reaffirm that the body is Spirit and the Spirit is body.

To affirm and seal this, I will draw a pentagram of light, tracing it from head to right foot, from right foot to left shoulder/hand, from left to right shoulder/hand, and from there to the left foot and back to the head. I make a sixth stroke by drawing a line of light from the head straight down over the body, over the feet, and then I swiftly and surely touch the Earth. This grounds the patient. By invoking the pentagram over the body, I call upon the knowledge that we are each a star and thus cosmically oriented and whole from self to Self.

When the patient is ready, I ask them to reacquaint with the surroundings, perhaps vibrating their name clearly within their mind three times to reconnect with identity, and gently but firmly patting down their own body. I also ask the patient to seal each chakra from crown to root by tapping the associated physical point three times with the intent to seal. This further grounding also ensures that the chakras will not leak psychic "fluid" and weaken the recharged being. I have been doing this for years and had never really seen or read about it anywhere else until my first Reclaiming WitchCamp experience, where it was a point of order to "dial down" the chakras before we all left the camp. This ensures not only the individual's psychic integrity and safety but also their emotional and mental balance equilibrium and creates a smoother transition from highly charged magical and mystical experiences to the "mundane" world.

Water-Blessing

The Water-blessing, in the form of the Rite of Self-Blessing previously described, works to reinforce the wholeness of Self after the "event" of healing. It is also an exercise or technique that the patient can take away and return to when needed through convalescence. Physically drinking fluid will also activate the bodily processes once more and serve to further ground (which is so important!). Kala, a Hawaiian and Feri technique, is another form of Water-blessing, which, in its simplest form, would also serve the purpose of this closing step beautifully.

A Simple Rite of Kala

You will need a glass of fresh water.

Align the Spiral Soul and hold the glass of water at the belly, place of Shadow Self. Consume yourself with all of the emotions, paradigms, memories, and attachments which hinder your flow and block you from being present and able to engage with the here and now. Indulge in the feeling of these things as they move through your being like wild animals, thirsty, hungry, and wanting. Take a deep breath and pull as much of this "stuff" as possible up through your throat, then out of your mouth and into the water as you breathe the vibration "Ha" (preferably elongated). Do this twice more until all of the "stuff" is in the water. Visualise or sense the water becoming murky, dull, and obscured.

Hold the water before you at heart level and simply connect with the power that sits in Own Holy Self. Radiate this outward to encompass the water. Watch as the water loses its obscuration and dullness; watch as it begins to shine with light. Say with conviction:

> *"Water is life, unbound and free;*
> *Water—this water—will cleanse and clean me."*

Drink all of the water as in the Rite of Self-Blessing and feel as it cleanses every piece of you, allowing you to vibrate with that same radiance the water possessed. It is done.

Shamanic Soul Retrieval

In *By Land, Sky & Sea*, there is a short section on soul retrieval. I relayed the story of one of my spiritual brothers and his revivification through the interface of the Goddesses. I did not refer to any particular technique for Shamanic soul retrieval, but I will offer my suggestions, frameworks, and personal understandings below.

In the aforementioned section of *By Land, Sky & Sea*, I refer to the power of memory and the act of remembrance, citing the Well of Memory, the World Tree, and how these things renew our underlying wholeness, allowing us to reclaim the sovereignty of Self and become Self-possessed. This is the aim of Shamanic soul retrieval: to aid another in recalling what seems lost (but isn't) and empowering them to accept the right and rite to wholeness/holiness.

The theory of Shamanic soul retrieval involves the idea that the soul complex (its underlying wholeness) can become splintered or fractured by both external and internal trauma. The psyche (soul) of the individual may break or snap forcibly and be lost to consciousness in a car accident, medical operation, physical/sexual assault, or something of that nature—sudden, abrupt, physically abrasive, and traumatic. The psyche may lose its integrity in less overt or instantaneous ways as well and be seen to be seeking refuge in the hidden away darkest recesses of our own Self.[62] This may happen due to enduring psycho-emotional belittling or bullying, child molestation (which, of course, fits into the above category as well), substance/chemical addictions, and mental illnesses or disorders such as anorexia nervosa (as these disorders are also products of soul loss).

There are actually many instances in Western societies where Shamanic soul loss or fragmentation can be seen as the cause of several states of mind and being, so Shamanic soul retrieval may be a useful remedy alongside other forms of psychotherapeutic modalities. Remember, all things are connected; what we might consider depression caused by a

---

[62] This is synonymous with the idea of the Underworld as a "realm." Like most dualities, the internal/external dichotomy is an unhelpful illusion.

simple chemical imbalance (though it's never that simple) will generally have deeper roots, as even the chemistry of our bodies is a signature of the Divine and thus is open to healing of and from the Divine.

It can actually be quite difficult to approach an individual who we believe suffers from soul loss; not only is the condition rarely heard of, but it also generally sounds out-of-this-world and thus not applicable to those in the "mundane." Many medical associations and professionals would either laugh at or condemn the notion as supercilious and ultimately dangerous to the patient's care and health. However, Shamanic soul retrieval in its varied original forms is actually an age-old, well-respected, and traditional technique of healing with enormous potential.

To effectively perform a Shamanic soul retrieval, the malady must be identified correctly. This can be diagnosed through communication with the spirits, guides, and totems of the patient or through divination (covered more in Chapter Eight). Another way to diagnose would be to perceive the energetic bodies or psychic signatures of the individual, either through auric analysis or the Sight in general. You may also simply know. Either way, make sure that you approach the patient carefully and considerately, especially if you have seen it initially and are wishing to communicate. Again, the notion may be completely rejected, in which case it is not up to you to convince them of it; the individual chooses their pathway with the information at hand. If someone approaches you and reports most (if not all) of the following, there is a chance of soul loss or fragmentation:[63]

- Disconnected
- Ungrounded
- Unfocussed
- Lost and uncertain
- Psychically disparate and splintered
- Energetically drained
- Irrationally frightened or terrified
- An unmistakable yet ambiguous feeling of "not being whole"

---

[63] I must remind the reader that many of these traits are symptoms of various mental illnesses and serious health problems. If you suspect mental illness consult a doctor, psychotherapist, or suitable healthcare professional.

While it may not appeal to the broader community, the concept of soul loss will definitely be approachable to those who either include themselves under the umbrella of Paganism(s) or who are mystically and magically oriented. It will be a much easier and more straightforward discussion for those who approach you from these backgrounds. Once the soul-loss phenomenon has been accepted as a viable explanation for the underlying condition, then the actual methodology (which is decidedly trance-based) can be implemented.

The Technique

To renew an underlying wholeness, the spiritual pragmatism that "you are always whole, you simply need to renew and reclaim your Sovereignty of Self" should be postulated and passed as a form of mantra or affirmation. The Rite of Divine Fire, Spiral-Soul Alignment, and the Three Realms Alignment are worth it to integrate into the patient's discipline for at least one week leading up to the soul retrieval itself. A form of water-blessing (Rite of Self-Blessing or Kala) should also be suggested and taught to the patient. The Rite of Divine Fire will wrap the patient in enduring and all-encompassing love, creating a strong foundation to carry them through the pain of soul loss. The practice of both the Spiral-Soul Alignment and the Three Realms Alignment will centre, align, cleanse, and balance the individual and create a point of continuum and connection between what is normally perceived as external and what is felt to be internal. Water-blessing provides a source of further energetic cleansing but also a spiritual sustenance which enriches and nourishes the patient.

Both the healer and the patient should be physically present for the technique (obviously). The patient needs to be as comfortable and warm as possible and is appropriate. For psychological reasons, it is best to keep the space dark (which also mimics the Chthonic realms, the Underworld, and Sea, where soul-pieces are apt to travel and hide) and then to create a lightness in the room (either through sunlight or candlelight) at the culmination of the rite (when the patient is reborn to light). The patient should also be in a rested state so that, when breathing and becoming entranced, they do not fall asleep. Generally, the rite should keep the patient alert enough.

Breathe. Perform the Spiral-Soul and Three Realms Alignment. Cast the Circle and honour the Directions and Sacred Elements of life. Call upon any allies that may be required for assistance or that the patient has asked to be called. Psychopomp deities and spirits are perfect for soul-retrieval work, as are the Chthonic deities, although they are rarely mutually exclusive. A rhythm-keeper (a drum or rattle is best) and one tall white candle and black stone (such as obsidian, jet, or onyx) are also required.

When you are aligned, prepared, and have directed the patient into a cycle of conscious, deep breathing, call openly for the light of the cosmos to dwell within the light of the candle. A prayer like the following will suffice:

"Holy light of the cosmos, spinning and spiralling into eternity.
I call upon thou to settle in the hearth-flame here,
which is also the Flame of the Heart.
Let there be peace and stillness in this place and presiding
over this time outside of time.
Let there be peace."

Light the candle and bow to the light of the cosmos.
Begin to drum or rattle and chant:

"Call Wild to Wild,
Call Self to Self,
In the Circle that lies,
Between the Worlds."

As you drum, allow your trance to deepen until you feel the ripple of the Veil. At this moment, slip between the worlds and follow the thread of light that you will see: it calls you to the lost soul-piece.

Race upon the wind, or dive through the water, or dance through the Fire. There may be many challenges to endure and realms to pass as you follow this thread of light; however, with your allies, you are strong. You will be able to accomplish this journey and undergo this feat of magical strength. At last, when you come to the end of the thread of light, you will find the refuge place of the lost soul-piece. It is not important whether this is considered a realm outside, broader than the autonomy of your single human patient, or whether it dwells within the patient's psyche. At this point, call to the black stone as an ally by name and attribute(s), for the stone will be the storehouse of the soul-piece. When the spirit of the stone arrives, charge the stone to accept the soul-piece, then take the stone in your power-hand and ride the rhythm through the worlds back to your body. Ground and centre.

Tell your patient that you have retrieved the lost soul-piece and that it is contained within the black stone (referring to the stone by its name and its attribute[s] again). Ask the patient to physically show you where on the body they feel the stone must be placed. The patient will know. When they have done so, place the black stone there, charging it by name and attribute to return the soul-piece to the wholeness of the patient by whatever name they have previously told you. The black stone ally will transfer the soul-piece, and the wholeness will be naturally restored.

To affirm and seal the renewal, instruct the patient in the Rite of Self-Blessing. After this has been completed, direct attention to the light of the cosmos and recite the following prayer (or something like it):

> *"Holy light of the cosmos, spinning and spiralling into eternity.*
> *Your presence has been felt and adored!*
> *Let there be peace and stillness in all places, in all times.*
> *Let there be peace."*

Self-Soul Retrieval

There are instances of soul-retrieval that do not require an external being to facilitate the healing and remembering process.

When we fall in love or create psycho-emotional bonds of any kind, we are apt to giving up what may be termed a "soul-piece" to our beloved(s). When we share a loving connection, a psychic cord or attachment is formed (depending on the nature of these, I sometimes call the cords "ego-attachments"). While some of these are simple, pure, and flowing well, some of them become channels which negativity pour through. I experienced this in my first serious romantic relationship.

My boyfriend and I lived together in a very small, confined apartment. We had been dating on and off throughout the last year of high school (both of us enduring Year Twelve in different cities but the same state), and when the first year of post-graduation bliss arrived, we found ourselves both moving to Brisbane and reforming our relationship. At first, this was a joyous and exhilarating thing; it gradually became, on the part of both of us, a very poisonous and co-dependent relationship. Towards the end of our relationship, I remember looking across the living room at my boyfriend. I thought to myself, "Who are you?" and then more startlingly, "Who am I?" I had completely lost myself, and our relationship had become senseless, absorbed in only one another (or the sum of one another), which I shudder at the thought of. I had truly lost myself, or at least pieces of myself.

A month after our official break-up, I was at my main altar conducting my devotion ritual when a presence filled the space. I was not familiar with this being, yet there she was in her golden majesty, stalking the bounds of my Circle and staring through me, daring me to surrender. She was a lioness, so I took her to be Sekhmet, lioness-headed Egyptian Goddess of rage, retribution, and cleansing. I welcomed the Goddess in my Circle, and then, just as suddenly, she began to swipe at me, claw at me, scratch, and sever the tension of my skin. I felt every blow.

At first, I was shocked and afraid, but I realised that Sekhmet was extracting the poison of my newly ended relationship and letting me bleed until I was clean of it. The psychic pus and fluid that poured out of me was not attractive and resembled a befouled green, oozing substance. This was one of those timeless experiences in which the process endured for a natural cycle until I awoke to myself and, somehow, the job of the restoration of my wholeness was mine to take on—of course! Ever since that day, over sixteen years ago, Sekhmet has been on the periphery, watching and waiting, guarding and protecting.

Sekhmet taught me a valuable lesson, which is echoed by a powerful Feri maxim postulated by the late Grandmaster Victor Anderson, "Never submit your life force." We may share it, and this may form cords and threads between us that aid and deepen our connections, but if the connections are soured or become unhealthy, we will all suffer the consequences. This is where the popular aphorism "the ties need to be severed" comes into play. Obviously (and more overtly), a toxic relationship with hate, jealousy, struggle, intimidation, or fear means the cords or ego-attachments will need to be either cleansed and released or completely severed.

Ultimately, it is up to personal volition as to how to confront the shadows amassing behind the cords, but the cords must be allowed to disperse before the work of confrontation can begin. These shadows are actually pieces of our soul(s) that have mutated from being distanced from one's personal integrity. They need to be confronted face-on, challenged (this goes both ways), accepted, danced with, and integrated in a pure way.

Following is a technique which involves scanning the bodies for these cords or attachments and applying intuition in regard to what are healthy or unhealthy attachments. If these are healthy attachments (such as between partners, siblings, parents, or children), they still need to be cleansed, but they will also still need to be watched in case they take on co-dependence or toxicity in any form. If the cords are vampiric, oppressive, draining, or destructive, then they must be severed to remove the core of connection from whichever "body" it is directly attached to.

The Technique

Perform the Spiral-Soul and Three Realms Alignments.

Breathe into your Holy Centre and find equilibrium. When you have reached the point of stillness, expand your consciousness to cocoon your body and being, and "scan" for any cords of attachments. These will generally appear as tendril-like channels. Some will glow with light, others will appear dull or murky, others will appear as almost pulpy, blood-filled veins (and then some). Wherever you find a tendril, cleanse it by directing light through it by connecting to the wellsprings of power from the Three Realms or the World Tree and drawing upon the light that radiates from or is present within. This light will purify and cleanse the cords.

During this process, some of the cords will naturally fall away and disappear or disintegrate. Let this happen. Others will remain and continue to shine, glow, or flail like enraged serpents. It is now time to follow each of the remaining attachments/cords to the points of connection or origin; remember that you may be responsible for the sending or forging of some of these cords, as it is sometimes complicit. At the other "end" will be one of several "things": a memory, a place, a being (human or non-human), or even a concept or belief. We share relationships with all (and more) of these things, and though we have already done the work of cleansing our connections, we now need to feel and intuit whether these are healthy and supportive connections or draining and compromising ones. Spend time working through these revelations and discoveries of what is on the other "side." Once you have found resolution (knowing that there is more work of confrontation and integration to be done), we must draw upon a sword of light.

Call for the sword of light from swollen darkness. Draw it forth from chaos. Open your hands (physically, energetically, or both) and accept the sword as it is conjured; grasp it, wielding it with force and intent. As you nurse the sword, open your awareness to its intelligence and listen to its wisdom. Take it and begin to sever the unhealthy, imbalanced, and poisonous cords and attachments. As you do this, banish the influence and let it be released. Wherever you sever a cord, ensure that you direct light to that place to remove the core of connection. Visualise the light amplifying in vivid brightness and see it coalescing in that place, cycling and spinning with a deep passion and ecstasy. It will disperse and disintegrate the core of connection, then heal the wound. Any psychic scars will be minimal, but if they do remain, the energetic imprint was so strong or enduring that the scar will provide a reminder of the dangers of toxic connections.

The sword of light will do its work and move around the bodies, severing attachments. While at first, you will find that your entire concerted presence of will is required for facilitating this, gradually and earnestly, the sword takes on a mind of its own and does the work for you. When all cords have been severed, and all wounds have been cleaned out with light, the sword of light is reabsorbed from whence it came. Thank the sword and be grateful. You will always be able to conjure it again for future work.

To seal this work, perform the Rite of Self-Blessing, and as you do so and the water rushes through your being, open to the lost soul-pieces. Gradually, they will return, one-by-one, and not always in drastic ways. Some of them may take longer and will be more difficult to merge, but they will do so in peace and balance. Light a candle and make the Rite of Divine Fire.

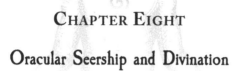

CHAPTER EIGHT

Oracular Seership and Divination

"Shamans were among our earliest diviners, and their many roles as diagnosticians, counsellors and healers demanded many methods. Most often they rely on their spiritual helpers or spiritual vision."
—Roger Walsh, M.D., Ph.D, *The World of Shamanism*

In *By Land, Sky & Sea*, I wrote two chapters which referenced what can be referred to as *Oracular Seership:* Chapter Twelve: To Journey and Vision, and Chapter Thirteen: To Channel. There is a rationale to the linear order of these two chapters. Channelling follows vision-journeying because we must attain a vision before we can communicate it. Therein lies Oracular Seership. Neither the vision-journey (which is not the same as a Native American vision quest) nor the channelling can be taken away from it. In this chapter, I will go into more detail on the art of Oracular Seership *and* divination and provide several techniques for approaching both in the Shamanic way. This chapter will, therefore, be broken into two major sections dealing with both topics separately.

Seeking the Vision

How is the vision sought? How do we perceive the "Other" reality or attain to what Core Shamanism refers to as "non-ordinary states of reality"? To perceive the Other in life is to become intrinsically and instinctually aware of its indwelling presence. However, it must be said that the Other is not necessarily better or more holy or sacrosanct than what we ordinarily perceive to be reality, and I am not simply referring to consensual reality either, which is a product of the overculture. The Other is simply that shade (and I use this word intentionally) of Reality we are not conditioned to, are often warned against, and may unsettle us regardless of any perceived or inherent "moralistic value."

Humans are creatures of habit, as the old saying goes. This seems to be an instinctual survival mechanism: routine creates confidence in certainty, and certainty breeds a belief in security. However, while routine may have its practical aspects of structure and security (making it worth it in many regards), risk needs to be considered, too. Humans are also creatures of risk. Through risk, we catalyse great change in our lives and the future of our species. When risk and routine are balanced, they create a powerful synergy for a life lived courageously and with conviction. By peering through the "Shades" (the Veil, the shadow) and seeing into the Other, we are able to attain the visions which we have opened consciously to. Visions may also choose to reveal themselves to us through patterns of synchronicity or spontaneous ignition.

My first spontaneous vision that I can clearly remember came in 2001 when I was in my first year of high school. During the September holidays, my mother, sister, and I usually traveled to Bali every year. I was now consciously practising Witchcraft, and I had just performed a ritual to make me more aware and sensitive.

One night in Bali, I woke up sweating and with a pounding headache. I screamed for my mum. My body was physically repulsed at the strangeness of what I had been dreaming/seeing. I saw two buildings (nondescript, as if this detail was not the important one) come crashing down, and I saw George Bush, though at the time I was thirteen and did not know who he was, I only recognised his face from somewhere. Bush was standing on what I realised later was the car Hitler would drive around in, waving at the people, pointing at the rubble, and laughing in a maniacal, frightening way. All night, I was tormented by this dream. My mother would try to get me to fall asleep again, and I would wake up either screaming or vomiting; several times during that night, I curled up on the tiled floor like a dog because it was so cold and I was completely overheated.

The next day, I awoke, still feeling incredibly sick. I rested and began to feel a part of the world again. In the early afternoon, my mother took my sister and I into the markets in Singaraja, a large city on Bali's northern coast where I was born. We spoke with a man at the markets, who told us the news about an attack on the Pentagon. Later, we heard the rest and watched the unfolding news reports at my uncle's house. I sat there, watching this all play out with a strange feeling. I turned to my mother and said simply, "Remember my dream?"

This is an example of both seeking a vision (although unwittingly) and having one spontaneously imparted, which are Shamanic initiations in a way. While I often emphasise the self-determined nature of the Witch (and Own Holy Self by way of the sovereignty of Self), the self does not exclude the fullness of reality and its experiential nature. There are many times in which it will not be the Witch who initiates the communication; it will be the spirits, the deities, and the powers that be. Therefore, think of the vision-journey as you choosing to seek and the vision choosing to be found.

It is a very fine line between unbidden and consciously called-for visions. The difference comes from the impetus of either the Seer or a spirit. A spontaneous vision is inspired by connective (whole) impetus, sent from a deity or other spirit to the Seer, or incited by a particular strand of the Wyrd vibrating and intersecting with one's own. A sought-for vision is inspired by personal (autonomous) impetus, and the volition is decidedly self-determined. How these two things can truly be definitively separate, however, is beyond me.

The Technique

As mentioned, I gave a whole chapter to channelling in *By Land, Sky & Sea*. For it, I channelled Divine or universal information and received an epic message, which, when analysed and deconstructed, embodied a methodology to become an open vessel to safely and successfully channel. All of these techniques, it must be reiterated, are simply stepping stones for a personal path of evolution; they are mine (or have come through me), and I am making them accessible to all as springboards in their whole or partial forms to inspire others to create and come upon their own ideas and ways of approaching the magical arts. In this vein, I will not reproduce the technique for channelling discovered in *By Land, Sky & Sea*; I will note, however, that the technique in my previous book is one that works effectively to energetically condition individuals to receive information, then communicate and express it. I have taught the following technique over the past decade, and it has always been useful. What I will offer here is a Three Soul-specific way to translate what I call "universal information" and spin golden threads of wisdom from it to convey to those who seek knowledge.

Align the Spiral/Triple Soul.

Focus on the person before you. Concentrate your awareness at your brow, the Third Eye, and open this chakra. From this point, send a soft, tubular tendril of light to the very edges of the person's aura, and ask that they begin to project any questions (or aspects and areas of life they feel need clarification or direction) to you. As you receive them through the tendril/tube, this will be transferred into Talking Self, then down through Shadow Self, only to be taken directly to Star Self.

Invest your presence and attention within your Star Self and open to the Divine wisdom or universal information that is coursing through the cosmos by knowing the ancient truth that you are profoundly All That Is (the Centre to the Circumference). Allow the Circumference of the cosmos to zero in on the point that is you and open your Star Self to channel that light.

Move the light through the body down into the belly, where Shadow Self is anchored. Feel the tension that emotion produces by its very nature but allow this to be naturally facilitated and transmuted by the "bridge" of the Three Souls. Through the emotional lens of the dreamscape, information is then channelled upward into the Talking Self, the soul which will communicate the information or vision. Remember and bless your open Third Eye.

Speak with ease; allow yourself to be free of judgement, criticism, analysis, and evaluation (for now). Leave this until after the experience. Indulge in the flow of information and the expression thereof. Either describe what you are seeing or feeling or simply speak to the person before you.

Before the vision-seeking and channelling, you should encourage your partner to also simply remain in a receptive state without judgement, criticism, analysis, and evaluation. Their job is to simply allow the information to enter through the filter of the Talking Self and then transmute to Shadow Self, only to be absorbed by Star Self and then have it returned in the opposite order. Talking Self will understand the words and freely welcome them. However, the portals from each soul must be wide open to ensure the information is not stuck in any one soul but experiences the lens and quality of each. As the information flows through Shadow Self, it will arouse certain emotions that are certainly associated with the pieces of wisdom. The information will return to Star Self, providing a polishing of the "gems," so to speak, so that when they rain down upon you again and filter back through Shadow Self to Talking Self, they will shine in truth and find the doorways to ignite your awareness.

In having taught channelling to many people now, it seems the first problem arises when speaking or conveying the information received. Many people stumble when they feel forced to express a vision or intuition in a way that will sound cohesive and coherent to their partners. The best way to ensure freedom of flow here is to not judge yourself as you convey. Simply go with the flow of whatever is received and understand that you do not have to sound like some archaic prophetess or Renaissance magician to be an effective vessel or channel. Be aligned within your Spiral Soul, know that you are the Holy Centre, and claim your worthiness to the innate title of Seer and Witch and you will begin to touch on the ancient and forever-renewing quality of our Wild magic. Unbidden, it will change our lives; bidden, it will shake and remake them.

The Rite of Cleansing and Opening the Eye

This succinct ritual is intended for the opening up of the "psychic" senses and faculties. Ideally, this ritual would be performed on the full moon. For this rite, you should either be skyclad or wearing clothes you are not afraid to get wet.

You will need:

* A ceramic or glass bowl of warm spring or rainwater (you may need to heat the water on the stove slowly)
* 1 teaspoon of dried mugwort
* 1 teaspoon of dried rosemary
* 1 medium-sized amethyst

Place the bowl directly in front of where you will be positioned. Place the rosemary on the lefthand side of the bowl and the mugwort on the right. The amethyst gem can be placed between you and the bowl. Breathe into the Holy Centre and align the Three Souls.

Gaze peacefully at the items gathered before you, and then bring your awareness to the water. Charge it with the light of the heavens and the Earth as you draw it through your being and down through your hands held open over the water. Chant:

> *"Water flowing,*
> *Water knowing,*
> *I am flowing,*
> *With the Water.*
> *Water shine,*
> *Open Mine,*
> *Eye is open,*
> *Water flowing."*

Once you feel the water is charged and blessed, take the rosemary in your left hand and speak with the spirit of the plant. The following formula is useful:

"Rosemary, cleansing herb of the sea, awaken thou spirit and enhance thou potency. Grant me your gifts, I pray."

To name the herb and then address the quality or aspect you wish to draw upon within the working specifically is to respect the ally and its gifts, not to mention good Witchcraft. It is simply polite to speak directly to the spirit and ask for its aid rather than assume authority over it.

You should feel the response of the rosemary spirit. Assuming this is positive and you are continuing with the rite, sprinkle the rosemary into the water, then wash your hands and face with the potion. This is to cleanse your senses.

Now, take the mugwort into your left hand and recite a similar formula over this plant-ally to invoke the gifts of the Sight. When you feel a positive response, take the mugwort between the fingers of your power hand and push it against your Third Eye as you chant:

"Witch's Sight, second Sight,
Enchant herein the powers raised!
Witch's Knowing, magic flowing,
Ignite in me the Seer's gaze!"

Repeat this as many times as needed to arouse the power to a surging peak, which, at the point of release, you should immediately direct into your newly cleansed and newly opened Third Eye. This will feel quite intense, but ride the tide and surrender to embrace the magic. When you have taken in the power, sprinkle the mugwort into the water.

Now, address the piece of amethyst in the same way you have done with the herbs. You may even gently tap the gem three times to wake up the spirit within. Again, assuming the amethyst spirit wishes to co-operate, pick the gem up and drop it reverently into the centre of the bowl through the water. Incant the following again aloud three times:

"Water flowing,
Water knowing,
I am flowing,

With the Water.
Water shine,
Open mine,
Eye is open,
Water flowing."

At the culmination of the third recitation, end with:

"Amethyst! Now heed my call!"

Quickly lift the bowl and upturn it over your head, letting the contents spill onto you. The rite is done, and the Eye has been cleansed and opened.

The Mythic Reality

When we vision and ignite the sight to perceive and receive, we open ourselves to the underlying forces which inform the manifest world. I would call this the Mythic Reality; I also tend to see no difference between the underlying forces and the manifest world, so perhaps it is merely a functional differentiation, but it is all the Mythic Reality. The dynamic, however, is evident within the apparent.

Of course, it would be far too cliché of me to claim this rested on the web of Wyrd—the vibrating, spiralling interconnections of the flesh of Spirit and the Spirit of flesh—but it is absolutely the truth as I know it. What does this mean for us incarnate beings participating within something firmly identified as consensual reality? Does the fact that I am a Witch imply that I am absolutely Other at all times and in every circumstance, especially in contrast to the "majority" of human beings populating our planet? Should I allow the archetype of the crazed Shaman or the Witch on the edge of the village to justify a martyr-like inclination to loneliness and emotional estrangement? How does one walk the fine line, straddling "both" the worlds but able to exist fully in each, whilst inhabiting and requiring that nebulous space in between? This is the source of panic most of the world feels towards the Other: a difference of context which discomforts our previously accepted notions and ideologies of reality.

As a Witch, I am fully submerged in the Mythic Reality, engaged with my own Soul-Story woven of my living myth. I am not enabled to see visions; I simply see them. I am observing, witnessing, waiting, watching, learning, listening, and growing with it all. I ride the currents that move, shape, and break the worlds; therefore, I am wild. I am strange to those who would cast me as delusional, sick, evil, or fanciful.

I was once at a youth interfaith training gathering in which a fellow participant of the Baha'i faith expressed to me that Witches didn't exist. She completely accepted that I was Pagan and understood the basics of what that meant for me, but Witches to her were fantasy figures from childhood tales and nothing more. I could have responded with anthropology, sociology, history, poetry, etymology, art, or simply religion and metaphysics to assert the valid and continued existence of Witches in the world, but I simply said, "I am a Witch." Therefore, Witches exist. It is no more delusional to state that about myself than for a Muslim accountant to refer to himself as such or for a non-binary person to embrace their genderlessness. I am not speaking to the postmodern ambiguity of constructed, and thus empowered, identity; I am speaking of the Mythic Reality that is alive and not separate from anything.

I mention this within the section on Oracular Seership because, without understanding this earnest truth, a vision is both baseless and useless. To vision-journey and then to obtain a vision is an unfolding process which occurs in synchrony with reading or writing a book, getting dressed, having a shower, or brushing my teeth. There is nothing that upholds its inherent worth above or out from the "rest." A vision is as relevant as I make all of my life.

A Shaman may dance around a campfire and drum and rattle all they like, and a Witch may peer into a dark pool of water and scry until their eyes bleed; the vision is not found unless we can see the forest for the trees. We behold the detail and simultaneously, without pause for thought, apply it to not just a broader matrix but an infinite boundlessness: the Mythic Reality.

Last night, the Feri Guardian of the East gave me an answer I asked him for that, of course, led to a new search for a new detail within an overall journey, started not by him but by my own yearnings as given up to Aphrodite, inspired within me because of my love for another. It doesn't stop there. I look for the detail because I know it swims within the wellspring I am diving into. Aphrodite, Persephone, my mother, the World Tree, the *Way of Wyrd* by Brian Bates, and the ice cream I ate and felt awful about all dwell together in the same house, the same forest, and the same living cosmos, that my Soul-Story unfolding inhabits. I search for details and seek visions not for the sake of solving anything but to create an enhanced awareness of my own Being and, therefore, to embrace the gnosis innate within me, constantly revealing the depth of my Divinity.

These are the secrets that are immortal and yet indefinable. Remember that the vision is a proffered piece; our job, once gifted with the piece, is to return it to the whole.

What is Divination?

Divination is the art whereby a skilled individual interprets symbols, signs, patterns, and/or omens in an attempt to read the processes and dynamics of Divinity as it expresses itself throughout eternity. A diviner (one who participates in divination) may also target a particular expression or manifestation of Divinity (a human being) to interpret their particular pure will and its orbit or current. At least, this is how I most broadly define divination.

To divine is to "plug in" to the current of the Divine and assess the quality of its presence at any given time or, as Persephone once said to me, "Wherever time has placed thee, and space has prevailed over thee."

Divination is a nearly essential component of any Shamanic craft or vocation, which echoes the charges of British cunning folk, Balinese *balian*, and Mexican *curanderas*. To think upon the old Witch at the edge of the village or the hedge is to think of a wise or cunning person who not only casts spells and speaks with spirits but also reads the signs of nature to portend the future, understand the past, and provide wisdom for the present.

In contemporary Witchcraft, many traditions suggest to its aspirants or students that they learn at least one form or medium of divination. For many of us, this will be the tarot; for others, the Nordic runes; and for some, astrology or palmistry. Ultimately, however, the technique and theory between the forms are similar or the same (though the attitude may differ, and sometimes this makes all the difference).

The Technique of Shamanic Divination

Shamanic divination is simply the concept of divination qualified by the Shamanic paradigm we have discussed. Shamanic divination honours the depth and infinite possibility of any particular individual, treasures the Mythic Life and Soul-Story of all beings, and understands divination to be a methodology through which we are blessed enough to witness, for a brief moment, an aspect of that unfolding legacy and mark it on the Wyrd.

The technique of Shamanic divination is not necessarily one discrete thing; the secret is in the attitude that manifests in how the reading (divination) is conveyed.

My preferred form of divination is the tarot. I have been working with a particular deck for several years now and it has passed through many hands. It has been a part of my cunning charge that divination is a skill of mine, especially as it relates to tarot and the signs of the palm. The last few times I visited my birthplace of Bali, I was inundated with requests of divination, as it is an art that is highly respected in the Balinese culture, and though the Balinese have not necessarily seen divination with tarot or even cards before, they are familiar with the concept and therefore do not falter at the appearance of the tarot. The indwelling concept, technique, and orienting attitude to the experience are familiar.

When I read the cards for another person, I breathe into my Centre and cleanse the cards (even if I had cleansed them after the last reading) to ensure that the energy of the previous querent (person being read for) is dispersed and gone, so that the energy of the new querent is not confused or "impure." I never perform a reading unless I know my cards are cleansed and blessed. To do this, I will shuffle my cards while focussing on channelling light into and through them and chanting:

"I bless, I cleanse, I consecrate, I purify, I charge!"

I then hold my cards up, blow on them, and draw a pentagram over and around them to seal the cleansing. If you are reading with the Runes, you might simply shake the pouch that holds them until it feels right. With dice, you might hold them in your hands, breathe over them several times, and then shake them to roll. With palmistry, the medium belongs physically to the person being read for, so it would be almost anathema to cleanse; simply centre yourself.

If you feel the need to create or affirm a space for the reading session(s), the following is a very succinct but potent way in which to do that:

1. Breathe. Align the Spiral-Soul.
2. Gesture to the ground and say, *"By the Land..."*

Gesture to the sky and say, *"By the Sky..."*

Cup your hands together at your heart and say, *"By the Sea..."*

Seal this Three Realms blessing with *"By the Ancient Trinity. So mote it be!"*

3. Touch the ground once more, focussing on the spirits of place, and say with conviction:

    "O Holy Spirits of Place, I honour your providence and presence.
    I work with you and not against you. May you welcome me as
    I welcome you."

    Hit the ground with your hands three times as if to vibrate the blessing into the Earth.

4. Stand and turn to the East and give peace to each direction (East, North, West, South, Above, Below, and Centre).

5. Return to the East and draw a Circle while chanting:

    "I cast this Circle to cleanse and banish all
    that hinders my limitless flow."

    Repeat this until you feel the area is cleansed of any vibrations that may have limited your work.

6. Recite the final prayer:

    "May my ancestors (and any other specific allies) bless me in this holy
    work of the Seer and guide and guard me in the fulfilment thereof.
    May there be truth, power, wisdom, insight, and clarity for all who
    come to share in story here."

Once the space has been created and affirmed, the reading may begin. When reading, open to the flow of the Divine. If you have laid down a spread or group of signs, do not attempt to interpret the cards, Runes, lines, or any other signs of the medium independently of one another. Read each sign within the context of an overarching theme, pattern, and story that will become apparent. Once the signs are revealed, do not simply confine your glance to the first sign "in order" and read each in isolated progression. Look at the totality and study the themes and patterns that emerge. For example, if reading tarot, this may be how many cards of which suit(s) or how many major arcana as opposed to minor arcana cards appear.

For the runes, if using the Elder Futhark, it might be significant if a disproportionate amount of a certain *aett* (eight) appear over other signs. These may constitute certain patterns, but when divining, you are also looking past the superficial and delving into the unfolding Soul-Story or Mythic Life as conveyed through the agency of the medium. This is where you must work with intuition and instinct rather than the simple "mechanics" or "constituents" of the divinatory medium. An example might be the following spread of tarot cards:[64]

- The Magician
- Two of Cups
- Three of Swords
- The Empress
- The Hierophant
- The Devil

Firstly, assuming the "order" of these cards wishes to be read in that direction of progression, I would open my awareness (and not just physical sight) to the spread of cards. Mentally, I would follow the intuitive flow and prepare to receive specific knowledge or facts and figures which either appear "spontaneously" in my mind or are heard or seen. Then, I will generally begin with the initial card (the card I laid down first), as this initiates the unfolding.

In this case, I would speak to the querent about the power of manifesting will through determination, conviction, and a quiet or innate understanding of the "fusion of factors," which enables a potent wielding of the force for and of change (the Magician). Then, the story flows on.

I might mention the cards by title or name and contextualise their presence or placement, but I am generally still attempting to remain fluid. To continue, I would caution the querent to be wary of using this Magician's gift to draw in passionate, soul-entwining love (at the present time), as the Three of Swords qualifies that, if this is to be the case, it will be underscored by emotional torment, manipulation, and entanglement. However, this also

---

[64] I actually don't use traditional spreads, although I find them helpful guides for beginners. I lay the cards down as they require or as I feel and generally refer to the first one lain down as the "pinnacle" of my" spread." I start from that point and move organically through the whole.

feels to me as if the love is already opening, and therefore, the following cards create a resolution within themselves.

The Empress and the Hierophant speak of abundance and the structure to contain and secure it. At this point, I would encourage the querent to understand that abundance, prosperity, and fecundity are all in store and in overflowing dimensions, but to respect and nurture this Divine blessing; one must ensure that balance and organic structure and disciplines (which reflect one's core values) are put in place to reinforce the blessings. Ultimately, it seems that the focus on creating a life that reflects one's values and honouring them by living in congruence with one's Self and pure will is the way to the light at the end of the tunnel and out of the implied emotional tumult. The Devil's message is that any binding we perceive or feel in our lives is actually illusory, and any limitation or emotional shackles we might feel locked into or cornered by because of the Three of Swords has a simple resolution: walk away and let it go. Focus on the cultivation of abundance and all will fall into place.

In reflecting on this process, I might also add that there are four major arcana cards to two minor arcana, so I would mention the "fated" implications of these events as a domino effect or chain reaction. Events which might also have the capacity to shift one's attitude towards life and all relationships thereof. The story as a holism is the significant thing, although attention to detail is also important. To balance both and convey a fully fleshed account, with considerate and deliberate effort underpinned by intuitive flow, is to provide a Shamanic reading in the truest sense. Remember that the majority of querents seek out diviners for clarity and direction—in that order.

Just Knowing and the Deep Well

Every now and then, I reflect on the process of divination and things such as the previous tarot session I was involved in. In retrospect, I realise that at least half of the information I expressed to the querent did not come from the cards themselves at all and not even necessarily from the relationship or the pattern in wholeness. Sometimes, I *just know*. Some might call this *claircognisance* (clear knowing); however, I feel that it derives from a strong connection with the Deep Well.

The Deep Well is sister to the World Tree, and though we could easily relegate the Well to the guardianship of the Wyrd Sisters and the province of the Underworld, it is something more than that. Cosmologically speaking, the Well sustains the strength, vitality, and growth of the World Tree. Without these nourishing, sweet waters of life, the Tree could and would not exist. The primordial waters of life are pre-existing in many creation stories. For example, when Eurynome dances with the North Wind Ophion (the Serpent) and mates with him to bring forth the Cosmic Egg from which all came, she dances upon the waves of the Sea. In Genesis, Yahweh hovers over the waters of deep seas before the God even creates the heavens and the Earth. It is by splitting the seas vertically that Yahweh creates the firmament, and by splitting them horizontally, Yahweh creates dry Land (Earth).

The Sea is the realm in between; it is the substance of chaos. The Sea reconciles the implied duality of the Sky and the Land, opposites in everything: above and below, etheric and solid, and masculine and feminine. This is also why the Sea is considered a frightening and hellish place in many mythologies, a realm of death, uncertainty, and chaos in the most feared sense. The sea is bitter and deadly, and yet it is the womb from which we came. To many, the duality of binary opposites and polarities formulates a safe and generic container, whereas it is the Shamanic prerogative to smash these illusions and remind everyone of the Centre which is Everywhere, and of the Sea that subsumes reality.

The Well lies in the heart of the Sea. The Well of the Underworld that lies beneath the World Tree, nourishing it, is one and the same with that realm I have identified as Sea. Sea is both the child (the Third Factor) of the alchemical love of the heavens and the Earth or Sky and Land, as well as the predecessor and origin of them both. The Waters, the Seas, the Deep Well: these are the powers of chaos which brought forth creation. It makes a great deal of sense when we consider the role water plays in the vast majority of the world's religious and spiritual traditions. Water is life!

I mention this because to simply know is to hover above the primordial waters and to behold the unfolding of creativity. It is to rest in the primal origin and flow from that place to that place, over and over. When I connect with the Underworld—my ancestors, that vast and unravelling lineage of legacy—I am tasting the salt and the sweetness of the Sea and drinking from the Well. This is how I just know.

A Prayer to the Deep Well

"Deep Well, Well Deep, though I rest, I do not sleep;
Thou art the mighty Origin, of all without, of all within;
And so I call for every wave of knowledge pouring from your cave.
I see the Holy Majesty of the wholeness of Infinity;
I dip my cup into your stream, and behold the unseen;
Before Time was, you were, and so I pray:
Deep Well, Well Deep, I am awake, I do not sleep."[65]

The Nature of Time

If divination is the art of interpreting the flow of the Divine (which is both immanent and sentient) and it can be accessed at any time, this implies that time is not so much a thing drawn out, differentiated, and named "time" (to be objectified as such). Time is not a law of the cosmos that must be obeyed; it is a quality of the living, limitless cosmos. It precedes the "creation of things," and therefore, is sewn into the very fabric of being. The Orphic cosmology paints the picture beautifully:

First, there was the Aeon (Infinity), an ageless and undetermined presence of Time (Kronos). Kronos dwelt with Ananke (Necessity) and two Serpents, breathing in the stillness of space. They came together, and from their sinuous union of undulating ripples came Bright-Shining Aether, Erebos (Darkness), and Kaos (Chaos), the primordial spirit and matter, with deep potentialities already dwelling within Time and Necessity. Time came together with Aether in raw and fruitful desire. Upon the dark chasm of Kaos, Aether spread open her wings, and from between her legs came forth the silver Cosmic Egg. When the Cosmic Egg cracked open, the top half became the heavens above the stars and the lower half the Earth. Protogonos (First-Born) stepped forth, androgynous and beyond gender. Protogonos is also Phanes (Light-Bearer) with golden wings shining like the Sun, four eyes, the voice of a bull and lion, and many-headed, invisible yet radiating light!

This myth continues to explain the sovereignty of certain gods through whom the passage of time moves. However, it is Kronos (Time) who is

---

[65] Gede Parma, Fio.

Infinity (also called Aeon) that clarifies the forethought and precludes the "creation." Time, necessity, and the dynamic tension they share propels the expression of desire and, thus, creativity.

We've all heard it said that time is an illusion or that Pagans and Witches do not necessarily subscribe to time as a linear concept (or even as a cyclical concept) but more of a spiralling flow. Is this enough? Should we look more incisively into "Time"? Time is one of the Orphic serpents who dwelt in the "time before Time." It is also Kronos, who manifests later as the same-named son of Ouranos, who castrates the Old King and then attempts to devour all of his children, passing through Zeus and then to Dionysos almost as progressive incarnations of the same spirit. How, then, do we relate to this force or idea? There seems to be one spirit swimming through this majestic river and manifesting as diverse expressions in apostolic succession. It is the Spirit of Time: Kronos, the Serpent. So, Time is a "thing." Time is a presence and a quality of the cosmos which we do not abide by, but partake in.

If Time is ever-present and is a being, idea, presence, and quality of the cosmos within itself, then *all* of Time is accessible at any "point." To see into any phase or part of Time is to recognise this principle and to cultivate such an attitude toward Time. In doing so, we are opened to the first Time: Aeon and Infinity.

Conclusion

The Soul-Story and the Mythic Life

"Guard the Mysteries; constantly reveal them!"
—Lew Welsh

"...I am that which is attained at the end of Desire."
—*Charge of the Goddess* (Doreen Valiente)

The material within this book has laid a framework for Witches to establish a Shamanic Craft practice held and nourished by an open and deep cosmology and philosophy. The art of altering consciousness is just as much about shifting paradigms as it is about inducing psychic trance. The Shamanic Witch ignites awareness, fulfilling the pure conscious state that is the gift of life in Mystery in its fullness. The All-Self is not merely a model or metaphor for the limitless Divine, it is the sacred reality and truth enlivening all to be as it will be. To initiate and receive initiation is to dive into the cosmic current and embrace the infinite depths: the potential you and the hidden potency. This is the distinct expression that creates identity and sings the song that blurs and breaks the barrier between so that all may be all together. The Web and its vibrating Wyrd are the mother and child of this communion.

In this conclusion, I wish to explore the notion of the Soul-Story and the Mythic Life. It distils the lessons of the whole and aims to offer delight, hope, presence, meaning, power, and magic to any individual who would aim to align the Spiral Soul and become the World Tree. There are no techniques or methods to be found within this chapter, but simple poetry which will serve as a good night kiss. When you rise to claim the new day, seize it with willingness and courage, and you will have found the fruition of desire which seeds itself.

Be free and hold your flame as the sacred illumination that shines forth from the stars in darkness before you as you journey. The depth of darkness breeds the bright light, and we will soon find that they ever court, ever dance, and ever spiral together.

The Well reflects you and all spirals to join the continuum together. We are initiates because we are humbled by witnessing wonder, and we have become worthy of the deepest of things.[66] Ignite consciousness like Fire in the head but remember to quell the flame and bring it to your heart and belly so that the Three are One. You are aligned to accept fully the essential. We are each an essence of the Essential; embrace your uniqueness.

I always say that once one is initiated, every day and every moment becomes an initiation; there is constant and changing reinforcement and actualisation of that primal communion with the source. To touch that source and to hold a living relationship with the Mystery is to flow with the rhythms and tides of what is, was, and will be in the eternity of space and time, unbound and free.

If the Mysteries are mysterious, then they uphold the original and intended meaning behind the word "mystery." *Mystes* in ancient Greek culture referred to the initiates themselves: those to whom the great and potent truths of the world(s) were revealed in splendour; those who had received gnosis and chosen for themselves to seek, wander, wonder, and discover.

To know the Mysteries is to surrender to the ever-secret. We are the holy ones: the children of Earth and starry heaven. We are not only houses of Spirit but expressions of Spirit, and thus, we are all children of God(dess). We are gifted with love, truth, and wisdom (the gifts of initiation) so that we may live, thrive, and flourish.

The Deep Well

The World Tree has a sister: the Deep Well. Though the Three Worlds are joined by the majesty of the Oak, Ash, and Mountain, it is the Deep Well which feeds and sustains the World Tree. We are, therefore, urged to look down and deeper than we could dare to conceive.

The Well says drink deep of me, but first, you must make yourself worthy, and only you can do that. You are sovereign over nothing and no one but your sacred self. Know the truth that Self is Self and hold the Grail,

---

[66] A saying of Jarrah Staggard.

the fulfilment of Mystery which is engendered by yearning, and you will have come home to the wandering centre—the initiate who lives in the Holy Centre—which dwells in all things.

To truly understand what is meant by Soul-Story and Mythic Life, we must reflect on She in whom we live, move, and have our being, from whom all things emerge, and to whom we shall return. I will refer to this Mighty One—this Holy One—by the title I first knew her by Grandmother Weaver.

Quite recently, I knelt in fellowship with other Wildwood Witches to be present with a dear friend. There is a ceremony within our tradition which is conducted with an aspirant who has been accepted into the Inner Court of Mysteries (whether this is into a coven or, more broadly, into the Fellowship of the Wildwood). As I watched this rite unfold, I realised that it embodied the true nature of our tradition. It is not a rite that we have received from the ancient past in a linear historical fashion, nor is it a rite that we wrote or devised in any intelligible sense. Like many "things" that are part and parcel of Wildwood Witchcraft, it is a rite that simply formed itself through a coalescing of spirit which came forth in communion and celebration, that self-sprouted and organically enmeshed into our lore and mythos, and that typifies the quintessence of who we are as Wild Witches and what it is we connect and commune with.

As the aspirant merges with the realm of Wildwood itself and perhaps explores it for the very first time in this incarnation and recollection, they touch the very core of our spirituality and its profound implications. In literally moving between the worlds (the pre-eminent Shamanic technique of ecstasy), we remind ourselves that we are bound by nothing and challenged by everything. The worlds form around an infinity that expresses its consciousness as Self. This All-Self, Great Cosmic Goddess Star-Born and unfolding into the limitless creation is my Grandmother Weaver.

As I witnessed the unfolding of this Wildwood rite for this Wildwood Witch, I felt both strangely distanced and wholly present. I believe that this strange paradoxical emotion was kindled because not only have I been involved since the "beginning" of the weaving of our Tradition, but I have felt every shift and change so viscerally that it is as if I have breathed through a greater being and lived by the Will of It. Is this a state that is spiritually and philosophically desirable? Is its absorption into the wholeness of reality? Or am I sacrificing my autonomous nature and Sovereignty of Self? Am I losing myself to the Self? I listen to the words of the Shamans and I remember that I am a Wild Witch and walk the crooked road, straddling the worlds and moving into and moving through.

As I walked home from that park, from that tree that has been imprinted into my Memory, I beheld Grandmother Weaver's voice, and she spoke to me:

> *"In the belly of the ocean is the Well of Creation. All rivers flow from the Well of Creation...All rivers return to the Well of Creation...."*

I realised then that if I call Her Limitless Being "Zero" (as T. Thorn Coyle does for God herself) to ensure that I do not refer to any numerical value and therefore draw it out, objectify it, and confuse it for infinity, I am surrendering to her circumference. If I surrender with consciousness, then I am aware of the deep love that saturates every piece of the body of God. If I ignite my awareness, look out upon the swollen darkness, and see myself in All, I become the Holy Centre that is ever-wandering and ever-wondering. I introduce myself for the first time to the Living Myth or my own Soul-Story, for I can truly look out and, in doing so, pierce the depth of my Mystery. I have seen that every single part of life is joined in the wholeness that surrenders to itself in infinite potential and infinite possibility.

If I choose to view the world through this paradigm-shattering paradigm and renew my sovereignty of Self from the place I call Own Holy Self, then I am capable of both writing and reading the Story that is encoded in my breath, beat, blood, and body.[67] I become cognizant of my pure will and reflect that, while all flow with the pure will, to embrace and re-sacralise our own pure will is to wilfully and with desire step into the momentum and moving current of will. To do this and invest every piece of awareness in the Mythos (Story-Reality) that lives in the nature of meaning is to make the pure, *pure*. I possess my Self through mastery of choice, and I determine to become the Centre to the circumference and the circumference to the Centre. All pure will is *the* pure will. Though they flow through different lands, all rivers are home to different creatures, experience different climates and seasons, represent the embodiment of different ecosystems, and return to the ocean from whence they came. These are the primordial Waters of life upon which the breath of the infinite ripples the surface of the Deep Well.

---

[67] Thank you, Dylan!

My Soul-Story

It is past midnight as I write this, and I am keenly aware of a shifting and changing inside of my being, catapulting me into the momentum of my pure will. I have struggled for so long in truly accepting this charge as priestess and Witch as my vocation in this life; and I will continue to struggle, but not without meaning. Yet it seems the spirits, as my equals and friends, would encourage nothing else. If I am to truly stand as I kneel and become both the World Tree and the Deep Well, I will surrender to the All-Self that is within me and that gave birth to me.

I am my own Divine Origin. I am my own seed and outcome. How do I choose to join the past to the future? What is the present but a fleeting moment which engenders itself continuously? Time is a serpent, a spiral, and a river through which life flows and shines its splendour upon us. When I say, "I was asked to take the sword (and I have) and crowned by the Mother of Angels (and I was)," am I speaking literally or metaphorically? For me, this dichotomy is a deeply misleading one, and I wish not to be trapped by its limits. My Living Myth has been shown to me at every point with every breath and every time I have forgotten and forgiven. In embracing my Living Myth, I begin to understand my Soul-Story and see it not as a pre-ordained destiny or fate handed down from "up above" but as a song of connection which pierces the very heart of me and opens me to the holy truth that everything that is possible is so because of my presence and participation.

T. Thorn Coyle asserts, "God Herself is the fabric of All. Change can occur in conformity with love and will. Our presence is required." For me, this means that I am God herself unfolding into the Holy Centre that, by my ignited awareness, has become illumined as the investment of my presence in the here and now. The realisation of the pure will as "stepping into the current and momentum" reflects to me that it is with love and will together that I open to the Great Mystery as All-Self and as my mirror. Without love, my will is void of meaning and spirit, and without will, my love is irrelevant and useless.

My prayer to Self is this:

> *"May my pure will be empowered and liberated; as I wander/wonder through the landscape of my Living Myth, may it be deepened and enhanced to my Own Holy Self."*

As a Shamanic Witch, I am a walker between the worlds and a healer, knower, wise one, singer, dancer, and vessel. I speak to the spirits, gather up power to make change, transform the essence of my soul to take on other guises, and open to receive the powers and forces of potent beings. To what end?

I am capable of infinite potential. By becoming the sovereign of my Self and igniting my awareness to cultivate initiation in each conscious moment, I share the power that is kindled within me with the All. I activate my hidden potency and engender the living potency. I truly become a God for a moment, and the spirit within me rejoices in the process. I am remembered, married to memory, and reborn through the dark cauldron of nature into the Spirit, which is my birthright/rite. I am truly the Holy Child, as are you.

Living Myth/Mythic Life

"All that wanders is not lost..."

—J.R.R. Tolkien

Life is neither literal nor metaphorical. It is neither a symbol of itself nor itself a direct embodiment of an answer. Life is Myth, and recognising this fact enables us to become the true voyagers and wanderers. We become enlivened to the charge of existence and stand to wander through the shifting paradigms and realities endlessly, dynamically dancing with the pure will of God herself. This pure will is seamless, and yet this mighty fabric, this woven tapestry, is eternal and undying. Our threads woven into this grand design are the details that meet with the infinity and make the darkness light and the light revealing.

In the centre of each of us is an unwavering Mythic Life that yearns for expression. I am not referring to any one archetype which may seem to reflect our life experience or embody our cause or principles. I am speaking of one simple and profound truth that the Shamanic Witch may embrace: "Nature is our sacred foundation. Magic is the essence of nature. Magic is our Sacred Charge." Put simply, "I am nature. Magic is my lifeblood. I am magic." If we are to be literal, now is the time. Literally, I am the magic that the eons have spoken of and shuddered and delighted at! Literally, I am the soul-spun story of the shimmering height and the darkest depth! Literally, I am whatever I behold and whoever I choose to be. My purpose, my woven Soul-Story, and my humming Living Myth is to take what is literal and transform it through the poetry of the soul into the wisdom and grace of the Divine. If I am able to surrender without losing my Centre and to glimpse the eternal within the sentient and the sentient within the eternal, then my pure will is flowing, and the mark of the Spirits has ignited upon my brow.

If you have read this book and your soul has stirred in response to the poetry of the tripartite cosmos, or your senses have been aroused by the ecstatic techniques and rituals, and you long for initiation into the Shamanic Craft, these are my hard-won pieces of insight and wisdom.

Humble yourself by doing the great work of knowing thyself, and in knowing thyself, become potent. In becoming potent, reveal the holiness of Self; in revealing the holiness of Self, revel in it. In revelling in it, claim and possess it; in claiming and possessing it, allow for freedom. In freedom, there is eternal responsibility, so you must do the Great Work of knowing thyself and seeking harmony with the Wyrd and Web. If you receive initiation in this way, then it is right and good, and you may celebrate this threshold moment (and there are countless and mark them all) by singing to the corners of the cosmos:

"As I stand, so do I kneel."

APPENDIX I

Shamanic Craft Terminology

All-Self: The totality of a self-aware being. In the Upanishads, this may be referred to as the Atman/Brahman—the Universal Soul—which the atman (little soul) reflects or embodies.

Being: All that is because it is.

Dark Cauldron of Nature: The dark, fecund void which nourishes being and recycles and renews all life. It is the womb of the Goddess and represents Spirit as predecessor, child, and alchemical Elemental fusion.

Great Mystery: A term used by some First Nations and Craft traditions to refer to the ultimately unknowable essence of life. This term has been absorbed into contemporary Paganisms and Witchcraft as a poetic reference to the Divine providence.

Here and Now: The Eternal Present as a concept stripped of any time-ordered meaning. The place one finds oneself is the immediate outcome of investing presence in one's consciousness, igniting it.

Hidden Potency: For the many forms of life to be expressed as beings, we must all be endowed with hidden potency. To live in alignment with one's pure will, from Own Holy Self, is to cultivate sovereignty of Self which activates the hidden potency. Thereby, we become living Gods.

Holy Centre: The place within that is beheld consciously as the centre to the circumference of the limitless, unfolding cosmos. As there is no end to the universe, there are no "physical" co-ordinates to arrive at a specific placed centre; this poetically and fundamentally enables us to affirm that the Centre is in all places. When we consciously embrace ourselves as a "centre," we become/arrive at the Holy Centre.

Living Cosmos: The world(s) in their power, wonder, terror, and infinity.

Living Myth/Mythic Life: The idea/truth that our lives are not linear, void of meaning, or obsolete, and that our lives are spiralling and therefore deepening into continued synchronicity, revelation, and liberation. Each of us is a traveller dreaming our existence into being, expressing the wonder-voyage of Own Holy Self.

Overculture: A term popular in the Reclaiming Tradition of Witchcraft. It refers to the monolithic societal paradigms which rule the consumerist, industrial, and heavily fragmented/compartmentalised human culture.

Own Holy Self: The embodiment of the totality of being within the Self. When we are at our pure state—with Talking Self, Shadow Self, and Star Self aligned and unified—we are greater than the sum of our parts and we come to our Own Holy Self. When we live from Own Holy Self, we cultivate sovereignty of Self and Self-Possession.

Pure Will: The flow of the good which each individual is charged to actualise. We all flow with pure will, but determining one's life-path through its unfolding is to consciously enter its current and momentum and to stand proudly in the river of Will, remembering that all rivers flow to the Sea.

Sovereignty of Self: The lifework of realising one's inherent Divinity and claiming it as sovereign right, therefore, autonomous—yet interconnected—rulers of our unfolding fates. Sovereignty of Self is to be in accord with Own Holy Self, enhancing and attuning it to the pure will of the living cosmos, while maintaining an equal balance of individuality as a unique expression of the Self. T. Thorn Coyle calls this "Self-Possession."

Wild Way: Another way to say "the Crooked Path." The Wild Way is the path that the Wild Witch walks; it is seemingly the middle-way between God and oblivion—the third or Faerie Way—and yet, by its own twisting and turning, it becomes all paths as woven into one. The Wild Way is ever-changing; it is the innate primal root of all things in existence.

Wild Witch: A Witch who pursues the Shamanic path.

By Land, Sky & Sea: Three Realms of Shamanic Witchcraft and the Context of the Shamanic Craft Apprenticeship

Within these pages, you will find references to my book, *By Land, Sky & Sea*. This was my third published book, released by Llewellyn in October 2010.

I began to create the structure of this book on my first pilgrimage through the sacred landscapes of Britain, Ireland, and Greece. This was a nine-week journey that I embarked on with two other Wildwood Witches, who have lived in Britain ever since. I recall writing preliminary notes in a three-person tent at one of the activist-occupying sites peopled by folk defending the ancient kingship grounds of Teamhair (anglicized as "Tara") in Ireland. I wanted to find the people who were blocking the building of the highway there, and we struck up a conversation with a ceramicist and spirit-worker who happened to be one of the activists. She took us to the campsite, and we helped out for a few days.

By Land, Sky & Sea is a phrase that is often spoken at Wildwood rituals. We might say it just after grounding and aligning, or after casting the Circle, or after acknowledging the country and the traditional owners. For our tradition, this cosmology has always been central.

The Shamanic Craft apprenticeship developed out of a personal need and desire to offer deeper, possibly initiatory Witchcraft work to spirit-workers I knew in my community. The first in-person group began at the Samhain of the Southern Hemisphere in 2011, so the first initiations happened at Samhain-tide in 2013. (These initiations were discussed with some graduates of the two-year apprenticeship.) This also coincided with my name change to Fio, which happened on the night of May 2, 2013, in my mother's house in a circle cast by my mother's hand with my own Witch knife.

This work was a distillation of my own harrowing initiation at the hands of the Spirits, my two Wildwood initiations, my service in that community, and my desire to help facilitate an awakening of ancestral charge in other Witches. The initiation that some people ended up going through was not into any formal tradition or lineage; it was into their own power as a Shamanic Witch and their own charge to service. In Wildwood Witchcraft, we sometimes speak of self/community/cosmos as three concentric rings that help contextualise one another. This was offered as a map and model to folks in the Shamanic Craft apprenticeship to help clarify their own service and celebration. Much of what was taught can be found in *By Land, Sky & Sea* and *Ecstatic Witchcraft*, but you'd have to read between the lines for the rest.

I have chosen to not have this book reprinted since it went out of print. It belongs to a specific time in my life and was a resource that many people I came across loved and used often. I am happy for this. I treasure the beautiful cover and the experience of writing the book. It opened the way for this very book—first published in 2012 by Llewellyn—and its new Crossed Crow edition. Occasionally, you may come across copies of *By Land, Sky & Sea* in the wild. If you do, cherish them for me.

Appendix III

More on Trance Possession

When I teach trance possession, I begin with this provocation: "We are never not possessed." When I eat rice, drink coffee, or devour chocolate, on some level, I am knowingly participating in certain partnerships and synergistic possessory covenants that are centuries or millennia old. These beings—the rice, the coffee, the chocolate—are saying, "Take us in, we will work with you, give us space…plant us, harvest us, and we will perpetuate ourselves." These are the old partnerships our ancestors forged.

Many in so-called Western societies fear trance possession. The notion that we might surrender the faculties of control and hand over to another being—another "centre-of-agency"—allowing the substance of self to be displaced or opened up terrifies those who are tied to certain models of "selfhood." There are certain ideas of the duality of "self and other," of "this is this, and that is that," that are reified by consumerist, capitalist, and industrialist modes of existence. When we work with aspecting, oracular prophesy, or trance possession, categories begin to move "too" sensuously and "too" ecstatically, and euphoric and ecstatic opportunities arise. We are afraid something might happen, that something may change! A similar anxiety and fear arises in people learning the sorcerous arts: what if something actually happens?! My response usually is that we are hoping it will! We desire these consequences, these experiences, and these encounters with the sacred.

The notion of "we" or "I" that many have been entrained into must be adjusted or confronted. After all, the "we" that we might think we are is literally saturated in deep and primal synergy with countless bacteria, fungi, and other ancestral powers uncountable and unnameable.

The arts of consciously, lucidly, and proficiently opening as a skilled and strong vessel to carry and be carried by a spirit, a god, or a Mystery is an initiatory experience that many crave. To face the fallacy of "control" and to realise that sovereignty implies an intrinsic belonging to the grounding of our own being—to the fabric of things—ignites an awareness of what is possible. In this way, training in the possessory arts, especially in the context of community and culture, reminds human societies of how significantly interdependent we really are.

Ecstatic states of oracular vision and visceral expressions of possessory power have been a part of my life since birth. In islands like Bali, we understand that there is an exquisite and sacred tension between the illusion and substance of Self and the collective and unfolding Self of Mystery. We know that agency is twinned with responsibility, so the possession of the human by the more-than-human is a crucial and ancient bond necessary for deepening engagement of biodiversity and custodianship in any given place and in any time.

Here are three techniques and processes I have developed in my work with aspecting and trance possession over the last fifteen years of community teaching.

Double-Headed Possessory Trance

I developed this technique after being inspired by the phrase "double-headed possession." It came rather readily as if I had simply stumbled upon it "in the astral," fully formed, so to speak. I have taught this technique since 2012.

The Technique

Acknowledge. Ground. Centre. Align.

Go to your working space. If you do not have a dedicated working space, cast a strong Circle with an emphasis on focus, containment, precision, and strength, or prepare the space in whichever manner aligns with your practices, ensuring you have also prepared yourself through communion with the deity or spirit you will call in.

It is important to always have at least one tender who is experienced with deep trance and possessory states. This person should ground the space and witness and hold space for the Witch or spirit-worker who is opening as a vessel.

1. Invoke Libra, the Scales, upon you. Open your arms to assume the right-angled praise posture, reminiscent of ancient Minoan and

Egyptian goddess statuary. (I have heard this pose called "the Epiphany of the Goddess.") Feel the beauty, harmony, and resonance of the Scales bless you and this work. Know that the Scales underscore this mystic, sorcerous, and devotional work. You may even ask aloud for the Scales to lay their blessing over you in the name of beauty, harmony, and resonance.

2. Fill your being and awareness with facts, figures, connections, and qualities of who you are, how you think and feel about yourself, and how you ground into core self and identity. Recite, feel into, and stir these aspects or qualities within to an almost "deafening" and overbearing point. This is to gather up the "substance of the self" as a tangible presence that you are able to perceive and move with your trained attention.

3. Conjure up the Blue Flame—the fetch of the Earth—from the core of the planet. Draw the flame up between your feet and up through your genitals, intestines, between your lungs, through your heart, throat, and up through the hemispheres of your brain. This flame is intelligent and aware, and it protects and blesses us and the work. It will form a profound membrane and delineation for what is about to happen.

4. Shift your weight and lean to one side of the body to pour the "substance of the self" into that side. The Blue Flame wall ensures it will not move back into the other half. You are now fully and vividly occupying one-half of yourself.

5. "Turn" to perceive the other half of yourself, to sense into the space and vacuum now created there, with your awareness. You will sense and perceive through the Blue Flame barrier. Feel into that sensation and bear witness to the emptiness there and how it has formed the perfect vessel. This can often be a very bizarre and surprising experience. It is also the key to this technique.

6. Call out to the being to fill this "empty" half of the body and to become one of two heads. Perceive and witness as the other half is filled with the presence of the spirit or deity.

A note of caution:

This technique allows for full consciousness for both deity and human to co-exist and hold dynamic tension in embodiment together; hence the term "double-headed." This will feel remarkably odd to some, and that is normal. Work with the breath and the grounding cord to support you as you move through the experience. A handful of the many people I have taught this technique to have experienced quite shocking effects in their nervous system or within their brain. If that is the case, send the Blue Flame back down into the Earth with love and care, and then imagine, feel, and perceive that you are being bathed in pearlescent lunar light. You may want to lay down in cushions and softness and just call upon that lunar light to saturate and shimmer through your being. Align your Three Souls and be with the breath.

When you wish to transition out of the double-headed possessory state, speak directly to the deity and communicate this. As per any previous negotiations and agreements you have already made with this being or in general, this ought to be swift and simple. If it feels complicated, ask for assistance from your human ally tending you within the space.

Some people report feeling completely capable of doing this work completely on their own, but my advice is to do this with another experienced in the room just in case.

When you feel that the presence of the spirit has fully departed, perhaps leaving a trace of blessing or an echo of power, draw the Blue Flame back through you down and into the Earth. Release and ground. Aligning your souls again in a methodical manner may help to further the grounding and sensation of belonging to oneself. You may need to physically lean into the other side of your body so that the "substance of self" moves back and through. Showering, bathing, or eating now is a good idea, followed by rest.

Give thanks to the ancestors and spirits of place.

Taking the Chair: Trance Possession Circle

I developed this technique out of a limited experience with reconstructed Seidr Craft rites of trance prophesy and spirit-flight that may take place in various Witchcraft and Pagan communities. This technique blends more of the possessory protocol and years of experience cultivated in the ecstatic rites of Wildwood Witchcraft.

In order to go ahead with this rite, you should already know who the deity or spirit you will be working with is and gather the necessary items and offerings to do this respectfully and well. You will need a group of people to perform this trance possession.

1. Arrange the space so that it is cleared out except for a solid chair in the centre of a circle of cushions and chairs in a surrounding circle for

those who want or need them. Build a shrine for the deity in front of the central chair so that the vessel is facing it when they take the seat.

2. The group may now acknowledge the land and first peoples, ground, centre, align, cleanse, and other opening actions. (The vessel should not be seated when this is happening.) Create the working space for the rite. A Circle would work well here, but the spirit you may be working with might require a distinct working space created in some other fashion.

3. Before the vessel takes the chair, all assembled may touch the chair and bless and charge it for the rite. You may wish to use this Wildwood blessing:

"We bless, we cleanse, we consecrate, we purify, we charge."

This spell may then be chanted several times to call up the Seat of Seers into this very seat:

"This seat is as strong as stone.
This seat is as old as bone.
This seat is a seat of vision.
This seat is holy precision!"

If appropriate or desired, you could anoint the seat and the vessel with charged waters and oils and smoke the space and one another with burning herbs and resins.

4. The vessel will take the seat and begin to slip into trance. They may choose to rock back and forth on the seat while building a strong sensation of being a vessel. Any anxiety, nervousness, doubt, fear, excitement, or whatever emotion the vessel experiences can be harnessed to build up the etheric vessel-shape—such as a cup, cauldron, or crucible—within the spirit-worker. A written contract may have already been drawn up regarding specific agreements and negotiations. Part of the magic of this ritual is that the vessel is anchored into the seat, and the entire possession will happen from that place.

5. All those gathered will be surrounding the central seat, kneeling, sitting, or standing. The group will start to collectively invoke, perceiving and imagining the vessel as a container able to draw in and hold the vivid presence of this being. Someone may be drumming

over and behind the head of the vessel or even at the feet or belly of the vessel while others speak invocations quickly and precisely over them or into their ears. This works wonders! Basically, a great deal of power is raised and then released into the vessel to open the way for the being to come in.

6. At this point, it is typical for the Great One to make themselves known through the vessel. They may speak or sing, or they may focus on individuals and speak directly to them. It is often true that the possession transforms the feeling, voice, size, and overall presence of the human vessel. Questions may be asked of the Great One, and offerings may be given. The rite unfolds as it needs to.

7. At a point deemed appropriate by the group, the spirit is thanked, honoured, and asked peacefully and powerfully to depart from the vessel. It may be said,

"Great One, we are so deeply grateful for your presence and blessing here at this rite. We ask that you now leave this vessel and leave them better than you found them, by which we mean,
Vital,
Centred,
Grounded,
Peaceful,
Fulfilled (and so on)...."

More offerings may need to be given afterwards in response to specific instructions from the being.

8. Once the spirit has departed, the vessel is helped off the seat and given the aid they need to ground and come down from the experience.

9. The Circle is released, or the space is dismantled in whichever way it needs to be. It is advised that the person who served as vessel leave the space and shower or attend to their needs in some way with a key trusted person. The group may debrief another day, or if the group is together for several hours (or stretching into the night), the group may debrief after the vessel returns. One important thing to note is that talking directly to the human person about the things "they/you" did is jarring and bad possessory protocol. The person who served as vessel will likely feel confused or dissociated from what is being said and not relate to it, as it was the spirit/deity/being doing and saying those things. Aspire only to say, "The spirit

did this, said this…the deity moved like this through the vessel…" and similar language. Always check in with one another before launching into a full debrief.

Enhancement, Inspiration, and Into Integration

This method is a perfect way to prepare for and experiment with levels of aspecting in preparation for trance possession or simply to experience the magics of enhancement, inspiration, and integration. You may do this alone up until inviting the Spirit to touch the gate of your heart. If you choose to go further than this, I advise you strongly to have a tender in the space with you.

1. Acknowledge country. Ground. Cleanse. Align.
2. Bring your attention to the space between your surface skin and your second/etheric skin. (Most people will perceive 2–3 cm of space here.) Breathe and direct life force through that space. Meditate on this for a few minutes. Notice how you feel and what sensations you have.
3. Expand your awareness through into your Breath-Body, your Breath-Soul, and Middle-Soul, which is the same as your aura. Find the edge of your aura. Once you've found it, get it to ripple. Some people will use visualisation and sensation, some will physically shake or sing, and others will stretch out their hands and arms and tremble these to get the aura to ripple or shimmer.
4. Now, you invoke the spirit. You ask the spirit to cover and cloak (what I call "mantling") the edge of your rippling aura. Ask them to cover and cloak you but not to pass through the aura. Hold this for several minutes. Experience the sensations of holding the boundary. This can be called "enhancement." If you are strongly invoking in ritual, you will naturally go into this state. All great actors and artists are in a state of enhancement when they are at work.
5. When and if you are ready and willing, ask the spirit to cross through your auric edge and come in to share your Breath-Body. This may be called "inspiration." Notice what happens here, paying attention for several minutes. This can be an amazing way to have a very lucid conversation with the spirit. If you watched a priestex in ritual invoking and they begin to seem fused with the spirit or deity, this is what is

happening. But remember, you still have your full consciousness and faculties; your hands are still on the "wheel."

6. To enact the beginnings of integration, bring your awareness to the Gate of your Heart. Some people will perceive a specific sigil here or hear or know a sound, signature, or something of note. This is important to remember and record. Invite the spirit to touch the Gate/the seal but not to pass through. Hold this for several minutes. Take notice and pay attention. If you were to go into a deeper state of integration, you would then ask the spirit to move through the Gate of your Heart into the Labyrinth of You, but for this, you will need a tender in the space with you.

7. Very methodically ask the spirit to withdraw their touch, then to step out of your aura, and then, finally, with reverence and love, farewell the spirit from your space. Pay attention once more for a few breaths to each state: beginnings of integration, inspiration, and enhancement. Notice how you are feeling and what sensations you are having.

8. Journal, reflect, meditate, stretch, or take notes. Ground.

APPENDIX IV

Medean Sorcery

Medea, the legendary enchantress, is infamous for the murder of her own children and famous for helping the so-called hero Jason with her wiles and sorcery. Medea is the granddaughter of Helios, the Sun God, via her father Aeëtes, King of Colchis. In the lore that we have been passed through layers of storytelling, we discover that Medea is considered to be a devotee or priestess of triple-faced Hekate. She calls upon this ancient Goddess in her spell-workings. She also calls upon Night and the primordial powers a Witch would call upon. Medea's magic seems to be accessed and worked by fully identifying with Wild nature, by surrendering to the reality of being powerful as such, and by allowing that power to surge and seethe through and as her. By claiming that power and wielding it, Medea is powerful.

In some magical traditions, the idea is that the priestex, the Witch, or the vessel draws in the spirits and the Gods and, in this way, conducts great power and mystery, but in Medea's case, she melts and melds into the rest of nature. She is able to ride Fate because she has become Fate. Many of my most magical experiences have been catalysed by simply deciding to act as if this could be. In the process of that acting, *as if* what I have experienced is that the powers, the magic which I desire to commune with, lean in and participate with me. Daring to occupy one's potential in this way is a hallmark of the Witch and certainly of Medea.

The following ritual process will enable a Witch who desires to step into and wield power to do so by invoking the aid of Medea and her court of spirits and beings. There is a particular order and methodology that, once entrained or integrated, will simply spill forth from you in the process of conducting this ritual. Step into this, and then step aside and allow the Medean presence to be potently channelled into the work.

Before you enact the rites, slowly and thoroughly read through each step, making notes, drawing diagrams if you need, and feeling and sensing into the unfolding of the magic described. Consider how you feel about it and what it provokes in you. If you come earnestly to this work, you may discover new alliances or affirm established connections.

Opening Rites

1. Place a black candle ("from darkness comes light"), a bowl of fresh water, and an incense stick or dry twig/branch small enough to be plunged into the bowl of water before you. Prepare offerings ahead of the working to give at the close of the rite.
2. Acknowledge country. Ground. Align.
3. Kneel in the North-East, between the Hinge of the stars and the place of the dawn. You may kneel in the South-East in the Southern Hemisphere if you wish to emphasise the place between the Midnight Sun and the dawn, though North-East may still be an option if you feel the morphic resonance there.
4. Light the candle and recite the "Orphic Hymn to Primal Fire" (fumigation of saffron):

> *"Primal Fire, ascend to us with the dawn, and rule the sky.*
> *Glory of the Sun, with burning luster illumine*
> *even the silver Goddess Selene.*
> *Aethereal Fire, radiant heat that inspires life,*
> *Light bearer, power of stars,*
> *Cause now the blooming of the iris and the rose,*
> *And to the grain, be kind,*
> *Hear our prayer of supplication,*
> *And be thou ever innocent, serene, and gentle to our Land."*

5. Take your Witch knife and hold it with one hand. Point the knife and the pointer and middle fingers of your other hand at the flame. Open your awareness to perceive the fire whirling through you and the space, releasing that which binds you against the full realisation of your deepest wealth and highest good. Chant fiercely at least three times:

> *"Hekas, Hekas, Este Bebeloi."*
> *Phoenetically: "Heh-kahs, O Heh-kahs, Es-tay bay-bay-loi."*
> *Translation: "Far, far be removed the profane."*

6. Drop into your breath and sink into the great dark. Visualise or imagine Hekate's firebrand—the flaming torch—as the strength of your spine and the power of your will. Merge with the torch completely, and at the crest of your crown, behold the flame ignite! This is Hekate's firebrand or torch; the light is of Helios—the line of Hekate—and Medea's Witch-fire! Say aloud or hold in heavy silence:

> *"All that is Above is as All that is Below.*
> *Fires of the starry crown come down!*
> *Hellfire arise!*
> *Fire where we are gathered, I exalt you!"*

7. Imagine and know that all of this is moving and flowing through the fire lit at your brow, at the crest of your crown. Take the incense or twig and light it with the flame, then plunge it into the bowl of water, saying:

> *"Kye-yer-neep-toe-may,*
> *May this water be purified by the holy Fire!"*
> *Draw the sign of the five-point star over it and say:*
> *"By the five-point star, so mote it be!"*
> *Travel anti-clockwise around the space, sprinkling the water over*
> *yourself, all gathered and the space saying:*
> *"O theoi genoisthe apotropoi kakon."*
> *Phoenetically: "O thee-oi ghen-oys-thee ah-poh-troh-poi kah-kon."*
> *Translated: "O Gods, turn away all evils."*

8. Turn to the North or South—the place of silence and darkness, depending on your hemisphere—and touch the edge of the blade to the flame lit before you. Say:

> *"This is Medea's knife!"*

Feel it as it is so. Turn to the direction of silence and darkness. Hold the knife high above you and pray for Helios' flame to enter your knife, as you are in the line of Medea as a Witch:

> *"Helios, sink the sun into this sword! Kiss my knife!"*

9. See and feel the sun enter the blade. From North or South, walk seven times around the space and, as the Circle of Arte is formed, chant:

"In the name of Helios and Medea, I cast this Circle of Arte."

10. Turn to the East and, this time, go with the Sun—clockwise or anti-clockwise, depending on the hemisphere—and call to the Four Winds. In the East, vibrate the name *Euros* three times. In the South, vibrate the name *Notos* three times. In the West, vibrate the name *Zephyros* three times. And in the North, vibrate the name *Boreas* three times.

11. Seal this by coming back to the centre and saying:

"The star in the stone,
The light in the bone,
Dove and serpent kiss,
Where egg is wreathed in mist!"

It is done.

The Working

1. Sink into the dark. Call out to Hekate and Hermes as partners in magic.
2. Recite the following words of power from Ovid's *Metamorphoses* to identify with Medea.

"O night, night, night!
Whose darkness holds
All mysteries in shade, O flame-lit stars,
Whose golden rays with Luna floating near
Are like the fires of day—and you, O Hekate,
Who know untold desires that work our will
And art the mistress of our secret spells,
O Earth who gives us bounty of weird grasses,
Your wandering winds and hills and brooks and wells,
Gods of the dark-leaved forest and gods of night,
Come to my call.
When you have entered me,

> *As if a miracle had drained their banks and courses,*
> *I've driven back rivers to springs and fountains,*
> *I shake the seas or calm them at my will;*
> *I whip the clouds or make them rise again;*
> *At my command winds vanish or return,*
> *My very spells have torn the throats of serpents,*
> *Live rocks and oaks are overturned and felled,*
> *The forests tremble and the mountains split,*
> *And deep Earth roars while ghosts walk from their tombs.*
> *Through crashing brass and bronze relieve your labours,*
> *Even you, O Moon, I charm from angry skies!"*

Call upon your Holy Daimon to descend and speak to you of the sorcery your deepest soul requires. Ask the guidance of the Gods and your Daimons/Spirits and Familiars.

3. Bring what unfolds to the altars of your Three Souls until you are vibrating with the power of an articulated and deepened intention. A word or sigil of power may distil in this time.

4. Build power from the base of your spine up to the flame at the crest of your crown. Feel the twin serpents of Hermes' *kerykeion* (caduceus) arise and wind up, raising the power up the spine to the fire at your head. When it reaches this place, the wings unfold on either side, and the fire blazes ever more incandescently.

5. Recite the spell (as many times as needed) to invoke Hekate to open the Gates of Power:

> *"I unlock the Gates of Magic,*
> *I untie the ties of time,*
> *I surrender to all space,*
> *Invoking power with this rhyme!"*

6. Now, already saturated completely with your will and on fire with the power, stir and raise it to form a great river of magic. You may chant:

> *"I raise the power, I raise the power,*
> *I raise it well, I raise it well,*
> *In this hour, in this hour*
> *For this spell, for this spell!"*

7. When you have stirred the power and are riding the rapture of it, sit down and come to stillness. Open to feel and perceive the river of power internalise and go within to settle into the song of the soul-story of you. Feel the sorcery settle and sink back into the darkness.

8. See and feel the wings of the kerykeion fold back in, and feel the serpents settle naturally. Allow the incandescent flame to dim a little as a way of returning to a middle-world state.

9. Honour the spirits and powers, perhaps making appropriate sacrifices or offerings here.

10. Go to the direction of silence and darkness, and then anti-clockwise to each cardinal direction and vibrate the name of power there once (for example, Boreas and North). Release the star-gates (pentagrams) in the four directions.

11. Honour Medea and Helios, and release the gathered-up tension of the Circle of Arte, walking in whichever direction feels natural. Loosen the anchored circle, chanting:

"I release this Circle of Arte in the Names of Medea and Helios!"

12. Feed any leftover power and resonance to the spirits of the place, the Holy Daimon, your fetch, or any other spirit you feel is appropriate, with breath and attention. Dedicate offerings to the spirits seen and unseen, known and unknown, after the Circle is released and unbound into Sea, into Sky, or into sovereign ground.

Bibliography

Adler, Margot. *Drawing Down the Moon (Updated Resource Guide)*. Penguin Group/Compass, 1997.

Anderson, Cora. *Fifty Years in the Feri Tradition*. Harpy Books, 2010.

Aswynn, Freya. *Northern Mysteries & Magick: Runes & Feminine Powers*. Llewellyn Worldwide, 2002.

Athanassakis, Apostolos. *The Orphic Hymns: Text, Translation, and Notes*. Johns Hopkins University Press, 2013.

Bates, Brian. *The Way of the Wyrd: Tales of an Anglo-Saxon Sorcerer*. Hay House, 2005.

Bhikkhu, Thanissaro. "Upajjhatthana Sutta: Subjects for Contemplation." Access to Insight, 1997, waccesstoinsight.org/tipitaka/an/an05/an05.057. than.html.

Coyle, T. Thorn. *Evolutionary Witchcraft*. Tarcher, 2004.

—. *Elemental Castings*.

Cummer, Veronica, and Jo-Ann Byers-Mierzwicki, editors. *To Fly by Night: The Craft of the Hedgewitch*. Pendraig Publishing, 2010.

Curott, Phyllis. *Book of Shadows*. Broadway, 1999.

—. *The Love Spell*. Gotham Books, 2005.

Danielou, Alain. *Gods of Love and Ecstasy: The Traditions of Shiva and Dionysos*. Inner Traditions, 1992.

Davies, Owen. *Popular Magic: Cunning-Folk in English History*. Hambledon Continuum, 2007.

De Angeles, Ly. *Witchcraft: Theory and Practice*. Llewellyn Worldwide, 2000.

d'Este, Sorita and David Rankine. *Wicca: Magickal Beginnings*. Avalonia, 2008.

de Lint, Charles. *Spirits in the Wires*. Tor Books, 2003.

Digitalis, Raven. *A Witch's Shadow Magick Compendium*. Crossed Crow Books, 2022.

Eliade, Mircea. *Shamanism: Archaic Techniques of Ecstasy*. Bollingen Paperback Printing, 1972.

Faerywolf, Storm. "A Conjuring of the Male Mysteries in Modern Witchcraft." Crafting the Warlock, 18 February 2010, https://faerywolf.com/crafting-the-warlock.

Farrar, Janet and Gavin Bone. *Progressive Witchcraft: Spirituality, Mysteries & Training in Modern Wicca.* New Page Books, 2003.

Gede Parma, Fio. *By Land, Sky & Sea: Three Realms of Shamanic Witchcraft.* Llewellyn, 2010.

—. editor. *Crafting the Community.* Conjunction Press, 2009.

—. *Spirited: Taking Paganism Beyond the Circle.* Llewellyn Worldwide, 2009.

Gerber, Richard. *Vibrational Medicine: The #1 Handbook of Subtle-Energy Therapies.* Bear & Company, 2001.

Goodman, Felicia and Nana Nauwald. *Ecstatic Trance: New Ritual Body Postures.* Binkey Kok, 2003.

Grimassi, Raven. *Hereditary Witchcraft: Secrets of the Old Religion.* Llewellyn Worldwide, 1999.

—. *Ways of the Strega: Italian Witchcraft: Its Legends, Lore, and Spells.* Llewellyn Worldwide, 2000.

—. *Witchcraft: A Mystery Tradition.* Crossed Crow Books, 2024.

—. *The Witches' Craft: The Roots of Witchcraft & Magickal Transformation.* Crossed Crow Books, 2024.

Hutton, Ronald. *Shamans: Siberian Spirituality and the Western Imagination.* Bloomsbury Academic, 2007.

Johnson, Kenneth. *Witchcraft and the Shamanic Journey.* Crossed Crow Books, 2023.

Keeney, Bradford. *Shaking Out the Spirits.* Station Hill Press, 1994.

Leland, Charles, Mario Pazzaglini, and Dina Pazzaglini (trans.). *Aradia, or the Gospel of the Witches: A New Translation.* Phoenix Publishing, 1998.

Morgan, Lee. *A Deed Without a Name.* Moon Books, 2013.

Mumford, John. *Ecstasy Through Tantra.* Llewellyn Worldwide, 2002.

Mynne, Hugh. *The Faerie Way: A Healing Journey to Other Worlds.* Llewellyn Worldwide, 1998.

Penczak, Christopher. *The Temple of Shamanic Witchcraft: Shadows, Spirits and the Healing Journey.* Llewellyn Worldwide, 2006.

—. *The Three Rays of Witchcraft: Power, Love and Wisdom in the Garden of the Gods.* Copper Cauldron Publishing, 2010.

Pande, Alka. "Mahashivratri - The Five Elements of Shiva." Times Now News, 9 Mar. 2021, timesnownews.com/columns/article/mahashivratri-the-five-elements-of-shiva/730234.

Polson, Willow and M. Macha Nightmare. *The Veil's Edge: Exploring the Boundaries of Magic.* Citadel Press, 2003.

Roads, Michael. *Journey into Nature: A Spiritual Adventure.* H. J. Kramer, 1990.

Starhawk. *Dreaming the Dark: Magic, Sex, and Politics (15th Anniversary Edition).* Beacon Press, 1997.

—. *The Fifth Sacred Thing.* Bantam, 1994.

—. *The Spiral Dance (10th Anniversary Edition).* HarperCollins, 1989.

Stein, Charles. *Persephone Unveiled: Seeing the Goddess & Freeing Your Soul.* North Atlantic Books, 2006.

Walsh, Roger. *The World of Shamanism: New Views of an Ancient Tradition.* Llewellyn Worldwide, 2007.

Wilby, Emma. *Cunning Folk and Familiar Spirits: Shamanistic Visionary Traditions in Early Modern British Witchcraft and Magic.* Liverpool University Press, 2005.

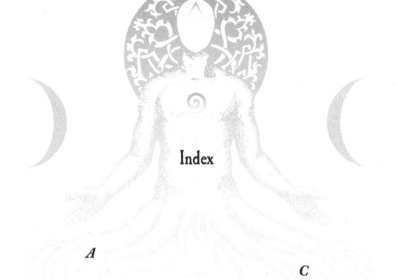

Index